More Secrets More Lies

A novel by J. Tremble

Also by J. Tremble
Secrets of a Housewife

A Life Changing Book in conjunction with Power Play Media
Published by Life Changing Books
P.O. Box 423 Brandywine, MD 20613

Library of Congress Cataloging-in-Publication Data;

www.lifechangingbooks.net

ISBN (10)1-934230-99-5 (13) 978-1-934230-99-2
Copyright ® 2007

Dedication

✳   ✳   ✳

I would like to dedicate this novel to my wonderful mother,
beautiful wife, and caring children.

I Love You All!

Power Play
Media

in conjunction with
Life Changing Books

Acknowledgements

＊   ＊   ＊

I would like to first thank my family and friends, especially my loving wife, whose support has made this book possible. Hats off to the staff at Benjamin Stoddert Middle School, in Temple Hills, MD. Your courtesy, support and feedback on this project were invaluable. A special thanks to Michelle Lewis, Kiniesha Abraham and Ronald Woodard, who's got the best creative talents in Maryland on lock. I can't forget Erika Jones, Shellie Davis, Tiedra Taylor, and Valerie Odom for their emotional support. Much love to Trina Johnson, Sharon Harper, and Porscha Baker for mental support. To the Rough Rider Flag Football Team, thanks for believing in me.

A special, special thanks goes out to the professional team who made it all possible: Leslie Allen, and Azarel, my publisher, thanks for believing in me and seeing my project through. Leslie, I can't thank you enough for all the late nights and hard work you put into this project. Hopefully, all the marks from your red pen will pay off. Nakea Murray, my publicist, thanks for keeping me connected. Vida, your graphics are top notch. Kathleen Jackson, thanks for getting the final editing done. Shout out to anyone else who has assisted me.

To my outside support squad: A special thanks to Cheryl Moody and Keisha George for your diligence in dissecting this book.(Smile) Ronnique, Lisa Williams, Tam, Rashaun and Emily, thanks for providing technical support on this project.

Thanks to all of the Power Play Media family, Darren Coleman (Do or Die, Don't Ever Wonder and Ladies Listen Up), Azarel (Bruised 1 & 2), Danette Majette (I Shoulda' Seen it Comin'), Tonya Ridley (The Take Over), Tyrone Wallace (Nothin Personal), Zach Tate (Lost and Turned Out), Tiphani Montgomery (The Millionaire Mistress) and Mike G (Young Assassin).

I especially want to thank all of my distributors who have sold copies of Secrets of a Housewife all around the world and the African-American bookstores. Last but not least, whether you've given technical, moral, or emotional support during this project, I still want to thank you.

Peace,

J. Tremble

Chapter 1

The steam crept into Tarron's bedroom, as he opened his eyes, startled by the soft voice singing in the distance. *Oh my God! I must have left the shower running all night,* he thought. Tarron quickly sat up and stretched his body. He anxiously hopped out of bed, and slid into his favorite navy blue slippers, headed toward the sensual sound.

As he walked toward the master bathroom, the singing grew louder and more enticing. Just as he pushed the door open, an enormous amount of steam filled the air. Searching through the midst, Tarron caught a glimpse of two silhouettes behind the foggy glass door. As he drew closer, he was able to make out two long seductive bodies and four erect nipples. He smiled. *My eyes must be deceiving me. It couldn't be.*

There appeared to be two women in the shower together. Tarron felt the front of his silk boxers begin to expand. His circumcised penis peeked through the slit as he became excited with anticipation. He walked slowly toward the shower and slid the door open slightly. His eyes almost popped out of his head as he noticed his wife, Secret, applying soap to another woman's back. Tarron began to rub his eyes, just to make sure they weren't deceiving him. He scanned Secret's hour glass figure from head to toe, and smiled as he heard her singing one of his favorite oldies, *Tonight* by Ready For the World. The hair on his arms

rose when a pair of caramel colored hands, with French manicured nails, slid up Secret's stomach, and rested on her breasts.

"I love your nipples," the woman said, in a seductive tone.

Tarron's mouth almost dropped to his knees at the sound of
the familiar voice. He had to know exactly who the other woman
was, so he discreetly opened the door a little further to reveal her
identity. Tarron couldn't believe what was going down. His heart
skipped a beat when he realized the other woman was Victoria,
his former mistress. He thought someone was playing a joke on
him. His wife of eight years held her head back, as Victoria made
circular motions with her tongue over Secret's nipples. He
blinked frantically, trying not to miss any more of the wild show.

A smile of undisguised lust spread over his face as he watched
Victoria and Secret lathering each other's body. Their bare hands
two stepped in perfect rhythm up and down their naked bodies,
while Secret continued to sing. Tarron's eyes widened even further as Victoria pulled on Secret's nipples and made seductive
noises. *Why wasn't Secret this freaky before?* he asked himself.
Was I the problem? Maybe I wasn't giving her what she needed?

The foam from the Sweet Temptation body wash began to
cover Secret's breasts. Tarron admired how her flowered tattoo on
her left ankle sparkled as the water ran down her leg. He'd seen
the tattoo many times before, but seeing her with someone else
made everything about her a turn-on.

Victoria's hands stopped at Secret's tiny waist as she pulled
her one hundred-thirty pound frame in close. She slowly licked
Secret's neck, causing her to tremor with excitement. Victoria's
long nails caressed Secret's back as she pressed her perfectly
formed 36B breasts firmly against her. Her right hand followed
Secret's spine all the way down until she reached the crack of her
ass.

Secret let out a load moan when she felt Victoria's fingers in
her forbidden zone. Victoria used this opportunity to grab Secret's
lower back and kiss her passionately in the mouth. Ironically,

Secret was a step ahead of her lover. She yanked Victoria's head back by her hair and hungrily sucked on her lips. Tarron stood amazed when he saw Secret use her tongue to outline the perimeter of Victoria's mouth.

"Your lips are so soft," Secret moaned.

The comment immediately made Tarron lick his lips, as he started to massage his fully erect dick. Suddenly, the water from the shower bounced off the women's naked bodies, and splashed into his face. They were so engrossed in each other, they didn't seem to notice Tarron standing there watching their every move with his dick in hand.

At that moment, Victoria turned her back to Secret and placed her hands on the rear shower wall. Tarron became overly excited. He panted like a dog in heat. He knew this position all too well. Victoria loved to be fucked doggy style. Tarron thought back to the many times she would arch her back, as a signal for him to provide deeper strokes. He could envision squeezing, then smacking her ass repeatedly. Tarron instantly stroked his dick faster, thinking of pounding her inner walls until her knees trembled. He thought about how Victoria was a pro when it came to tightening and releasing her pussy walls against his dick, and she knew that always made him cum. His jaw dropped when he saw Secret bend over to lick Victoria's love nest from behind.

"That's right bitch, eat this pussy!" Victoria said, with authority.

Tarron stroked his dick even faster, as he watched Secret's tongue play with Victoria's bright pink clitoris. The sounds of Victoria moaning with pleasure almost gave him a heart attack. He could no longer control himself. It was time to join in.

Opening the door with force, Tarron stepped into the shower still wearing his silk boxers, which clung to his body like fitted biker shorts. He didn't care. He just wanted to be involved in the erotic scene before it ended.

"What took you so long, baby?" Secret whispered.

"We knew you were standing there watching us the entire time," Victoria added. "Did you enjoy the show?"

"Hell yeah!" Tarron responded. "But don't stop on my behalf," he stuttered, half-shocked.

"Oh, don't worry, we're not done," Victoria said, as she grabbed a ten inch dildo that was lying on the slippery shower floor.

"What are your plans for that?" Tarron asked, with concern. He was down for whatever, but he wasn't into any gay shit.

"You'll see. Turn around, baby," Victoria ordered to Secret.

Like a little girl in school following the teacher's instructions, Secret slowly grabbed her ankles as Victoria inserted the dildo in her pussy. *Damn, when did she become so flexible?* Tarron thought. Victoria pushed the rubber dick into Secret with rapid strokes, as Tarron watched in amazement. He couldn't believe his wife was allowing this to happen, but he was glad she did. *Maybe if she had done this months ago, we would still be together,* he thought. Just as he was about to join the fun, Victoria took the dildo out of Secret's pussy and inserted it into her mouth. Tarron jumped back!

"Umm…you taste good, Secret," Victoria moaned.

Before Secret could respond, Victoria had decided to perform on the real thing. She slowly lowered her body to a knee position, and used both hands to turn Tarron around so that his erect dick was directly in her face. She used her teeth and nails to rip his silk boxers, which had shriveled up like a prune. Tarron's wet body shivered involuntarily with excitement, as his manhood sprang free from its cage. The feeling of the warm water running down his back increased his rising desire. Tarron had a dazed look of pleasure when he felt Victoria's soft lips wrap around his dick and began to suck with the force of a Hoover vacuum.

"Can I join in?" Secret asked, as she began squeezing Tarron's chest.

She licked his back with long vertical strokes. Tarron looked down to watch Victoria insert more and more of his shaft into her mouth. Instantly, thoughts of her leaving him for his brother, Jay, made him angry. He began pushing his dick deeper into her mouth, causing her to choke. Victoria tried to pull back, but he grabbed the back of her head and pushed even deeper.

He paused his thrusting when he felt Secret's descent behind him. *Oh shit, what is she doing?* he thought. Tarron looked down at Victoria, who was still giving his dick a full workout despite him trying to take her tonsils out.

Instantly, Secret pulled his boxers from the bottom of Tarron's legs, tossed them from the shower, and watched them land on the edge of the sink. She stared at his firm ass only inches from her face. Secret remembered all the times he wanted to do freaky moves to her virgin ass, but she resisted. She was ready to reverse the play.

Tarron clinched his entire body as he felt Secret's tongue teasing the sensitive area around his ass. He tightened his cheeks as she started to tease the area with puffs of cold air.

"Loosen up, baby!" Secret said playfully, as she smacked his right hip to relax his muscles, just as he had done to her many times in the past.

He ignored the painful slaps, and kept his tight hold. At that moment, Victoria stopped the head bangin' session to help Secret with her target.

Victoria reached both her hands around Tarron's chiseled body, to spread his ass wide open. His heart began to race uncontrollably. Even though a part of him wanted them to stop, he had to admit it felt good. Tarron decided to give in by bending forward, allowing easier access, which caused water to fly everywhere. The mirror fogged, as the heat from their bodies steamed the bathroom.

"Doesn't that feel good, daddy?" Victoria asked, in a childish tone.

The feeling of being on cloud nine prevented Tarron from answering. As Secret continued to give her cheating husband pleasure from behind, Victoria grabbed his dick to finish her job. Secret became more aroused while playing with Tarron's ass, so she reached around and began to play with Victoria's hardened nipples.

The sensation of having his salad tossed and his dick sucked with such intensity, was too much for him to handle. The feeling of tiny needles began to curl his toes. He was close to exploding in Victoria's mouth. He reached down and grabbed the back of her head for the second time, so that she could take all of him and swallow every ounce.

Tarron let out a loud moan, as he unloaded a large amount of warm thick cum into Victoria's mouth. There was no need to force her head down any longer, because Victoria had grabbed his thighs from behind, so that his dick was totally in her mouth. She continued to suck forcefully without ever missing a stroke.

A few seconds after his first orgasm, Tarron started to receive a tingling feeling from behind. He felt another surge of heat rushing from his feet to his head. This was a new feeling of sensation for him, so he didn't know what to. His legs started to become extremely heavy, as if blocks of concrete were tied to his ankles. He became weaker by the second, as large goose bumps floated back and fourth through the hair on his arms.

Tarron thought he was about to cum again, but quickly realized that the feeling was a little different. The numbness he experienced immediately came from his backside, and his butt got wetter as the tingling stopped. His entire body began to shiver and shake.

Damn, did I just cum from my ass? Tarron wondered, as his eyes rolled back in his head. His self pleasure abruptly ended as Victoria pushed him aside to embrace Secret. She locked her lips onto Secret's and shared ounces of Tarron's man juice.

"Secret, don't you just love the taste of his sweet nectar?" Victoria asked.

"Mmm, every ounce of it," Secret replied, as she licked the cum dripping from her mouth.

Astonished by what he was hearing and seeing, Tarron watched in amazement as Secret and Victoria engaged in freaky, erotic sexual acts that he didn't know were possible. The longer he watched, the faster his dick began to rise again. Victoria gave Secret a few more small pecks on the lips, before looking deep into her eyes.

"Enough foreplay! Let's take this into the bedroom. We're ready to do all kinds of things to you, baby," Victoria said to Tarron.

Tarron stared like a malfunctioned robot, as Victoria and Secret's wet naked bodies stepped from the shower, and walked into the bedroom with joined hands. Just as Victoria shot him a welcoming look over her shoulder, he noticed how similar their figures were. Both women had athletic bodies that were in great shape. *I should know, I paid for both of their gym fees,* he thought. Victoria's ass and breasts were slightly larger, but Secret wasn't far behind. They both had long wavy dark hair, except Secret's had an auburn tint, and a far better grain. However, Victoria's beautiful long and firm legs made up for that.

Tarron turned the stainless steel knob to the off position, and stepped out of the shower, anticipating what was about to go down. Just as he put his feet on the marble tile, he lost his balance on the wet floor. His legs were still weak from the double orgasm. He tried to regain his balance, by reaching out for the sink, but instead his hand caught the ripped silk boxers, which couldn't stop his fall. He fell to the floor, hitting his head on the toilet.

With his hand pressed against his temple, Tarron managed to

get up, and staggered into the bedroom covered in blood. When he got through the door, he lost his breath. Secret's body was stretched out on the floor with blood all over her. Both her wrists were slit!

Their children, Terrance and Tika, were by her side, yelling and screaming, Get up, Mommy! Get up!"

At that moment, Tarron touched his head and realized that it was Secret's blood covering him, not his. "

What the hell is going on?" he shouted. He looked around the room, and saw Victoria in the corner holding Jay's hand, and they were laughing out loud. Tarron repeated, "What the hell is going on?"

Terrance rose from his mother's side, holding a razor blade in his right hand. He walked very slowly toward Tarron shouting, "It's all your fault! It's your fault. I can't stand you! I hate you! I hate you!" Terrance raised the blade, and swung the sharp edge across Tarron's neck.

Tarron woke up, yelling and waving his hands. His body was drenched in sweat. He couldn't believe that the entire episode was just a terrible dream. *Even the sex.* He looked around and heard his mother, Motherdear, laughing with the children. Tarron quickly realized that he had fallen asleep on his old sofa, after dropping Terrance off from football practice. *Damn, it feels good to be home again,* he thought. He looked at the clock on the wall and saw that it was 7:15 p.m. *Visiting hours will be over by the time I get to the hospital to check on Secret, so I'll go early in the morning. I can't believe that woman actually slit her wrists because of me. Damn, I never expected her to go that far.*

Tarron tried to roll over, but was stopped by his stiff erection. Staring at the ceiling, he also began to think about Victoria. Tarron knew he shouldn't blame her for everything, but he couldn't help it. The woman he had left his family for was now fucking his punk ass brother. He wondered if Jay's sex was better than his. Tarron continued to stare at the ceiling for the next hour, and finally realized that he couldn't go down without a fight. *I can't let shit go on like this. Brother or not, I got something for his ass.*

Chapter 2

David walked confidently through the automatic doors of the hospital with a dozen roses in hand. The strong smell of disinfectant was repugnant to him, as he stopped at the information desk to ask for Secret's room number. He was immediately attracted to the young lady sitting behind the desk, who reminded him of Halle Berry.

"Hello, gorgeous, can you tell me what room Secret Jenkins is in? Oh, and give me your number while you're at it," David said, looking into her beautiful grey colored eyes.

"I can help you out with your first request, but you're out of luck on the second one," the young lady replied.

"Come on, beautiful. I came to visit my sister, but that visit can wait, if you'll allow me to stay here and talk to you. Actually, these roses were for my sister, but now I want you to have them," David said, placing the glass vase on her desk.

"Thank you, they're beautiful," she said, standing up to smell the roses. "I'm sorry, but I'm not allowed to have visitors at my desk. Besides, you look a little too old for me, I'm only twenty one," she ended, with a slight grin on her face.

The comment made David's smile turn into a cold stare.

"Umm…Mrs. Jenkins is in Room 310," the young lady said, as she sat back in her chair, pretending to read a piece of paper.

David began to walk away, but quickly turned around and snatched the vase from off the desk. "Tell one of your young broke ass boyfriends to buy you some flowers then."

David was furious. He hated being turned down by any woman. He really wanted to reach around the desk and choke the shit out of her, but he tried to be on his best behavior whenever possible. *Besides, I'm on my way to see my future wife. I don't need anyone messing that up,* David thought, as he looked for the elevator. He wondered if the girl really believed that Secret was his sister.

David's Gucci shoes clicked on the shiny tile, as he walked down the long white hallway. He waited patiently in front of the elevator, visualizing Secret's face. Suddenly the doors opened, and a pregnant woman walked out with a man rubbing her back. *One day that will be me and my Boo,* David thought, as he stepped into the elevator. He had only one thought in mind as the doors closed and he pushed the number three button on the panel. *Please Lord, let her be alright. I don't think I could handle losing her. I know it was foolish to let her go, but this time, I'll make things permanent.*

The door to Secret's room was slightly ajar. His shadow fell across her bed as he tipped into the room toward her. The squeaking sound of the opening door made Secret turn her head. She slowly began to smile, as her eyes locked onto David's light complexion and his six foot-three frame. Secret moistened her dry lips with a few sweeps of her tongue.

Oh my! Here comes my big boy toy. Secret's long stare gave her time to entertain the nasty thoughts that flooded her mind. It had been about a month since she'd seen David, but his good looks hadn't changed. She'd always been attracted to El Debarge look-alikes, and David fit the bill perfectly. *I guess what some comedians say is true, light skin is back.* Secret let out a small giggle. David stopped and gave her a look that asked, *what's that laugh for?*

Secret continued to check him out. Studying his frame from top to bottom, she shook her head at David's athletic two-hundred and twenty pounds, that were chiseled to perfection, as if God had done it personally. She loved his dark wavy hair that hung just over his shoulders at the base of his neck. Secret giggled again when she remembered being with David in the company's limousine, and how his mustache and the small beard covering his chin had tickled her neck when he began his foreplay.

"Okay. Do I have food on me or something?" David asked.

"No, baby, why do you say that?" Secret replied.

"What is it then? Why do you keep laughing at me?"

"I don't know what you mean?" Secret let out another little giggle, realizing that she had been caught. "I'm just looking at how much weight you've put on, that's all. You're such a butterball now."

"Yeah, I've put on several pounds. That's a good thing though, right? It's more of me to love now," David said smiling.

Secret was no longer listening to David, even though his mouth was still moving. Her eyes watched his full lips as they opened and closed. She smiled again, showing even more teeth, as two cute dimples appeared at the corner of his mouth.

"There you go again," David said.

"What?"

"Never mind!" David shrugged his shoulders and shook his head. He pulled the dozen of white roses from behind his back. "These are for you," he said, walking over to the window to place them on the ledge. The moment David spotted other roses, he tried his best to get a sneak peak at the name on the cards. *I wonder who gave her those flowers? She better not be fucking anybody else,* he thought.

"So, what brings you here?" Secret interrupted.

"You, of course." David pulled a chair close to the bed and took a seat.

"Thanks for the flowers, but there's no need in getting comfortable. Visiting hours are almost over. You'll have to leave soon."

"This won't take long. I just need to know what that no good nigga did to make you do this to yourself?" David lifted her hands and examined her bandaged wrists. He stroked her right hand before releasing it.

"Don't blame Tarron for everything. I blame myself as well," she replied, as she pushed the button on the remote to raise the back of her bed.

"What happened? I need to know why you did this to yourself, baby."

Secret cleared her throat. "Well, nigga, don't think you didn't have anything to do with this either!"

"What are you talking about? I've never done anything to hurt you," he said defensively.

"You decided to leave me when I was at my lowest point! That's what I'm talking about."

David started to feel bad about telling Secret that they needed to chill for awhile, until things cooled down with Tarron. He remembered how he thought giving her space was the right thing to do, but obviously that wasn't the case. David really loved Secret, so he instantly regretted giving them that time apart.

"I'm so sorry, Secret. I never thought I would cause you more pain by doing that."

"Well, I know you thought what we had was just a fling, but I really care about you and enjoyed the time we spent together."

"Now you know I care about you too. I just didn't want to share you with Tarron, so I took the punk road. I said let's chill for a while, but I'm back now. Ready to love you like you need to be loved."

Secret shot David a funny look, as he stared at her with dreamy eyes.

"Damn, Secret. Please accept my apology." He kissed the palm of her hand like she was the Queen of Sheba. "I promise, I'll never leave you again."

Secret couldn't help but think how crazy her life was at that very moment. "I could really use a friend right now. I've been so depressed since Tarron found out that Jay was the biological father of Terrance." She breathed a heavy sigh. "Up until that point, Tarron thought so highly of me. But I guess when you find out that your son is really your nephew, that would mess with any man."

"What about the affair he was having? Didn't that bother you?"

"Of course it bothered me! I think a part of me actually died inside when I found out he was cheating." Secret wiped her face, as a single tear raced to her chin. "Can you believe he allowed that bitch inside our home for a family gathering? Not only that, but I found out later, he actually fucked her in our basement. There's a dent in the damn wall to prove it!"

"That's fucked up, Secret," David said.

"Well, hold on to your seat because I'm not finished!" Her voice became louder as she continued to talk. "The thing that hurt me the most about this whole ordeal, is that he left me and our children for this bitch. He even had the nerve to call her his soul mate."

David rubbed Secret's arm as she stopped to wipe her face again. He knew she needed to get this off her chest, so he was willing to suck it up and listen to her say Tarron's name over and over.

"To make matters worse, my affair with you didn't even work."

Several of the monitors began to beep and flash. The nurse's station was alerted when the signals went off. A middle aged nurse working the evening shift rushed into the room.

As the nurse walked over to the monitors, she eyed David with an accusatory glare. "Is everything okay Mrs. Jenkins?" she asked.

"I'm fine, Shelly," Secret replied.

Shelly walked to the monitors, pushed several buttons, and then made notes on different clipboards that hung on the sides of the machines. Shelly walked over to the bed and checked Secret's vital signs and recorded them on another clipboard. Just as she was about to leave the room, she watched as David wiped the beads of sweat from Secret's forehead. Her stance softened.

"Visiting hours are almost over, Mr. Jenkins."

Before David could correct her, she closed the door. David turned and looked at Secret with a smirk on his face.

"Where was I?" Secret asked, as David wiped her forehead again.

"You were having an unsuccessful affair," he reminded her.

"Oh, that's right. But even though I was doing dirt myself, I decided to write Tarron a letter from my heart, exposing my deepest emotions at his family reunion. I thought if he read it, he'd come to his senses, and we'd be able to put things back together. You know, for the sake of the children."

David gave Secret the same cold stare that he had given the young lady downstairs. "Do you still love him?"

"Not now." She lied for the sake of saving David's feelings. "Prior to me slitting my wrists, I still loved Tarron, and wanted to give our marriage another shot, but what did that bastard do. He chose a ho over a housewife."

David didn't comment, he just stared at Secret as tears began to fall for the third time.

"Now, to complicate matters further, at this point I don't know what I want. I'm so confused about my life."

"Oh yeah, well I think you really want to be with me, but just don't want to admit it," David said, with a little laugh.

"Now is not the time to be funny," Secret said, while rolling her eyes. "I just couldn't take it anymore, David. I just wanted to end it all. My life was spinning out of control, and I didn't have emergency brakes. But I really messed up when I tried to take my own life. My little attempted escape from reality has given Jay the ammunition to try to gain custody of my son. But I'll kill him before I let that happen. However, karma is a bitch, because now Tarron's little ho has left him for his brother." Secret displayed a huge smile.

David leaned back in the chair and took a deep breath. He knew she couldn't be serious about killing Jay. He took an even longer look at the woman he loved. She had never looked more beautiful than she did at that very moment. Her rich tan complexion and honey colored contacts mesmerized him. Psycho or not, he still loved her.

"I think I love you," he whispered.

Secret turned to look at David. "What did you just say?"

"I think..." he took another deep breath, "nothing."

Secret had heard every word very clearly, but she just knew that her little freak toy wasn't about to try and catch intimate feelings for her. *Damn, didn't he just hear me say that I cared about him? I don't think I ever used the word love.* She wasn't in any position to handle anymore drama in her life. Things were already hectic enough, and he wasn't about to make them more chaotic by expressing some bullshit love for her.

David appeared to be the entire package. He was rich, confident, very attractive, and a great sex partner. He would be perfect for a woman who needed a man, or even a husband, but Secret definitely didn't fit any of those categories right now. She was only interested in David because she was able to be a totally different woman around him without being judged. There were no hurdles to jump, no barriers to hide behind, and especially no rules to follow. Because she didn't love David, her heart, mind, and soul were not at risk. He was a distraction from all the chaos that was currently in her life.

David leaned in closer to her ear. "Secret, I won't just stand on the sidelines and watch that man keep hurting you."

"Don't worry yourself with Tarron and me. Everything between the two of us will work itself out in the end. It always has." Her tone became lighter, and her voice sounded smooth like silk. "What you should really worry about are all the different ways you can please me all over. That's your role in this drama, my little sex toy. The toy I can pull out of my bag whenever I need some sexual healing." Secret let out a little laugh and began humming the chorus to Marvin Gaye's, *Sexual Healing,* in a seductive manner.

David had heard enough. He thought to himself, *she really doesn't mean that. I know she loves me, and really wants to be with me.* He began to reflect on all the long conversations over nice dinners they'd shared, the long walks on the waterfront, and the times they'd made love for hours. He also decided the sneaking around was over. He wanted to air out their dirty laundry, even to his employees at VIAX.

At that moment, he thought about Nurse Shelly and what she'd said about visiting hours. He stood up in preparation to leave, when Secret grabbed his arm.

"I know I'm in the hospital, but will that stop you from satisfying me, baby? Why don't you put those magic fingers under the sheet and play in my valley for a second or two? I need some relief…please," she begged.

In spite of his annoyance, David smiled as he sat back down. He looked both ways, as if someone else was in the room, then slid his right hand under the sheets. His hand started at her knee and tickled its way up her inner thigh until he got to the juicy lips of her pussy. Luckily she wasn't wearing any panties. Using his index finger, he stroked long and hard until Secret closed her eyes and arched her back. He inserted his finger quickly. He could feel her tightening, as he continued to probe like a doctor performing a routine pap smear. David swirled his finger around the pool of her womanly juices, and decided that one finger wasn't enough. He slid in two more fingers, until Secret began to moan. His dick got hard as he watched her head rock back and forth. He clamped his three fingers firmly against her pelvic bone and held it tight.

"That's my good toy. Make me cum, baby. Make me cum," Secret moaned.

She was getting close to that peak that was desperately need-ed when the door opened, and Nurse Shelly came rushing in, car-rying a tray with her medication. David jumped, and tried to snatch his hand from beneath the cover before the nurse suspect-ed anything.

"Oh my, I'm so sorry Mr. and Mrs. Jenkins. But it's time for your medication. Besides, visiting hours were over five minutes ago." She purposely went in the bathroom, to give them one last private minute.

David looked at Secret and gave up a small smile. He slowly raised his fingers to his face and placed them in his mouth. David began to suck the juices off each finger, in hopes of keeping her in the mood.

"I love the way you taste. I can't wait until I have my tongue fully inside every inch of you," he whispered.

Secret didn't crack a smile. The moment was lost. She was mad as hell at being so close, and not reaching a climax. It had been a long time. Too long. The tingling was right at the tip. Secret rushed to take her medicine, in an attempt to rush every-one out the room, so she could finish what David had started.

David stopped at the door to get one last glimpse of Secret. "See you tomorrow," he called out.

"Yeah tomorrow," she responded, without enthusiasm.

David's facial expression quickly changed. He could hear the sarcasm in her voice. He knew she was pissed about not being able to cum, but he hoped that she didn't take it out on him.

The hospital corridor seemed deserted, and David could only hear his footsteps as he walked down the long hallway to the elevators. When he got downstairs, he headed for the exit. David went through the automatic doors with his head down. He had so many emotions running through his mind, as he made his way to the garage. *Somehow, I have to make her realize that it's me she really loves. I'm the only one who should have her. That motherfucker Tarron had his chance, and he blew it. I don't even know what she saw in his ass.*

When David got into his car, he sat for a while. He couldn't decide what to do or where to go, so he started driving around town to clear his head. Sitting at a red light, he looked at the dark sky and counted the stars. The light turned green, but he didn't move. Suddenly a broad smile spread across his face as an amazing idea began to take shape in his head. The car behind him started blowing its horn. He whipped his black 745i BMW around, making a u-turn, and sped off for the firm. *I'm going to make that nigga's life miserable,* he thought, as he raced down the open road.

✳   ✳   ✳

Tarron had been working in the company library for a couple of hours, when the sound of the elevator doors opening startled him. It was late, and he should've been alone at the office. The cleaning crew was not scheduled to begin until after midnight, and the security guard, Stanley, had just done his rounds. He thought about calling Stanley, just to be on the safe side, but decided to check things out himself. Looking in a few offices, he didn't notice anything out of the ordinary, but he continued to walk around the floor to investigate, and to stretch his stiffening body. When Tarron reached his office door, he found David searching through the files in his credenza.

"Are you looking for something in particular?" Tarron asked, suspiciously. He wondered what in the hell David was doing.

David jumped. "Tarron, you scared the shit out of me."

"What are you looking for?" Tarron asked again, in a firmer tone.

"I'm looking for some information about an account that I thought you might have," David replied, without cracking a smile.

"Which one?" Tarron folded his arms.

"That's okay It's late, don't worry about it. We'll talk later," David said, as he turned to leave. He brushed past Tarron, like no other explanation was necessary.

Tarron and David locked eyes as he exited the office. Tarron couldn't tell if he had been intentionally bumped as David left. *It was probably an accident, since I was standing in front of the door,* Tarron thought. He walked over to close the drawer that David had left open and paused. Several of the folders, which were out of place, were old accounts that David had given to him during his first year at the firm.

Tarron's attention was diverted when his computer chimed the familiar notice; YOU GOT MAIL. He walked over to his computer, and clicked the mouse to activate his mailbox. He was shocked when the message entitled: *Victoria Gone Wild* flashed on his screen. A part of him wanted to delete the e-mail, but in a crazy sort of way, he still had feelings for Victoria, which he couldn't seem to shake. Another click of the mouse, and his stomach dropped to the floor. Victoria's large B cups seemed to stretch across the screen in 3-D. Tarron wasn't used to receiving video clips via e-mail, but this one he had to see.

<Click>

Chapter 3

Tarron fell back into the chair, closing his eyes tightly. He desperately wanted to shut out Victoria's body movements on the screen, but he knew he had to look. His large manicured hands covered his face slightly. When he opened his eyes, Victoria was dancing provocatively to the beat of R. Kelly's hit, *Keep It On The Down-Low.* Tarron's pulse rate began to sky rocket as he noticed her wearing the sexy black laced bodysuit that he ordered from Tanga last Christmas.

Victoria began to twirl around with her arms stretched out to her sides, and her palms rotating up and down. Her firm breasts wiggled, as her upper torso glided to the beat of the music. He watched closely as she moved around the room, doing the exotic moves of a Hawaiian belly dancer. Every part of her body glistened from a thick coating of shimmery baby oil. Tarron eased to the edge of the chair in anticipation, as heat shot through his body. It traveled like fire through his entire body, but settled directly in his dick.

Victoria danced over to a leather chair and sat down. She seductively opened her legs to expose her freshly manicured vagina. *Damn, she probably did that shit on purpose. She knows I like a neat pussy,* Tarron thought, as his eyes watched her every move. Victoria slowly slid her right hand between her legs and started to tickle her wet lips with two of her fingers. She decided to make the movie even more exciting by lifting her left leg high in the air, and inserted the head of a large dildo inside her pussy. She used her other hand to lift one of her breasts and sucked her erect nipple softly.

Victoria's moans were so loud, Tarron quickly scrambled to turn the volume on his computer down. He scuffled with the speaker momentarily, unable to grasp the knob to control the volume. Nervousness took over as Victoria's moans grew louder. At that point, he didn't care how loud the video clip sounded. His erect dick began to firmly press against his pants, and the urge to set it free took control of his hands. He rubbed himself up and down before unfastening the top button of his jeans. The more Victoria pushed the dildo inside, the more excited he became. Tarron rapidly pulled his dick out and began to stroke it back and forth, as he watched Victoria please herself on the monitor. Victoria's moaning suddenly turned into yells as she reached her climax, and dug her long fingernails into the chair. Tarron had to look closely onto the screen, because it seemed as if the dildo had disappeared. Victoria had shoved the fake dick so far that it was barely noticeable.

Within seconds, Tarron's cum began squirting all over his desk and landed on a picture of Motherdear. Tarron sat back in exhaustion, as he watched Victoria dance around in her birthday suit and six inch stilettos. He grabbed a piece of tissue from inside his desk drawer to wipe the cum from the palm of his hand, and gently placed his shaft back into its home. When he looked at the monitor, Victoria's gyrating body passed in front of a mahogany framed full length mirror that was located beside her bed.

Suddenly, a familiar face flashed on the screen, causing Tarron to sit straight up in the chair. He hit the rewind button and paused the screen once he reached the designated spot. He blinked again, just to be sure his eyes were not playing tricks on him. His suspicions were confirmed. Jay's reflection was there in the mirror, holding the camera, with a wide sinister grin. As Tarron reached for the mouse, he could hear Jay smacking Victoria's ass.

Just before Tarron could slam his fist on the keyboard to end the porno clip, Jay shouted, "Wish you were here, bro."

Tarron's eyes turned into a fiery rage, and he lost it. The chrome pen holder on his desk was the first object to fly across the room. With a quick and powerful swipe of his arm, everything else on the desk smashed to the floor. He kicked his waste basket and it sailed into the air, raining papers all around the room. *I can't believe I was sitting here jerking off to that shit! That fucking bitch!* Tarron repeatedly stomped on the waste basket, crushing the smoky glass and wire mesh into splinters.

He stopped suddenly when he noticed David and the security guard standing in the door, both staring at him like he was crazy. Tarron lowered his leg slowly, and the sole of his shoe gently touched the thick brown carpet. The embarrassment on his face caused him to hold his head down, and he noticed that he hadn't buttoned his jeans. Tarron quickly buttoned his pants and began to smooth imaginary wrinkles from his clothes. No one said a word as he calmly walked to the window. David and the security guard surveyed the office, nodded to one another, then turned and walked away in different directions. Tarron watched his audience leave in the reflection of the window. Both of them had the same thought; *that motherfucker is going crazy.*

Tarron glanced around his office and realized it was time for him to leave. Losing control was not a part of the persona he had worked so hard to portray. After shutting down his computer, he reached into his office drawer for a another piece of tissue to wipe the visible cum off his desk. He grabbed a Post-It and wrote a note for the night maintenance crew.

To Whom It May Concern:
Don't touch anything! I'll clean it up when I return later today.

Thank you,
Tarron Jenkins

He secured the note to the door, making it clearly visible to anyone entering his office. Tarron grabbed his briefcase, and stopped to take another glance at the mess he had made, before he left the office. All he could do was shake his head.

*   *   *

The phone on David's desk rang. He reached over and grabbed the receiver, "David Jordan speaking."

"Mr. Jordan, this is Stanley at the front desk. You asked me to inform you the minute Mr. Jenkins left the building. Well, he's exiting the building as we speak," the security guard reported.

"Thanks, Stanley. Remember, this is between the two of us."

"Yes, sir."

David hung up the phone and walked down the hall to Tarron's office. He immediately began going through the files. *All this mess, he'll never even know that the files are missing until it's too late,* he thought. *What in the hell was he doing in here with his pants unbuttoned anyway.* David walked around Tarron's office like a chicken with its head cut off, so he could get out as quickly as possible. Even though he was the CEO, and dared anyone to question him, he still didn't want anyone to know what he was up to. David accidentally bumped Tarron's desk as he quickly walked pass, causing his pictures to fall over. As David picked up each frame, he glanced at the photos, hoping to see one of Secret. When he picked up the picture of Motherdear, his thumb landed in Tarron's thick cum. The slimly liquid instantly made David drop the frame. *What the fuck,* he thought, looking at his finger as the cleaning lady rolled her cart into Tarron's office.

David instantly walked over to his briefcase and started inserting files. She looked around the office, and then at David. He continued to stuff his briefcase.

"There's a note for you on the door," David said, without looking up.

The cleaning lady read the note and shook her head to acknowledge that she understood. She kept her eyes on him as she slowly backed her cart out the door. He hurried to catch her.

"No one needs to know that I was in here," David said, as he peeled off three one hundred dollar bills.

"That's quite alright, sir. I don't want your money. You can call me Bennett, because I ain't in it," the cleaning lady said.

He walked around the cart blocking her path. "Do you know who I am?" David asked.

"I think so," she replied.

"My name is David Jordan, CEO of this firm. I'm giving you this money as a tip for all your hard work and nothing else." He peeled off two more hundred dollar bills and placed the money firmly in her hand. "You'll hurt my feelings if you don't take this tip."

The cleaning lady hesitated for a second, and then nodded. David walked next to her until they reached the elevators. He pushed the down arrow, and watched as the cleaning lady continued her route. When she turned the corner, David yelled one last time.

"Remember, you didn't see me in there," he said, with a threatening tone.

Chapter 4

Fearing he would lose control again, Tarron worked from home over the next few days. He was pretty sure word had gotten around the office about his little episode. Stanley was known to hang around when his shift was over, and gossiped like a bitch with the other security guards. He wasn't in the mood to deal with the drama, so he informed his secretary, Shanice, to forward any important documents to his house.

Tarron was on a conference call with an overseas client, when the sound of, YOU GOT MAIL chimed in.

"This must be your document coming through now, Miguel," Tarron said.

"I hope so, because I've resent it three times," Miguel responded, sounding frustrated.

When Tarron clicked on the little envelope at the bottom of his screen, the bold black letters entitled, **MY PUSSY NEEDS A NEW HOME,** caught his attention. He shook his head as he immediately recognized who the sender was. Victoria had been sending him e-mails everyday, and always managed to use the word pussy in the title. *This crazy bitch needs to get a life, and leave me the hell alone,* Tarron thought, as he clicked on the message. Let's see what bullshit she has to say today.

More Secrets More Lies

My Dearest Tarron,

I'm so sorry that I hurt you, but you have to believe me when I say it was never my intention. I wish I could go back in time and do everything differently, especially the way we had sex. I do have an idea of what it would be like if we were able to press restart. I've been e-mailing you for days, because I have something very important to tell you... It's over between me and your brother, so now we can be together again. Open my e-mail entitled: POWER OF THE PUSSY, it should explain everything to you in more detail.

"Tarron, did you receive the files?" his client asked.

"No, Miguel. Please send them to me again. I'll check it out and call you tomorrow," he replied.

Miguel made a heavy sigh in the phone. "Alright, but I want to move on this as soon as possible."

"Not a problem. I'll talk with you soon," Tarron said, hanging up the phone before Miguel could respond.

He knew it was wrong to rush his client off the phone, but he had to find the e-mail from Victoria. Tarron felt stupid for falling for her games again, but the curiosity was killing him. He silently cursed himself for needing to see it. Tarron could feel his temperature starting to rise as he scrolled down the subjects in his inbox. Let's see...*Best Pussy in Town, Pussy Madness, Juicy Pussy*. Finally, the one he was looking for.

<Click>

Tarron,
If you're reading this, then maybe you still have love for me somewhere deep inside your heart. I knew Jay wasn't the man for me, and it was you who I've loved all along. Now, if we could go back in time and do things differently, picture a night of passion like this:

You walk into my house and a romantic atmosphere is created by the soft glow of candlelight. You continue into the dining room, and the table is filled with all your favorite foods. You hear my voice coming from the kitchen, telling you to have a seat and relax yourself. A shot of Patron Tequila is waiting for you as you loosen your tie and undo the top buttons of your shirt.

As I enter the room, carrying a tray of hors d'oeuvres, you become mesmerized as you stare at me with lustful eyes. I walk up to you and the scent of my vanilla body lotion drives you insane. Your dick immediately becomes hard and stands at attention, as you notice that I'm completely naked with a lady bug vibrator attached to my clitoris. I know you remember the little black and red sex toy we bought from the Treasure Palace. In case you forgot, it's the one that I step into and wear like thongs, but has little ticklers that vibrate against my clit. Damn, I know you miss what we had. Just face it, Tarron, I'm the only woman who can satisfy you. Lust

and desire quickly replace any thoughts of
food as you lift me up and shove all the
dishes on the floor. You throw me on the
table and decide to go straight to dessert.
I feel your tongue rolling around my inner
thighs, and you roughly kiss your way
toward my erect nipples.

   I tell you that I have a surprise,
and lead you into the bedroom, which surprisingly is empty except for a chair, and
a large white fur rug. You slowly take a
seat and I whisper, "I'll be right back,"
as I disappear into the darkness. Your
heart starts to race as you wonder what
freaky things I have in store. Suddenly you
hear Maxwell's sexy voice blasting from the
loud speakers. You begin to rub your hands
together and smile, as the anticipation
continues to build. Just as you're about to
call my name, you see a small remote with
one button on the chair. When your curiosity has peaked, you press the magic target.
You become shocked as the floor to ceiling
black curtains automatically open, and a
glass wall is revealed. Wow… that's some
James Bond shit.

   On the other side, you see me bent
over, holding my ankles. I watch as the
glass becomes fogged from your heavy
breathing. Thoughts of you ramming your
big, thick dick into my dripping pussy
becomes too much for you, as you begin
banging on the glass. I turn around to give

```
you one final look, when suddenly, my baby
walks out with his dick swinging, your
brother, Jay...
```

"What the fuck!" Tarron shouted, as he quickly hit the delete button, and almost dropped his laptop.

Sweat poured from his face as he rubbed his temples in anger. *Why does she keep doing this shit to me?* Tarron thought. Victoria was driving him crazy, and he needed someone to talk to before he went to the closet for his nine millimeter. That would surely get rid of her. He reached for his cell phone and dialed Pretty Boy Ray. They had been friends since elementary school, and Ray always knew how to make him feel better. As he dialed the number, he quickly thought back to their childhood. Ray had been a womanizer his entire life, and that's how he even got his nickname. Tarron quickly remembered being a lookout for him in the ninth grade while he had sex with two girls in the boy's locker room. Tarron had actually experienced his first threesome because of Ray, so he was very grateful for their friendship.

"Yeah!" Ray said, sounding impatient when he answered

"What's up, man? It sounds like you're busy."

"What's up, Tarron? Can I call you back? I'm on the phone with Dan Snyder. We're trying to work out a deal, so The Lion's Den can hold a Redskin's fan appreciation party."

"Damn, Ray, you're moving up in the world, anytime you're talking to the owner of the Skins. Call me back so I can get all the details."

Tarron smiled as he hung up the phone. Ray really had come a long way since opening the club, and Tarron was glad that he was partly responsible for Ray's success. He could remember when Ray used to jump from one labor job to the next, but now things had changed. They were like brothers, and shared a special bond. A bond that he and his real brother never seemed to acquire.

Tarron decided to call Kurt, who always answered on the first ring.

"Slim, why does your pressed ass pick up the phone so fast?" Tarron said laughing, as Kurt answered quickly.

"Because, it might be one of my bitches," Kurt responded.

"Oh well, I don't fit that category. Man, I still can't believe your ass got a divorce after only being married for eight months."

"Yeah, I know, but that shit just wasn't for me. What's up?"

"Actually, I need to come holla at you for a second. Are you at the Rhode Island Avenue store today?"

"Yep, are you coming through?"

"Yeah... I got a lot of shit on my mind right now. I'll be over there in a few."

Tarron thought about his dilemma as he hung up the phone. Although Kurt was another one of his good friends, talking to him wasn't like kicking it with Ray. Sometimes Kurt could be a little too judgmental, which pissed Tarron off, but he had to talk to someone.

Tarron drove down 16th street, and decided to stop at Ben's Chili Bowl. It had been hours since his last meal, and a chili-dog sounded really good at the moment. While Tarron waited for his order, memories rushed in like a flood. He and Secret had shared many of their dates at Ben's. This most significant D.C. landmark was even where Tarron got down on one knee and asked Secret to marry him. As cheesy as that was, Secret never complained about not having an over extravagant engagement. That was one of the reasons he had fallen in love with her in the first place. She always appreciated what he did for her, no matter what the price tag was. At that moment, Tarron realized that he was on an emotional roller coaster, because part of him wanted his family back, and the other part still wanted to fuck Victoria.

His food was still hot when he walked through the doors of Kurt's clothing store. "I know you brought something for me too!" Kurt yelled, when he smelled the delicious aroma.

"You know I did. If I hadn't, you'd just stick your nasty ass hands in my food," Tarron responded.

The guys walked through the back room and down the steps to Kurt's office. The small space was overcrowded with several video monitors. Kurt was so paranoid, that his shop was set up like a Las Vegas casino, with him acting as the eyes in the sky. The only thing missing was a pit boss.

"Man, what's up? I don't think I've seen or talked to you since all that drama went down at your family reunion," Kurt said, scooping up a large spoonful of chili.

"You're right." He turned to Tarron and gave him a light punch on the arm.

"Are you holding up, or holding on?"

"What's the difference?" Tarron asked.

"Well, Tarron, if you're holding on, then you must be going crazy. People that hold on, keep having thoughts of, *what if.* What if I did this? What if I did that? What if I didn't do this or that? It's hard for a person living like that to get through the day."

"Okay, Kurt. What about the holding up person?" Tarron asked, while stuffing some chili into his mouth.

"The holding up person has all the drama; the hurt, the pain, and everything else, hanging up like a wall behind them. It's there as a warning not to do it again, but it doesn't stop them from living."

"Kurt, you're on some other shit. Holding up, holding on, what in the hell are you talking about? That's why the boys hate your ass."

"You guys hate me, because I'm the voice of sanity. I'm the only one living in the real world. I understand that for every action, there must be a reaction."

"Anyway, Kurt, I came here to talk because Victoria is driving me crazy. She keeps sending me e-mails about us getting back together, but then she'll torture me by talking about fucking Jay.

She even sent a video clip of them in the act."

"You're bullshitting. Come sit at my desk and log on into your e-mail. I need to see this shit." He laughed a wild and crazy laugh. "I'm serious as hell. How am I gonna help you if I don't see the evidence!"

"Hell no!" Tarron responded.

"See! Speaking like a man still holding on. If you were holding up, you would've called a special poker night, and put that shit on the big screen."

"Victoria is different!" Tarron shouted.

"What? No, she's not. That homewrecker broke up your marriage, and left you for your criminal-ass brother. Nigga, are you still pussy whipped or something?"

"Hell no!" Tarron said, trying to display a convincing smile. *Shit, at least I hope not,* he thought. "Yeah, you're right. Come on, let's watch."

Tarron and Kurt sat in front of the computer, watching the video clips. They even read all the letters. The e-mails were really getting to Tarron, but he remained strong in front of his friend. He didn't want to admit that he really was holding on.

"That is one sick bitch. It may not feel like it now, but you're lucky to be rid of her," Kurt said.

"That's the problem. I'm not rid of her. She's hounding me almost everyday!" Tarron shouted, as he punched the wall.

"Watch it, man! Don't put a hole in my wall. My office may not be as big as your corporate shindig at VIAX, but it's all I've got," Kurt responded.

The sound of Tarron's cell phone ringing interrupted the porno session. He looked at the caller ID, and RAY popped up on the screen.

"What up, Slim?"

"I got the deal. The Lion's Den is going to be the official host of the first fan appreciation party for the Washington Redskins!"

"That's good news," Tarron replied.

36

"What good news?" Kurt asked.

"Ray just closed on the deal to host the Skin's party."

"Where are you, Tarron? Who's in the background?" Ray asked.

"I'm with Kurt at his shop."

"Oh, tell him I said what's up!" Before Tarron could relay the message, Ray kept talking. "Tarron, when you get some free time, I need your input on the proposal that I've been working on for opening two more clubs in New York and Atlanta."

"Sure, I have some free time now. I can come to the club if you want," Tarron said, looking at his watch.

"Cool, I'll be in the office when you get here."

Tarron closed his phone and gave Kurt some dap as he headed out the door. He smiled when Kurt had to get the last word.

"Keep on holding up."

Tarron had to admit he was feeling better, like maybe survival was possible.

Chapter 5

Pretty Boy Ray had just finished fixing two victory drinks, when Tarron pushed open the office door. He raised his glass as he thought about how the club was exceeding expectations.

"Tarron, let's have a toast to the future," Ray boasted, as he held up both glasses.

"Ray, I think you found your niche, that thing you were meant to do," Tarron responded. He grabbed hold of the glass tightly, like he desperately needed the drink. He fell back onto the plush leather sofa while Pretty Boy Ray jetted to get some papers from his desk. Tarron sipped his drink, while listening to Ray's ideas about the club's expansion and the Redskins' party.

"Ray, if we can come up with an award winning presentation, VIAX could be persuaded to provide the funding for your next venture."

He was interrupted by a knock on the door. Ray opened it, and in walked a beautiful woman carrying a huge folding table and pulling a small rolling case.

"You didn't forget our appointment, did you, Mr. Ray?" she asked.

"I can't lie. I did forget, but it's cool," Ray answered.

"Should we reschedule for another day next week?" she asked, in a succulent voice.

Ray thought for a second, then turned to her and said, "How about my associate take my session, while I handle some last minute details? Reschedule me for the same time next week."

"Your associate?" she said, with a hint of sarcasm.

"My bad, I'm so rude. Tarron, this is Monica, my massage therapist. Monica, this is my best friend, Tarron. He's the General Manager of The Lion's Den."

Tarron got up and walked over with his hand extended. A slight chill rushed up his arm as her soft hand touched his.

"Nice to meet you, Monica," he said.

"Nice to meet you, too."

"Tarron, there are some clean towels in the bathroom cabinet, and my robe is on the back of the door. If you get cold, or if you're shy, you can use it. I've got to run, so hit me on my cell if you're leaving once she's done. Monica, put it on my tab," Ray said, as he walked to the door. "Don't worry, Tarron, we'll discuss that presentation later."

Stretching his shoulders in an upward position, Tarron rushed into the bathroom. The moment he entered, he snatched his shirt over his head without even shutting the door tightly. The door slowly crept open as he finished undressing. Monica was busy setting up her table and arranging a variety of oils and lotions, when she looked up and caught a glimpse of Tarron's naked body in the bathroom mirror. His mocha colored skin and muscular body reminded her of a twenty year old. As Tarron looked in the mirror, he noticed Monica watching his every move. Quickly, he wrapped the towel around his waist and held his head up. Monica smiled as she finished her preparations.

Tarron stuck his chest out as he exited the bathroom, knowing that she was watching. He went straight to the table and removed the towel taking a seat on the edge of the table.

Monica smiled seductively. "You're in great shape. I don't see very many abs like yours. Let's begin with your back. Just relax. Lie face down."

His muscles tightened when the warm drops of massage oil touched his skin. Her hands were very strong. He moaned slightly as the tension began to recede from his body. The moaning turned to growling sounds of sheer pleasure, as Monica dug the heels of her hands into his lower back. She climbed up and straddled Tarron in order to gain more leverage. She needed to press harder, so that the remaining stress she felt in his muscles could be released. He could feel himself begin to relax. Her hands were like magic as she touched all the tense areas. It was as if she'd made all his troubles disappear. As Monica leaned forward to rub his back, her inner thighs massaged Tarron's hips. Instantly, his 'ole boy' jumped to attention.

For every action, there really is a reaction, he thought. Tarron tried to reposition his pelvic area now that his penis was awakened from its nap. Monica laughed.

"I guess you're used to guys getting aroused when you sit on their back, rubbing them the right way?" Tarron questioned.

"I wouldn't say that I'm used to it, but it does happen from time to time," she responded.

"Not to be rude. What else happens from time to time?"

"Well, nothing happens normally."

Tarron struggled to lift his head hoping to make eye contact.

"What does nothing normally mean?" He slipped his hand onto Monica's thigh, just to see her reaction.

"I've never found myself attracted to any of my clients in the past. So nothing has ever happened. But I do find that I'm attracted to you, and my body is on pins and needles right now." Monica's cheeks began to turn red.

"Are pins and needles a good thing?" Tarron asked. She remained silent.

Monica climbed to the floor and positioned herself beside his left leg. She pushed the towel up beneath his buttocks. Feeling the tension in his upper thighs, she began to massage them. Monica let out a small giggle as his toes began to curl.

"You're not going to answer my question?" Tarron moaned, struggling to look back at her again.

"Not necessary. Your session is almost over. Once I do the other leg, we'll be finished."

She walked over to the other side and massaged the right leg. Monica bent over and slowly slid her tongue up the middle of his back. Tarron closed his eyes, anticipating what was going to happen next. When she finished, she smacked him on his butt and walked to the bathroom to wash the oil from her hands. He was disappointed. *Why would she start something and not finish the job,* he thought. Tarron rolled over and hopped off the table. As his towel dropped to the floor, Monica stepped from the bathroom and stared hungrily at his body and erect dick.

"Is this your idea of a seduction tactic?" she asked.

"This is no seduction tactic. The little towel won't fit."

Tarron was about to pick up the towel when the door opened, and in walked Pretty Boy Ray, several of the bartenders and two dancers. All he could do was cover his penis with his hands. He was slightly annoyed and embarrassed.

"What's going on, brother?" Ray asked.

"Where do we put the dollars? I'm next! I'll buy that for a dollar," one of the dancers shouted, reaching into her Fendi handbag.

Tarron kept a little grin on his face as he bent over and grabbed the towel. He wrapped the towel around his hips and walked to the bathroom. His smile grew larger as he heard whistling and cat calls from the women watching his exposed muscular ass walking away.

Monica, on the other hand, was really embarrassed. At the intrusion, she had jumped back into the bathroom and locked the door. Tarron couldn't get in. He knocked until she finally opened the door and walked into the office.

"Oh, we're truly sorry. Did we interrupt something?" Ray

asked smiling.

"No you didn't," Monica said, in a harsh tone. She packed her things as the others in the room watched. On her way out, she heard someone say, "I need to learn how to massage a man the way she does." When Tarron came out the bathroom, all the women gave him a standing ovation. He played along and took a little bow.

*   *   *

David sat in his office reviewing the files he had removed from Tarron's credenza. He was really impressed with Tarron's work performance, and thought he was an excellent investor. He brought plenty of money into the company, and clients were in awe over him. He possessed an uncanny ability for choosing the right portfolios for each client, a real gift, one that could never be acquired solely from his Ivy League education.

As David perused the files, he decided that billing fraud would be the best way to frame Tarron. In the world of investment, David knew that everything revolved around the money. Clients never remember all the millions you might have made them in the past, when they find out they're being robbed of pennies. The only problem with David's plan was that this type of crime required time. And time was something he really didn't have. He had to take Tarron down before he and Secret could rekindle their fire, but he needed to be very creative; and being careful was a must.

David's smile preceded a devilish laugh. He was enjoying himself so much that his dick got hard. He reached for the phone and called the hospital to surprise Secret. He thought that maybe a little phone sex would help relieve the ache in his groin.

"Shit," he uttered. The line was busy. He quickly redialed the number like an overly jealous boyfriend.

43

His taste buds came alive when he heard Secret's sweet voice say, "Hello."

"I really needed to hear your voice," David said.

"Sometimes the littlest things in life can make a person's day, huh?" she replied.

"A little dirty talk would make my week right now."

"Maybe - maybe not," she said, with a laugh.

"You better stop playing, Secret. Maybe - maybe not my ass. I'm so hard, my balls ache."

"Wow, now that was really raw," Secret said.

David sat up in his chair. "I remember many occasions when you begged me to be raw. We would be in the middle of a love session and you would yell, 'Talk dirty to me, daddy, louder papi, or yes my mandigo!' David laughed loudly.

"Yes Mandigo? I don't think so. You must have me mixed up with one of those stink ass white women that fuck successful black men to ease their conscious of racism."

"I threw that last one in just to make sure you were paying attention to the conversation and not watching television," he responded, with another loud laugh. "Besides, I know you like to talk dirty. It makes you feel young again. Doesn't it? See, with Tarron, you had to be the happy housewife. You know…walking the straight and narrow." He grinned. "With me, I want you to be freaky…real freaky.

Damn, he's right, she thought. *I can be as freaky as I want to with David.* "I bet you only called me because your horny ass has a pitched tent, and you wanted to jerk off to the sound of my voice, huh?"

"You know me well," he replied.

"Too bad, my nurse is here to change my IV," Secret quickly replied.

"That's okay. I need to pack up my notes for this big case. I have major plans for this client. If he's not careful, he may lose everything."

44

"Don't remind me about losing everything. Tomorrow is my son's custody hearing. I have to call his father to make sure he's ready. Thanks for the call."

The phone went dead. David held the phone out and thought, *shit, that's cold.*

More Secrets, More Lies

Chapter 6

Parking near the court building was next to impossible. Tarron circled several blocks, and passed three public garages with a *full* sign posted out front. He had fifteen minutes remaining to get to the Family Court on Indiana Avenue, before worrying about a bench warrant being placed on his record. D.C judges were known for no-nonsense when it came to children. The city had relocated various divisions of the court into several different buildings in an effort to reduce the traffic problems outside, and increase the safety of employees and citizens inside. Tarron didn't think they had achieved the desired outside effect. Out of his peripheral vision he thought he saw Victoria and Jay coming off the Judiciary Square metro station elevators.

"I hope those motherfuckas get run over!" Tarron said, gripping the steering wheel. Tarron looked at his watch, and realized he only had ten minutes to find a parking space. "Shit, why didn't I take the subway?"

His phone vibrated. When he looked down at the number, which he didn't recognize, he almost ran into the back of a cab that had pulled over to pick up a fare. Tarron was still trying to get to his phone when a police car pulled into the lane behind him. The new cell phone law was strictly enforced, so he decided not to answer without his hands free device. Seconds later it vibrated again, but he ignored it. He didn't think the call was worth the hundred dollar fine, or the precious minutes he would lose being pulled over. Finally, he spotted a car moving from a parking space near 4th and H Street. Once he parked, he returned the call to the unfamiliar number.

"Boy, where the hell are you?" Motherdear shouted.

"Whose phone number is this?" Tarron asked.

"It's my new one. You know how your children are. Tika was playing with the old one, and the damn thing fell in the toilet. Forget that, where are you?"

"I had a little trouble finding a parking space. I'm only a couple of blocks from the courthouse. Where are you?" Tarron asked.

"I'm standing in front of the court building with the kids and your lawyer. You need to hurry, because I think I saw Jay and that no good slut going through the glass doors when we got out the cab."

"Yeah, I saw them, too. I'll be there in a minute." Tarron said, closing the phone. He wished he didn't even have to think about Victoria. And he definitely wasn't prepared to see her.

As he approached, his five year old daughter, Tika, ran into his arms. His son, Terrance, was too cool for that type of greeting, and settled for a nod of the head. I guess eight year olds didn't do that type of thing. Tarron hugged Motherdear and shook his lawyer's hand, Steven James. Tarron and Steven attended undergraduate school together, and had remained friends even when they started pursuing different careers. Fortunately for Tarron, Steven went on to law school.

"What's up, Steven? I brought the documents you asked for. Secret is pretty organized with all the family records, so everything should be there. All of Terrance's school and health records are there too," Tarron said.

"Good, I'll make copies and return the originals. Remember, this is only an informal meeting with the judge today. Your brother hasn't officially declared the name of his attorney to the court, so I don't know who we'll be up against. Furthermore, I've never litigated before this judge. I want you to understand, this will not be an easy case. Today we'll introduce some facts to the judge, clarify any questions he has, and receive a court date. He may also give some interim instructions."

"Such as…?"

"He may assign temporary custody for Terrance," Steve said quietly. He directed Tarron and his family toward Judge Willis' courtroom on the second floor.

Tika was in Tarron's arms, talking as if she hadn't seen him in years. As the group turned the corner, they saw Jay standing outside the women's restroom holding a purse. *I suppose he's waiting for that bitch,* Tarron thought. *She got his ass trained.*

The brothers stared at each other with intense animosity. Motherdear waved the others on ahead while she stopped to speak with Jay.

"Son, why are you doing this? You know you're in no position to be that boy's father. I'm so disappointed in you. How could you take up with that little slut, and put your brother and his children through all of this mess?"

"Sweet Motherdear, are you referring to me as a little slut?" Victoria asked, appearing out of nowhere.

Jay recognized the warning signs as Motherdear opened and closed her hands, never taking her eyes off Victoria. He quickly stepped between them.

Motherdear looked over Jay's shoulder and whispered, "Victoria, remember this as the time my son saved you. You have found a way to mess with both of my boys. Trust me child, another day will present itself, and nobody will be able to stop me from giving you the ass whipping you deserve." She looked at Victoria and shook her head." Your breast are about to fall out of that shirt. Didn't your mother teach you how to dress like a lady?"

"Out of respect for my elders, I won't even answer that. The only thing I will say is you're right, my sweet Motherdear, the time will come. Only when it does, I don't think you'll want to whip the ass of your daughter-in-law, the mother of your future grandchildren, and the love of your baby boy's life," Victoria said, stroking Jay's face.

Before Motherdear could say anything, the bailiff from Judge Willis' courtroom called for all persons in the informal hearing of Terrance Jenkins to enter. Jay grabbed Victoria's arm and quickly pulled her away. He didn't want to cause a scene, and risk the opportunity to gain custody of Terrance. Victoria never even glanced at Tarron while they were in the hallway. It wasn't until Tarron was seated at the table with his attorney, that he actually made eye contact with her. There was no warmth in the look that passed between them either.

Tarron wrestled with so many emotions---his internal battle with lust, the deep hatred he felt because of her betrayal, and the threat to his son. He thought, *I usually concentrate on the tiny features that make Victoria beautiful. Everybody can admire the total package, but the little things brought out my smile: The way she used concealer to hide the birthmark on her left cheek, whether her eyes were in seductive play, or tough negotiating mode, by the arch in her eyebrows that she drew on with her eyeliner pencil. But today I can't find any beauty in her. She's just evil and hateful...but why? Why does she keep sending me e-mails like she still loves me, and now she's acting as if I don't even exist?*

The Judge cleared his throat, "Bailiff, before we begin, please take the children to the outer room with one of the clerks. I'll also need everyone to identify themselves when they stand to speak. I will now hear opening remarks in the custody case of Terrance Jenkins."

Victoria jumped up proudly. "Good morning, Judge Willis. My name is Victoria Smiles, and I'll be speaking on behalf of Jay Jenkins while he is seeking appropriate legal representation." Victoria walked around the table and continued speaking. "Mr. Jenkins is the biological father of Terrance Jenkins and is seeking full custody of his son from his brother, Tarron Jenkins and the child's mother, Secret Jenkins." Victoria turned to look Tarron directly in his face. She gave him a slight wave with her hand.

"Ms. Smiles, I must be missing something. Why does Mr. Jenkins need to come to court to get custody of his son if he is the biological father?" Judge Willis asked.

"Well, Jayson Jenkins is not on record as the child's father. The mother never told him that he was the biological father. In fact, she allowed the brother, Tarron Jenkins, to believe he was the father of the child. She lied to both brothers, which is what brings us before you today."

"Mr. Tarron Jenkins, is this correct?" the Judge asked.

"Not exactly, Your Honor..." Steven interjected, "Your Honor, my name is Steven James, and I'll be representing Mr. Tarron Jenkins for this case. May I continue?"

"Yes, Mr. James."

"Your Honor, even though those things happened, it was not quite the way Ms. Smiles alleges. Initially, Mrs. Jenkins didn't know that Jayson Jenkins was my client's brother. Nor did she know that my client wasn't the biological father."

"Umm... interesting. Thank you, Mr. James. Okay Ms. Smiles, you may continue."

Victoria rolled her eyes slightly before continuing. "It wasn't until recently that Jay Jenkins discovered the truth. His son had a horrific accident, due to the negligence of Tarron and his wife." She looked in Tarron's direction with a slight grin. "The boy nearly died, and needed an emergency blood transfusion to save his life. Jay Jenkins was the only family member who could give this transfusion, and this is how everyone learned the truth. After all of this was revealed, the mother attempted suicide. The children had to witness their mother being rushed to the hospital. The list goes on, but I think I've said enough for now."

"You sure as hell have," Motherdear mumbled.

Tarron whispered in his lawyer's ear. Steven stood and shouted, "I object!"

"On what basis?" Judge Willis asked.

"Sir, Ms. Smiles may have ulterior motives in this case because she is, or has been, intimately involved with both brothers. In fact, she was instrumental in the marital break-up between Mr. and Mrs. Jenkins."

"Is this true, Ms. Smiles?"

"Well, there was a time I was romantically involved with Tarron Jenkins, and it is true I am currently in a relationship with Jay Jenkins..."

The Judge leaned forward and spoke with authority. "Wouldn't you consider that a conflict of interest?"

"Maybe. But I'm required to answer your questions honestly, no matter which side of the court I'm sitting on. Besides, I'm only here because Jay Jenkins asked me to speak for him. He didn't want to delay these proceedings because he hasn't found legal representation just yet."

"I'll let Ms. Smiles continue to speak, Mr. James," Judge Willis said.

"But Your Honor," Steven replied.

"This is not a trial, Mr. James. I just need to hear the facts in this case. Please sit down."

Steven sat down next to Tarron. "Don't worry, we'll deal with this later if we have to." he said, writing on his yellow legal pad. Tarron smiled and shook his head. He turned to Motherdear and gave a small wink which said, "It'll be all right."

"May I continue?" Victoria asked, in an irritated manner.

"Yes, go ahead, Ms. Smiles."

Tarron watched Victoria's every move as she laid out the details of his brother's claims. He stole a quick glance at Jay, noticing that he was also watching Victoria in the same way. As Victoria bent over to pick-up a sticky note that fell from her clipboard, her red panties were exposed from the tight mini-skirt she wore. Tarron knew he had to concentrate on being a 'holding up' brother.

Victoria concluded by saying, "Now that Jay has a steady job and a nice place to reside, I believe he deserves the right to raise his son. That's all, and I thank you for allowing me to speak."

"Where is Mr. Jay Jenkins residing and employed?"

"He lives at 9910 Connecticut Avenue, N.W., and works at Jackson and Shaw Law Firm," Victoria responded.

Tarron immediately recognized the address, it was Victoria's condo.

"What does he do at Jackson and Shaw?" Judge Willis asked.

"He's one of the leading package coordinator's at the firm," *she lied.*

Tarron let out a sarcastic laugh, then looked over at Jay with an expression that said, "What the hell is wrong with you? You lying ass bastard." He used his fingers to form a L-shape that was the international symbol for LOSER.

Jay held up his middle finger, and his lips mouthed a nasty, fuck you.

Judge Willis made a notation on his pad. "May I ask what a package coordinator is?"

"Umm…the mail boy," Victoria responded quickly.

"Oh, that's what it is. Thank you, Ms. Smiles," the Judge said, sarcastically. "Your turn, Mr. James."

Tarron's lawyer took a sip of water from a glass on the small table next to his chair. He stood slowly, fixed his tie, and began his opening remarks. "Tarron and Secret Jenkins petition the

Court to retain full custody of their child, Terrance Jenkins. While the circumstances of his birth are somewhat confusing and unfortunate, he has known only love and stability his entire life. His parents are prepared to provide the Court with records from birth to date, that will show how Terrance has been raised. He only knows Jayson Jenkins as his uncle. To change the dynamics of the relationship with his father and uncle would do irreparable harm to the child. We can show that there was not an intentional attempt by Mrs. Jenkins to deceive either man. Tarron Jenkins understands and accepts this fact."

"Where is Mrs. Jenkins?" Judge Willis asked.

"She's in the hospital at the present moment."

"Will she be able to appear at the formal hearing?"

"Yes, Your Honor. She will be released from the hospital in a few days."

Tarron glanced around the courtroom to see who was witnessing his family falling apart. There were quite a few people sitting in the room, but one person stood out. A man sitting in the last row wearing sunglasses and a baseball cap immediately caught his attention. Something about him seemed very familiar. Tarron decided to return his attention back to the proceedings. As he looked back seconds later, Tarron noticed the courtroom doors swinging back and forth. The familiar man had disappeared.

Out of the blue, an unknown female bailiff walked towards the front of the courtroom, carrying a yellow envelope. Tarron watched as she took a seat behind Jay and Victoria. He studied as the bailiff handed the envelope to Jay. His brother looked puzzled as he studied the contents.

Within seconds, he passed the document to Victoria. A huge smile spread across her face and she quickly wrote Jay a note.

Where did you get this?

Jay shrugged his shoulders. He took the pen and wrote back.

The bailiff just brought it to me. What does this mean?

Victoria grabbed the pen.

We have the ace card now. This information will not only ensure that we get Terrance, but it will destroy Tarron.

What the hell is going on? It has to be something good, Tarron thought.

"Mr. James, where is Terrance Jenkins currently residing, and who has custody of the child?" the Judge asked.

"Terrance Jenkins and his sister are staying with their grandmother, Mrs. Marchelle Jenkins. Mrs. Jenkins has moved into the family home of Mr. and Mrs. Tarron Jenkins until their mother comes home. The children are living in the same home where they have resided their entire life," Steven remarked.

"Well, this case will be continued. My clerk will schedule your next court date, and all parties will return with appropriate legal counsel. I'm going to grant temporary custody of Terrance to the grandmother, Mrs. Marchelle Jenkins. Until the next hearing, Jayson Jenkins will be allowed to visit his son if he chooses to do so."

Even though Motherdear smiled as she looked at him, Jay knew showing up at his brother's house would not be wise. The Judge struck the desk with his gavel.

The clerk moved to the Judge's bench to confer with him regarding his calendar. When that business was complete, the clerk called out, "All rise." The entire courtroom stood as the Judge rose and left the courtroom through the door leading to his chambers. Just before the Judge exited the courtroom, the bailiff passed him a note that Victoria had given him when no one was looking.

Steven and Victoria organized their paperwork. After they received the court date, everyone headed out of the courtroom. The two women filed out last.

Motherdear stopped Victoria by placing a hand on her shoulder and spoke defiantly, "Victoria, do you realize all of this is your fault? I won't let you get away with messing with my boys. Your ass better step lightly, cause you on dangerous territory."

Victoria experienced a sensation that she had only heard about---real fear. A chill zipped through her body, and her face became very pale. She tried not to show how much Motherdear had frightened her.

"Old woman, take your hands off me. I'm not bothered by your threats. You're through controlling Jay. That power belongs to me now," she smirked.

When Victoria looked at Motherdear, she knew she had gone too far. Plus, the look Motherdear gave her confirmed it all. With squinted eyes, and small slits in her forehead, a vein was seen throbbing in Motherdear's temple. Victoria felt pain shoot from her shoulder all the way down to her waist as Motherdear applied pressure by tightening her fingers. Tears formed in Victoria's eyes from the pain.

"Hussy, you better realize who you're dealing with," Motherdear said, pushing Victoria aside as she made her way to the door.

You old ass prune. I'll find a way to get you back too, Victoria thought, as she rubbed her shoulder.

In the hall outside the courtroom, the hostility between the brothers threatened to erupt into violence, as well. At one of Jay's taunts, Tarron grabbed him by the lapels of his suit, and pressed Jay's body against the wall. His grip tightened until he recognized the suit as one of his own that he'd left at Victoria's condo. At that moment, Tika ran to her father's side and hugged his leg. Surprisingly, Terrance decided to jump in between Jay and Tarron to stop the commotion.

"Why are you fighting? Please stop," he pleaded.

Motherdear walked out the courtroom and commanded Tarron to release Jay. She lifted Tika into her arms and began to comfort her. Regaining control of his temper, Tarron roughly released his grip on Jay's clothing. Jay stared coldly at Tarron before moving to check on Victoria, who was still rubbing her shoulder.

Tarron looked at Terrance and lowered himself in order to make eye contact. He hugged him tightly. At first, Terrance resisted, but finally returned Tarron's strong embrace.

"It'll be alright, son, trust me. I love you so much. You know that, don't you?" Tarron's voice trembled.

"Yeah, I love you too, Daddy," Terrance said, through his tears.

Jay looked back when he heard Terrance's reply. He could only watch as they continued to embrace. His eyes shifted to see Motherdear comforting Tika. Finally, he looked at Victoria who was looking through her purse for an aspirin. *Is she worth all this? I never meant to hurt the kids, or my mother.*

When she saw the defeated look on Jay's face, Victoria reached for his hand and motioned with her head toward the yellow envelope in her briefcase.

"It's not over yet, baby. In fact, it's just the beginning," she said, with a vindictive laugh. Her eyes narrowed to a squint, and fixed in the direction of the group still huddled in the hall.

Chapter 7

Birds chirped outside Secret's window as she finished packing her bags. Tarron was late, but since the hospital computers were down, Secret hadn't been discharged.

Tarron quietly stood at the doorway, observing how great Secret looked. The rest did her well. The bandages on her wrist were hidden beneath a long sleeved white blouse. Tarron could tell Secret had lost a few pounds. *She lost them in all the right places. There's no better diet than hospital food,* he thought.

"Instead of standing there staring at me like I'm a fish in a bowl, you should show that you have manners and say hello," Secret said, without looking up.

"How did you know I was here?" he asked.

"After waking up next to the same person everyday for so many years, you just know the smell when he walks into a room. The same way she can tell he's been with someone else, or when he tries to sneak in bed beside her late at night."

"Don't start, Secret," Tarron said, as he grabbed her bags.

"Do you really think it's that easy to forget?" she questioned, sitting on the bed. "Why are you here anyway?"

"Man! Why would God create such a beautiful woman with such an ugly attitude? I'm here to pick you up. You know you don't have any other family, so I had to be here."

Secret put both hands on her hips. "So now I'm ugly, huh?"

"That's not what I said. If you're going to act like this, you can take a cab home. I didn't come down here to have you yell at me, change my words, and put me down."

"Boy, stop being so sensitive! I was just messing with you. You used to know how to take a joke," she replied. "Thanks for coming, but I had someone else lined up anyway." She smiled.

"Keep on playing. I'm about to walk out that door without you," he responded, after throwing her bag onto his back.

The nurse rolled a wheelchair into the room, and rattled off a list of at home responsibilities before giving Secret the final clearance to leave. Secret plopped down into the wheelchair as the nurse pushed her down the hall, headed to the elevators. As she passed the nurse's station, several employees waved goodbye, but one woman stood out in particular. The problem was, she wasn't staring at Secret. Her attention was focused directly on Tarron. He smiled when he noticed the beautiful woman staring. All of a sudden, Secret jabbed her fist into Tarron's chest.

"Boy, you are so disrespectful. You've cheated on me so much that now you're looking at women right in front of me."

"Stop, Mrs. Jenkins. You'll open your stitches if you keep doing that," the nurse scolded, in a soft island accented voice.

"I'm not going to discuss this with you right now," Tarron said, trying to block some of Secret's punches without hurting her wrists. "It was nothing, just a look," he snickered. Tarron made sure he turned around one more time for a quick look at the tall model-like figure in the distance.

"Yeah, that's right! I forgot how you try to ignore or cover up the shit you do wrong."

"Whatever, Secret, you act like I was a horrible husband the entire time we were married. I didn't hear you complaining when we used to make love back in the day," Tarron said smiling.

"You're right, I didn't complain, but who's to say I wasn't faking it. Don't pat yourself on the back too much, because I've slept with a man who gave me a real orgasm." Secret smirked, as she rolled her eyes at Tarron. She had to say something to make him feel the pain she was currently going through.

"Who, Jay?" Tarron asked quickly.

"No, nobody you know."

The nurse laughed and shook her head, as she dropped Secret's bags into the elevator. "I see you two have some issues," she said, half-laughing.

Tarron's expression changed immediately. People could tell that the two of them were pissed. Their faces appeared to be competing for the most evil look possible. Finally, the doors closed and they rode to the first floor in silence. When the doors opened, Tarron grabbed the bag and walked out first.

Tarron pulled his navy blue Lincoln Town Car around the semi-circle under the awning. He got out and snatched the back door open on the passenger side with an angry look. Secret and the nurse exchanged a criticizing smile.

"I guess I'm riding like a superstar," Secret shouted out.

"Maybe the nigga who gave you your first real orgasm will let you ride in the front of his car," Tarron remarked, and strutted around to the driver's side.

Secret gave the nurse a wink as she closed the door. She settled comfortably into the plush leather seats and listened to the music as Tarron pulled off. The sounds of Mtume's *You, Me and He* played softly on satellite radio. Secret enjoyed the relaxing moment, as they rode in complete silence for the next forty minutes.

The moment they turned into Secret's suburban neighborhood, Terrance and Tika raced out as soon as they saw the Lincoln approach the driveway. The minute the car stopped, Secret tried to open the door to greet her excited children, but Tarron wouldn't release the locks on the back doors.

"Will you stop being an asshole, and open my door," Secret demanded.

Tarron ignored her and remained still. The same strange feeling that he'd experienced over the last few weeks had him spellbound. He still seemed to feel like a stranger in his own driveway. It was weird. He still paid the mortgage, spent time at the house with his children, but felt like he didn't belong.

"What are you thinking about?" Secret asked, in an irate tone.

"I'm just thinking about my first real orgasm." Tarron pressed a button on the steering wheel and the sounds of Escape's, *You're My Little Secret* filled the car.

Secret sat very still for a moment. Her anger subsided just a bit, even though the children had their faces plastered against the back window. It was the song Tarron chose for the first dance at their wedding reception. She moved up behind Tarron and started playing in his hair.

"You know I still love you, right?"

Now, that's more like it, Tarron thought. He tried to turn slightly to look at Secret eye to eye. Before he could free himself from her love clutch, Secret snapped.

She snatched his head back, with her arm tightly around his neck. "Sucker! Now open my door right now so that I can hold my children."

"Okay, okay. Give me a minute."

Secret didn't want to wait any longer. She released him and climbed over the front seat. Terrance and Tika knocked on the passenger window as Secret opened the door. They hugged her tightly and smothered her with kisses.

"Thank you, Daddy, for bringing Mommy home!" Tika yelled. She crawled across the front seat into Tarron's lap.

Motherdear watched from the door, with a smile. Secret continued to embrace Terrance. Tarron opened his door and walked towards the door with Tika in his arms. Secret and Terrance slowly walked hand in hand behind them.

What a wonderful sight, Motherdear thought. "Hey, it's nice to see you two like this. Come on in here, and stop providing neighbors with so much drama!" Motherdear shouted, as she rolled her eyes at the neighbors next door. Tarron stepped into the foyer, kissed Motherdear lightly on the cheek, and put Tika down.

Secret and the kids hugged again. Tarron went back to the car to get Secret's bags. She pulled away from the kids long enough to give Motherdear a hug, but they immediately started to cling to her again. She kneeled to their level and embraced them. She knew they needed the comfort and reassurance that she would not leave them again.

Secret looked up at Motherdear. "I'm so sorry."

"Child, don't be sorry. God let you remain on this earth for a reason. I'm in no position to judge you," she responded.

"I'm still sorry that I disappointed you. You wouldn't have let everything get you so turned around," Secret said, shaking her head.

"Hell naw! I would've boiled me a kettle of water until it whistled. And as God is my witness, I would've gone across the hallway to where that husband of mine was sleeping with his heifer, and given them both a full body make-over."

Secret threw her head back and roared with laughter. "It's good to be home." she sighed.

"You see, Secret, nothing makes you feel better than watching bad people rolling around, screaming in pain from scolding hot water."

"I'll keep that in mind for the future," Secret said, with a slight laugh.

"No, baby, you keep that to heart. But keep in mind that I will cut you if you ever throw hot water on my baby. You can burn the no good heifer, burn her to the bone. However, burning my child is an entirely different matter. Motherdear will never let anything ever happen to either of her babies. No matter how bad they deserve it. You got that?"

As Tarron walked up the walkway with a bag in both hands, a car pulled into the driveway. He looked back and realized it was Victoria's cherry red Mercedes CLK. The driver's side door opened, and Victoria jumped out carrying a small shovel. She wore a black velour sweat suit, Timberland boots and a camou- flage scarf on her head. Tarron frowned at her attire, because Victoria wasn't known to dress like that.

"What are you doing here? Have you lost what little mind you have left?" Tarron shouted.

"I'm here to get my shit!" Victoria shouted, marching toward the house.

"Get what shit? You must be high. You don't have anything here."

Victoria walked across the grass to the flower garden. "When we were at Home Depot, you didn't have your wallet, so I used my credit card to buy all these flowers and shrubs." Victoria dropped to her knees and started yanking flowers out of the ground.

Tarron was getting ready to stop her, when the front door swung opened and Secret strutted out. Her expression seemed to turn into rage, as she saw Victoria snatching flowers out of her garden.

"Bitch, you better get the fuck out my yard!" Secret shouted.

"Hell no, I'm not going to allow you to decorate your fucking house with the shit I paid for!" Victoria yelled back, still pulling flowers out the ground.

Secret started walking toward Victoria, but Tarron ran over and grabbed her by the forearms. He was careful not to grab her wrists. Motherdear heard the noise, and directed the children to go upstairs to their room. Secret began calling Victoria all sorts of names and pleaded with Tarron to let her go. Victoria stood in the yard with her dirt stained hands on her hips.

"You can call me whatever you want, bitch! I'm still not leaving until I get every last one of these flowers." Victoria started chanting like a crazy woman. "Roses are red, violets are blue, I fucked Jay and Tarron too."

Motherdear stepped out the front door. "I just called the police, Victoria. You better get your crazy ass out of here."

Victoria laughed, throwing a hand full of flowers at Tarron and Secret. "This shit ain't over!"

"If you come back to my house, around my children, I swear to God I'm going to kill you!" Secret yelled.

Victoria pointed at Tarron with her long fingernails that were filled with dirt underneath, "You miss this pussy, don't you?" Before he could answer, she turned and quickly walked to her car. "I'll be back, you can count on that!"

"Does Jay know you're here?" Motherdear asked.

"Yeah…he sent me, old heifer!"

At that moment, Secret broke away from Tarron and picked up the small shovel Victoria had left on the ground. Victoria ran at full speed to the other side of her car when she saw Secret coming toward her like a lion ready for attack.

"Oh, you need a weapon, huh? Put that shovel down and fight me fair. Fight me like a woman!" Victoria shouted.

"Fuck that. You came to get your shit. I'm just helping you!" Secret shouted, as she scooped up a small pile of dirt and dumped it into the sunroof of Victoria's car.

Tarron ran over and grabbed Secret. Victoria jumped into her car on the passenger side, crawled over to the driver side, and started her engine. She rolled down her window as she backed out the driveway in a zig-zap motion.

"It's on now. You better watch your back, bitch!" Victoria yelled, as she peeled off down the street like a stunt driver.

Secret and Motherdear gave each other a long, silent stare as

Tarron released his grip, picked up her bags, and walked into the house. Motherdear signaled for Secret to go ahead of her. She looked around and noticed several of the neighbors standing in their yards.

"The show's over!" Motherdear yelled, as she quickly walked to catch up with Secret. "Honey, I know you're hurt, but remember, don't even think about hurting my son. That crazy bitch is the one you need to go after."

Secret decided not to concentrate on Motherdear's comments. In her heart, she loved Motherdear like her very own mother, especially since her own mother was dead. Even though she knew Motherdear's love for her son was true, she knew from experience that her words were much worst than her bite.

The incident outside had Secret's mind wondering as she walked into the house. Her attention was brought sharply back in focus when she realized her house had been redecorated. She grabbed her chest and tried to hold her emotions at bay.

"What happened to my house?" Secret asked, in a shocked tone.

"When I moved in, I had a lot of free time on my hands. You know I love to decorate. So, I just did what came naturally," Motherdear replied.

"What do you mean…you moved in?" Secret asked.

"I've moved in for a while. Who else was going to take care of these children?"

"Thanks," Secret said, with a blank look. "But why did you have to move into my house? Their father should have come back home to take care of his children." Secret's voice strengthened.

"My son works crazy hours. Besides, he doesn't live here anymore. He only visits, until we get all of this mess situated. Somebody had to look after these children while you were off getting yourself together," Motherdear said, in a harsh tone. "Do you see anyone else who has stepped up to the plate?"

Secret looked around, like she was trying to figure out the most appropriate way to respond. "Off getting myself together? Well, I'm together now, so you can move back into your own house."

Motherdear grabbed Secret by the arms, and shook her side to side with a big smile on her face. "No child, I'm ordered by the court to be here. I have temporary custody of Terrance."

"What? Tarron!" Secret screamed.

Tarron didn't answer. He was upstairs in their room, searching through Secret's dressers and closet. He had already quickly scanned the notes and cards attached to the flower arrangements that were sent to her at the hospital. *That nigga with the first orgasm better not be in one of these cards,* he thought.

Tarron carefully perused the names of the senders. He read only the cards that had unknown signatures. He recognized the majority of the names, but one large vase had a card signed: You know who! *Who the hell could this be from!*

"Tarron, get down here now," Secret shouted, for the third time. She was at the bottom of the stairs, yelling with all her might.

What now? Even though Secret's tone displayed her agitation, Tarron marched out the bedroom, mimicking a soldier in *The Nutcracker.* He came to a halt at the top of the stairs and clicked his heels together. Raising his hand in salute to her, he said, "Yes, Captain?"

"You're not funny. Why does your mother have temporary custody of Terrance?" she asked.

Tarron began walking down the steps. It was apparent that his mood had changed. "Because I'm not Terrance's biological father, so I don't have any say in the legal matters dealing with him."

"You're the only father he knows. How can you say that you have no say when it comes to his life?" Secret responded sharply.

Tarron's hands wiped over his face. He appeared weary. "Jay

and Victoria are really trying to gain custody of Terrance. They made a major case against the living conditions around here. They made us out to be terrible parents."

"Jay and who?" Secret asked, in a rage.

"Jay and Victoria." Tarron said, in a low tone. "They have a strong case to gain custody of Terrance."

Secret hit the wall. "Why didn't you tell me all of this in the hospital?" she asked. "I would've beat that bitch down the minute I saw her today!"

"I didn't want to upset you in your condition. The Judge made it clear that the biological father carries a lot of weight when it comes to the law. I think the Judge was so confused, he continued the case and gave my mother temporary custody until Jay could get a lawyer. We have about two months before we return to court to have our case heard. Things are really messed up, Secret." Tarron brought her hand up to his cheek. He needed to give, as well as receive, comfort. He drew her close and they held each other.

"Mommy, can you come up and help us finish our puzzle?" Tika asked from her bedroom.

"Go spend some time with the children. I should be leaving anyway. I have a lot to do. Something strange is happening at work, and I'm getting concerned," Tarron confided.

"Is there anything that I can do?" Secret asked.

"Yeah, just get yourself together. Don't worry about anything else. My mother is here to help with the children, and I'll take care of all the bills. All you have to do is just get better," Tarron responded, with his usual bravado. His lips touched her hand softly, just as he turned to blow his mother a kiss. "I love you Mom," he said, before leaving. "You too, Secret."

Secret nodded, turned, and headed up the stairs.

Chapter 8

Secret sat in Tika's room, still shocked at how much the children's rooms had changed. The flowery printed drapes and the old fashioned bedspreads left a nasty taste in her mouth, but she didn't want to hurt Motherdear's feelings. She felt like a visitor in her own home as she laid across the plush carpet. Secret played with the children for hours, thinking about how much time she'd missed out of their lives. She reminisced about the times she shared with both Tarron and the children. Luckily, Tika's bedtime approached, so she began reading one of her favorite books, *Three Birds and the Bear.* Secret was halfway through the book, when she realized they were both asleep.

Instead of trying to move Terrance, she let him lay in the comfortable spot he had made on the floor. Secret grabbed a blanket out the closet, and placed it over her son's body. She was so glad to be back at home. As she walked to her bedroom, her mind raced, *please, let my room be untouched.* A long sigh of relief escaped her lips when she realized her room had avoided the Motherdear homely makeover.

The moment she entered her bathroom, a wide grin spread across her face; it also had not been touched. The master bathroom had always been her place of escape. The shower was spacious, with a built-in seat and special features that adjusted water temperature and texture, including a sauna. Several automatic dispensers held a variety of soaps, lotions and oils, including her favorite bath crystals. The large bathtub had a Jacuzzi that was big enough for two or three people. Tarron had even installed a waterproof sound system and aroma therapy to help provide total relaxation.

Secret remembered the first day after they signed the final papers for the house. She and Tarron entered the house to do a final walk through of all the rooms. When they got to the bathroom, Tarron couldn't control himself. Instantly, he began pulling off her clothes until she stood naked, wearing only a pair of white footies. Tarron bent down on his knees and kissed her stomach. His tongue slid slowly down between her thighs and found its way to her clitoris, until the juices from her pussy ran down her leg.

Secret's body shivered as Tarron forcefully pulled off his pants, and exposed his rock hard dick. She instantly decided to turn around, so he could fuck her from behind, but Tarron lifted her into the air and walked over to the shower. He sat on the built-in seat and slowly lowered Secret on top of him, inserting his pulsating dick into her throbbing pussy.

Secret clinched her teeth at the thought of Tarron dick pounding her with deep thrusts. She remembered digging her nails in his back, as she felt him going deeper. Secret began to bounce faster, like a jockey riding a horse. As an orgasm approached, Secret raised her arms, and accidentally turned on the shower. The cold water was a pleasant surprise, but it didn't stop the amazing feeling they both shared.

Tarron raised Secret's right leg and pressed her firmly against the back of the shower. He pushed his swelling dick as far as he could, and held it in that position, twitching the head of his dick back and fourth across her deepest wall. As Secret yelled with pleasure, Tarron turned Secret around and bent her over.

Tarron played with the tenderized lips of Secret's pussy, as he slid his dripping dick back into her wanting pussy. His hands smacked both of her ass cheeks like he was a star congo player. The tempo sped up, and Secret pressed both hands against the shower wall, pushing her ass toward him. There were a couple of times when her hands slipped, causing her head to bang against the wall. She didn't mind. Tarron's dick felt so good, that even a slight concussion wouldn't be enough for her to stop. Tarron took control of her pussy and made her experience multiple orgasms that day.

Oh, how I love this bathroom, Secret thought. She moved slowly toward the medicine cabinet and yanked it open. She wanted to make sure Motherdear hadn't invaded her space. "Whew," she sighed. All her things were in place and accounted for.

At that moment, Secret decided a bubble bath would be perfect. She wanted to get the scent of the hospital off her body. Secret undressed, ran her bath, and slipped into the tub. During her bird baths at the hospital, she often thought about the pleasure the entire family shared in their bathroom get-away. When Terrance and Tika were small, they used to pretend the large tub was their indoor swimming pool. She knew that all their current troubles would have to be dealt with, but for just a brief period, Secret only wanted to think of a time when everything seemed perfect. Suddenly there was a knock on the door.

"Who is it?" Secret said, irritated that she was being interrupted.

"Is everything alright? You've been in there for quite a while," Motherdear inquired.

"I'm fine. I'll be right out," Secret replied.

I just want to make sure your crazy ass didn't try to kill yourself again, Motherdear thought. "Okay Sweetie, just checking on you."

Secret looked at her water wrinkled hands, and realized she had lost track of time. She got out of the tub and quickly finished her nightly regiment. In the bedroom, she found that Motherdear had turned down her covers and placed a cup of hot tea on the night stand. *This may not be too bad after all,* she thought. The hot tea was soothing, but it didn't make her sleepy.

As Secret lay in the bed trying to read *Promise of Paradise* by Zack Bright, she heard voices and laughter. She put her book aside and went down the hall to investigate. There was light coming from beneath the guest bedroom door. She tipped to the door and tapped lightly.

"Come in," Motherdear said. Secret could hear the sounds of the *The Flip Wilson Show* as she entered the room. "What's wrong, child?" Motherdear asked, with concern.

"I can't sleep," Secret replied.

"Come on in. Watch a little television with me."

Secret walked over and sat down on the bed. They sat in silence, except for Motherdear's periodic outburst of laughter. Motherdear knew something was bothering Secret, but she thought, *I won't pry. The girl will have to make the first move.*

"You know, Motherdear, I still love your son," Secret said, when the show ended.

"I knew something was wrong," Motherdear murmured, as she turned off the television.

"I'm at a lost. Part of me is mad as hell because he left me for another woman. The other half feels terrible because I was out doing my own dirt." Secret leaned over on her side and curled up in fetal position. "Tarron wasn't the only one in our relationship who was cheating. He stopped paying attention to me a long time ago, and that hurt. Our sex life was almost nonexistent, so I went somewhere else to spice up my life."

"You children amaze me nowadays, in how easy a woman goes outside her marriage and shares her body with another man. In my day, women had more respect for their bodies and the holiness of marriage. We didn't cheat just because our lives weren't perfect. Lord knows my sex life wasn't perfect." She laughed.

"What's so bad about today's women wanting perfection? Why should we settle for less? Our husbands don't. They go out and have relationships, keep women all over town, and some even have extra families."

"I never lived for the sole purpose of matching my no good husband tick for tack. He was a part of my life, but not my whole life. When I stand in front of the pearly gates and the Lord asks me why? I'm not going to scream, because my husband was doing it," Motherdear said, with a slight laugh.

Secret rolled onto her back, closed her eyes, and continued to talk. "Tarron and I were perfect together. The thought of another man never entered my mind. He always had his time with the guys, and I never worried or asked about what they did. But about a year ago, he started to stay out late, and he began acting distant. Eventually we stopped talking all together. When the spontaneity disappeared, our marriage became routine and boring. Tarron shut me out, without me knowing what I had done wrong."

Motherdear leaned back and sighed.

"Then one day, I connected with someone who made me feel desirable again. When a man awakens the lust that has been building up deep inside you, you just explode," Secret continued to say.

"Why didn't you explode for Tarron?" Motherdear asked.

"I used to explode for him. Actually, we used to explode for each other. Then he became distant and so damn cold. What was I supposed to do? I have needs too. The other man made me feel like I was ten years younger. He brought out the other side of me, that had been bottled up for too long. I hate being this honest with you, but he brought out the freak in me."

"Did you love this man?" Motherdear asked, with a look of concern.

"No, there was no love in this relationship. He was just a sexual toy, to be put away when not in use. I didn't have to look at him daily after doing things that would make a prostitute blush." Secret let out a laugh.

"Doing all of those Debbie Does Dallas tricks, how can you say that you love my son?"

Secret snickered. "Because I do, with every breath I take. I honestly feel that without Tarron, I'm not whole."

"Baby, you need Jesus to make you whole. Not my son." Motherdear began tapping on Secret's forehead.

"How is it when old people get close to their *check-out-meet-Jesus time,* they always forget what they did when they were young? They start giving all this advice that will get them into heaven. They've lived their life of sins, and now what everybody else does is wrong," Secret said.

"Who the hell you calling old?" Motherdear asked, as she raised herself to a sitting position.

"I didn't mean *old,* but *older.*" Secret tried to clean it up, but it was too late. Motherdear had already swung a pillow at her. It struck Secret's head, then the left side of her body.

"Can an older woman do this?" Motherdear said, causing both women to break out into laughter.

They were still laughing when Secret stood up to go. She kissed Motherdear on the cheek, "Thanks for listening to me. I don't how, but Tarron and I have to work this out."

As she walked back to her bedroom, Secret's apprehension grew. *How can I tell Tarron that I slept with his boss, who may be in love with me, and out to get him? That will definitely push him over the edge,* she thought.

Chapter 9

Tarron continued to do all of his work from home. David had not seen him since the incident in his office a month ago. Tarron's absence provided David with the time, and ample access to the files he needed in order to carry out his plans. David had set up several phony offshore bank accounts with, of course, Tarron's name attached. He had been around long enough to understand that people never remembered what you've done for them in the past, if you were ripping them off. People definitely didn't play when it came down to their paper. Changing the information on the documents was so easy, that David found it comical. He was able to make an honest man appear to be an embezzler with an erase here, and an extra zero there. His final task was to get into the accounting system and change some numbers, but he hadn't found a way to do that without anybody catching on. He did however flag all Tarron's accounts with ACCESS DENIED on the screen. This way nobody could touch anything.

David unlocked a small drawer in his oak desk and stared at the many pictures of Secret. He had hired a private investigator a month ago just, to take pictures during her everyday activities. There were pictures of her while she shopped at the mall, loading groceries into her car, and even ones of her going to the dentist. However, the pictures he loved the most were of her working out at the gym. He loved looking at the sweat on her chest as she ran on the treadmill. He stared at the pictures, as a huge smile spread across his face.

"It won't be long now, my love. We'll have that fake ass nigga out our way for good," David said, as he began wiping the small particles of dust off her face.

He went to the back of the drawer and pulled out a pair of Secret's pink lace panties that he'd kept from one of their many rendezvous. He held them to his face and took a long deep sniff.

At that moment, Tarron's secretary, Shanice, walked by his office and heard him saying, "Damn, you smell good." Shanice shook her head, wondering what was going on with her boss. She often heard him talking to himself in Tarron's office, and noticed that he spent way too much time in there. He always seemed to have a hand full of files on his way in or out, and she couldn't understand why. Tarron wasn't dead, he was only working from home. She remembered mentioning this to Tarron during a conference call the other day, and neither of them gave it much thought. *David is the CEO of the firm. I guess he has every right to see the files in Tarron's office,* she thought.

After playing his part as the panty patrol, David put all his secret's away, and decided it was time for him to turn up the heat. He turned to his computer and hit the new mail button on the screen. He decided to send an e-mail to all of Tarron's clients, requesting that they review their billing statements, and to notify the firm if they believed any irregularities had occurred. David also decided to attach a few billing statements to really grab their attention. He displayed a devious grin as he hit SEND. *Now, let's see how that motherfucker gets out of this.*

✳   ✳   ✳

Tarron walked into his apartment, tired and sweaty, after dropping Terrance at home, following football practice. He had just turned the television to CNN's *Business in Review* and got a beer from the refrigerator, when the first call came in on his business line.

John Swanson was one of his oldest clients, and Tarron had helped his company show remarkable gains over the years, through well developed marketing and investment plans. John's own portfolio had increased by a couple of million dollars. Their relationship had gone way beyond business. He and Secret had visited John's home, and even attended his daughter's wedding.

"Tarron, how could you do this to me and my company?" Swanson shouted, as soon as Tarron answered the phone.

"Do what to your company, John?" Tarron replied, immediately feeling alarmed.

"Your firm sent an e-mail, along with copies of statements, to all their clients, asking us to check for any irregularities. When I checked my statements, it appears that you've been over billing me. That prompted me to check even further, and I came up with the same thing. How could you do this to me?"

Tarron took a deep breath. "I have never over billed you, or anyone else," he retorted.

"Numbers don't lie, Tarron. I'm looking at my statements right now. They're indicating that you've stolen about eighty thousand dollars from me over a two year period," John said.

"There must be some mistake. Numbers don't lie, but someone can make numbers say just about anything they want when no one is around to catch the lies," Tarron responded, in a thoughtful voice.

"I can't believe this. I thought we were friends, and I've always trusted you. But I'm going to give you the benefit of doubt. I still have faith in you, but this statement tells me a different story."

"Let me go through my records, and I'll get back to you,"

Tarron said, still sounding shocked.

"Fine. Make it soon," Swanson said, before he disconnected.

Tarron immediately tried to access Swanson's account on his computer. His eyes bulged as the words ACCESS DENIED popped on the screen.

"What the fuck is going on!" Tarron shouted. After several more attempts, he decided to go through the paper files. Luckily Shanice had just sent him a few client portfolios in the mail the other day. Tarron recalculated the numbers and the billings several times in order to be certain he didn't over bill. He wasn't able to find any discrepancies. He was still on one account when client after client started to call with the same problem. Tarron was dumbfounded at all the accusations, and his suspicions were growing.

He decided to call Mr. Swanson back. "John, I can't find any discrepancies, but something is terribly wrong. Can you overnight me the billing statements that you're reviewing? I'll check it against my records and get back with you."

"Fine, but try to get this straightened out, Tarron. My partners are having a fit right now."

He gave Swanson the address to his post office box before hanging up. *What the hell is going on? Anybody could make a mistake on a bill for one client, but no one can inadvertently make errors on all of the accounts. Even if I missed something, Shanice would have caught it. Obviously, somebody is playing games. But why would anyone at the office have it in for me?* Tarron knew his thoughts would plague him throughout the night, so he continued to review all of the data on his clients that he could access from home.

✳ ✳ ✳

J. Tremble

The VIAX Accounting Department was housed on the first floor of the building. Tarron entered the department through the double glass doors, and an expression of tension and anger seemed to accompany him. He was not his normally cheerful self as he headed toward Gregg Porter's office, the President of Finance. Everyone's attention was focused on him as he walked passed the receptionist and approached Gregg's secretary.

"Where's Gregg? I need to see him right now," he insisted in a loud voice. Tarron's presence was so intimidating she couldn't answer. Somehow she felt Gregg might be in danger. Tarron pounded on the desk with his right hand. "Where in the fuck is Gregg? I need to see him right now!"

The secretary picked up the phone and began pushing buttons. Tarron paced back and forth in front of the desk, until Gregg entered through the glass door.

"I need to talk to you right now!" Tarron shouted, pointing his index finger at Gregg.

"Calm down, Tarron. Let's take this into my office," he responded.

Tarron turned to follow him, and two large security guards ran into the accounting department just as he entered. The secretary had called for help.

"Is there a problem, Mr. Porter?" the security guards asked, at the same time.

"Everything's alright," Gregg said, looking at the guards.

Tarron didn't say a word. He looked around the room and continued to pace. Gregg asked the guards to close the door as he sat at his desk.

"Now, what can I do for you, Tarron?" Gregg asked.

"Over half my clients are threatening to leave the firm, or requesting a new executive because of some over billing bull-shit!" Tarron shouted.

"Tarron, please lower your voice. Let me check the records,"

Gregg said, as he turned on his computer.

He grunted, mumbled, and blew out air, while reviewing the information on his monitor. He picked up the phone and asked his secretary to bring in the accounting files for Tarron Jenkins' clients.

The secretary's face still showed anxiety when she entered the office carrying the documents. Tarron didn't speak, but his expression said, *you really don't want to piss me off right now.* She backed out the office, never taking her eyes off of him. Gregg continued to make the annoying sounds, as he perused the pages in several of the folders. Tarron's patience, like the heat from the water at the end of a long bath, had completely evaporated.

"What the hell are all the noises for?" Tarron asked.

Gregg tilted the screen towards Tarron. "You need to speak to Mr. Jordan. I've checked the numbers, and the records indicate that you've been over billing your clients. The accountant who was assigned to your accounts has been transferred to a mentoring program, so I'm not sure how he missed this."

Tarron could only focus on the blaring capital red letters that flashed across the screen: ACCESS DENIED. SEE DAVID JORDAN.

Tarron's anger was potent as he stormed from Gregg's office and through the accounting department. Everyone quickly stepped aside to clear his path. He uttered a steady stream of profanities under his breath as he forcefully pressed the up button to the elevator. When it arrived, Tarron stepped in, and began pacing back and forth in the tight little space. An elderly woman stood shivering in a corner probably thinking, *this young man is about to go postal.* She decided to get off on the next floor, even if it wasn't hers. He was the only person on the elevator when it reached the top floor. Tarron's steam could almost be seen coming from his ears by the time he entered the Executive Suite and approached David's secretary.

"Karen, tell David that I need to talk to him right now," Tarron said.

"I'm sorry, Tarron, but Mr. Jordan is out of the office for the rest of the day," she replied.

I know she's lying. I should just walk right past her and burst into the office, he thought. Instead he asked, "Where did he go?"

"I'm not sure where he went. However, he did ask me to leave an envelope for you on your desk," Karen told him.

Tarron's anger increased as he once again stormed off in a fury. Most eyes watched as he angrily made his way to his office. He strolled past Shanice without greeting her, which was odd. He had always been nice to her, and this was way out of his character.

Before entering his office, Tarron stopped, looked back at everyone watching, and yelled, "Get back to work!" before slamming his door.

Tarron paced back and forth, trying to relieve some of the anger and frustration. He knew he needed to calm down in order to gain some perspective on the situation. He didn't respond to several beeps on his phone. Finally, Shanice knocked on his door, and opened it without waiting for a response.

"Excuse me, Mr. Jenkins. Are you alright?" she asked.

"I just don't want to be bothered right now," he answered.

"I know, but a man from your bank is on the line, and he says it's very important that he speaks with you right away," she responded.

"Which line?"

"Line three."

"Thanks," he said, picking up the phone. "Hello, this is Tarron Jenkins. How can I help you?"

"Hello, Mr. Jenkins. My name is James Montgomery. I'm the manager assigned to your accounts here at Washington Bank."

"What can I do for you, Mr. Montgomery?" Tarron asked wearily.

"Well, sir, I hate to inform you, but the FBI has put a freeze on all your accounts and credit cards."

"What?" Tarron yelled. "How in the hell can the FBI put a freeze on my accounts? There must be some kind of mistake. Why would anybody freeze my money? How will I pay my bills if I can't get any money out the bank?"

"I'm sorry, sir. The government didn't give us an explanation. They just presented a legal document, instructing us to freeze your accounts and all assets you have," the bank manager replied.

"Who do I need to call to clear this up?" Tarron asked, in a more professional tone.

"I'm not sure. I'd talk to a lawyer. You should be receiving a letter from us in five to six business days with information regarding this action, and the status of your accounts with us," he responded.

"Five to six business days?" Tarron roared. His professional tone was gone again.

"I'm sorry about all of this. Good day, Mr. Jenkins," the manager said, before hanging up.

Tarron banged the receiver against the desk a couple of times before he put it back into the cradle. *What could Mr. James Montgomery possibly think is good about today? What the hell is going on,* he thought, as he sat in the chair and closed his eyes. Tarron remained very still for a few minutes, hoping that sanity would return to his world. When he opened his eyes, the letter from David Jordan was the first clue that things were not going to get any better. He used his sterling silver letter opener to open it.

Dear Tarron,

Let me begin by saying that the firm holds you in its highest regards. However, we are quite disturbed by the recent accusations from several of your clients. They are outraged over what appears to be over billing practices performed by you.

The firm has also received a letter from the Federal Bureau of Investigations, stating they are investigating you in connection to these same illegal activities. They have informed us that all your accounts have been frozen until this matter has been fully investigated.

We have no choice but to place you on immediate suspension without pay until this matter has been cleared. If you're found to have been using illegal billing tactics, you will be terminated and legal avenues will immediately be taken against you.

You have always been considered a major employee of this firm. We have experienced phenomenal growth because of your dedication and hard work. We are hopeful that this matter can be cleared up expeditiously and you will be able to return to your position. If you are innocent of all the charges, the truth will come out. Keep your head up.

David Jordan
CEO, VIAX-Shin Investment Firm

All Tarron could do was laugh. He balled the letter up into a make believe basketball and aimed for his waste basket. He missed. *The story of my day.* He picked up the paper ball and unraveled it, realizing that he might need it at some future date. Tarron gathered a few things from his office and headed for the door.

Shanice looked up as Tarron walked passed. "Is everything alright, Mr. Jenkins?" she asked.

"No, I've been suspended from the firm for over billing my clients. My accounts have be frozen by the FBI, and my brother has either fucked or is fucking every women that I've ever cared about." He gave her a long stare. "What do you think, Shanice? Should everything be alright?"

"Wow! That's a lot of stuff for anybody to have on their plate," she responded.

"Wow is right. I have more on my plate right now than a fat man at an all-you-can-eat buffet. But don't worry about me, I'll work everything out. I loved having you as my secretary. You're one of the main reasons I was so successful here." Tarron walked over and gave her a sincere hug. "When I start my own firm, I hope you'll come join me again," he whispered into her ear.

Shanice couldn't believe he was talking this way. "Just let me know when, Mr. Jenkins," she whispered back. She felt so badly for Tarron, but she knew that pity was something he didn't need and wouldn't accept right now. She sat quietly as she watched him walk toward the elevator. It didn't even bother her that he never looked back. Shanice assumed it meant, *we'll see each other again.*

Chapter 10

Tarron sat in his car staring at The Lion's Den. He didn't even remember driving to the club, but he did need a few drinks, and needed to talk with his best friend. Pretty Boy Ray was in his office going over manifests with the distributors when Tarron walked in. He watched as Tarron went to the private bar and made himself a glass of Hennessey, and downed it within two seconds. Straight no chaser. Ray knew immediately that something major had happened, because Tarron rarely came to the club in the middle of the afternoon unless they had scheduled a meeting. He called his assistant and asked her to take the distributors out to complete their business. As the men left the room, Ray grabbed a glass and the bottle of Remy Martin from the bar and sat beside Tarron on the leather sofa.

Tarron's shoulders were slumped and his eyes were focused on the empty glass. He had carelessly tossed his jacket over a chair, his tie was loose, and his very expensive Hugo Boss shirt was wrinkled and damp with perspiration. Ray's expression asked the question, and Tarron told him about his day. The more he talked and drank, the worse he felt.

"I thought getting things off your chest was supposed to make you feel better," Tarron said, when he reached the end of his story.

"It will," Ray responded.

"It's not working. I still feel like shit. And you know the worse thing? I have no idea how I'm going to meet all my financial obligations with the bank holding all my money in limbo."

"What you need to do is move out that expensive apartment and go back home. If you need to save money, that's the best thing to do," Ray advised.

"I know. Paying for two places is going to kill me. Not to mention all the court cost," Tarron complained. He poured himself another drink. "But that's not going to work, because everybody's at my house; Secret, Motherdear, Terrance, and Tika. I couldn't go there even if I wanted to."

"You know what you could do?" Ray asked.

"What?" Tarron inquired, drinking the smooth tasting liquid.

"You could always move in with me. I'm at work down here so much that I'm never really home anyway. You'll be doing me a big favor by moving in," Ray urged.

Tarron began to think back to when they were younger, and stayed at each other's house on the weekends. They used to sneak girls in through the basement windows and have threesomes all night long. Tarron's mind drifted back to the best years of his life.

"Hey, Tarron, what you think about that idea?" Ray asked, for the second time.

Tarron drifted back from his trance with a laugh. "Huh, think about what?"

"Haven't you heard anything I said? What do you think about moving in with me?" he asked again.

"That might work," Tarron answered, still smiling at yesterday's memories. "I'm about to bounce. I have to talk with Secret and Motherdear. And I need to see my kids."

"You'll have to rent one of those storage places, because my place is already furnished. I'll have a key made for you and leave it under the mat, just in case," Ray said.

＊　　　　　　＊　　　　　　＊

Tarron left the club, still unsure about what his next move should be. He decided to drive over to the place he once called home. He turned off the engine and sat thinking about his predicament for a few minutes. Visions of he and Secret bringing Terrance and Tika home for the first time caused his eyes to fill with tears.

Secret was on the phone talking with David when she heard Tarron's car door close. She looked out the window and saw her husband walking toward the door.

"Shit, Tarron's here. I have to go," she whispered, into the phone.

"Wait! I want to tell you something before we hang up," David said, feeling like he was being brushed off again. But Secret had already hung up. "Fuck! I'm not going to keep allowing this bullshit."

Tarron entered the house, to find the children baking cookies with Motherdear in the kitchen. He walked past the phone and saw a red light which meant someone was on the line. He picked up the receiver from the base to check, just as Secret walked around the corner.

"Excuse me, why do you have my phone in your hand? Hold up, I know you not spying on people?" she said, with her hands on her hips.

"I believe this is still my house, and I still pay the bills. I can use the damn phone anytime I feel like it!" he replied.

"That's funny. This stopped being your home the minute you packed your bags and left us for that no good ho."

"That's enough," Motherdear interjected. "Both of you need to take that nonsense into another room, where busy eyes can't see." She looked at Tarron with motherly eyes. "Tarron have you been drinking?"

87

Tarron and Secret turned to see Terrance and Tika staring back at them. Tarron put the phone back on the base and walked into the living room without answering. Secret was right on his heels. He paused at their wedding picture and mumbled, "Best day of my life."

"What was that?" Secret asked, in a sarcastic tone.

"Nothing."

"Let it out, Tarron. You got the gift of gab. I want to know what you just said," Secret nagged, as she poked him in his back.

Tarron spun around. His reddened eyes glared directly at Secret. "I don't need this right now, Secret. I was just suspended from my job, and to make matters worse, the feds put a freeze on our account. I'm not in the mood to play who's the better spouse."

Damn! I was just on the phone with David. Maybe that's what he wanted to tell me before I hung up on him. She knew David was planning something, but she had no idea he would go this far.

Tarron sat on the sofa, and closed his eyes. He let out a long deep sigh, and moved one of the many pillows Motherdear had added to the sofa so he could get more comfortable. When his eyes closed again, Tika came into the living room with a plate of hot chocolate chip cookies.

"Daddy, Mommy, try my cookies!" Tika shouted.

Secret sat next to Tarron, and each of them ate a cookie as Tika watched with eager eyes.

"Mmmm, baby. These are the best cookies I ever had," Tarron said.

"Yes, they are," Secret added.

"Wait until you try my cookies," Terrance giggled, as he entered the living room with a plate of cookies he made.

Secret and Tarron took cookies from his plate and bit into them. Seconds later, they both frowned. The more they chewed, the hotter the cookie got in their mouth. Terrance started laughing.

"Oh, my word," Secret moaned.

"What the heck did you put in these cookies, boy?" Tarron asked.

"I call them the Atomic Bomb chocolate cookies," Terrance responded.

"That boy soaked his cookie dough in hot sauce before he baked them," Motherdear said, laughing in the doorway, holding two glasses of ice water.

Tarron took a glass and dipped his tongue into the cold water. Secret watched with a huge grin as she fanned her tongue. When Tarron saw the look on her face, he got very creative with his glass. He lowered his tongue into the water, slid it up and down against the glass, and twirled the water around in a circle. As the water turned faster and faster, he pressed his tongue against the side of the glass again.

I love that long, thick tongue, Secret thought.

Tarron's erotic exhibition came to an immediate halt when Motherdear smacked him on the back of his head. "Boy, there are children and your mother in this room. Take that mess upstairs with your nasty behind. You're just like your father," she said, laughing as she walked back into the kitchen with the children following her.

Tarron's cell phone began to vibrate. Secret moved quickly towards him to try to see the number over his shoulder, but he blocked her view with his arm as he answered it. He said yeah a few times, okay, that's a bet, and I'll see you then. He hung up the phone, grabbed his keys, and headed for the door.

"Where are you going? We need to finish our conversation. What are we supposed to do about money?" Secret shouted.

"We'll talk later. I have something to do."

"And what's that?" Secret inquired.

"You're no longer in a position to ask *that* question." he said, as he left the house.

More Secrets, More Lies

Chapter 11

It was a beautiful Saturday morning, just right for moving. Tarron had decided to accept Ray's offer to share his two bedroom apartment in order to save money. Tarron rented a U-haul truck, so the guys could help him move his bigger items into a storage facility near Ray's apartment.

Kurt almost broke Tweet's wrist when he lost his grip carrying Tarron's huge cherry oak dresser and mirror. Tweet held his side carefully, because he knew if he didn't, Tarron would be on his case, and surely curse him out.

"Man, watch what you're doing!" Tweet shouted. "I'm not trying to hear Tarron's mouth for messing up his expensive furniture."

"Shut your crying ass up, Tweet! You know I hate fucking manual labor," Kurt responded, as he sat the dresser down to wipe the beads of sweat off his forehead.

"Don't get mad at me. Your ass should've told Tarron that you didn't want to help him move."

"Told me what..." Tarron asked, walking into the apartment.

"Man, don't pay Tweet's ass any attention. He's just bitching as usual," Kurt said, picking up the dresser. "Let's go, nigga, pick up your end!"

Tarron shook his head as he put plastic on his prized possession; a 52-inch Plasma television that he would truly hurt some body over. Tarron was a huge Redskins fan, and watching the games on his television was a must. He even made special arrangements for a moving company to take the T.V. to his new home. He didn't trust his crazy ass friends to do the job.

The rest of the move went fairly smooth. Everyone worked hard to get all the furniture out of Tarron's apartment and into the rental truck, except Pretty Boy Ray.

He was too busy getting a buzz from all the beer Tarron supplied. Every now and then, Ray would emerge from the apartment with a lamp shade, a couple of shoe boxes, or something small and light. The guys were used to him being a slack ass, so no one was surprised. At least he had showed some improvement since high school.

Ray had matured since his involvement in The Lion's Den, but only in a few areas. He was still anal when it came to the cleanliness of his home. The fact that he allowed Tarron to move in with him was unbelievable to everyone. Ray had strict rules for his friends whenever they had a poker night over his house, so it was no surprise when he made up a list of rules for Tarron to follow once he arrived. He even called the list *Ray's Commandments,* and made Tarron sign the bottom to show that he was in agreement.

Tarron wasn't used to depending on other people, but he knew he had to make this move because money was going to be tight until the mess at his job was sorted out. Tarron had tried to get a head start on his new unemployment role by sending out a few resumes, but so far not even one firm had expressed interest. Even his contacts were drying up. It seemed as if the entire world was turning their back on him. Tarron went from being the most sought after investor, to an outsider. It was much easier for people to believe the bad things than to entertain reasonable doubt.

He often prayed that someone wasn't out to tarnish his character, and that this whole ordeal was just a big misunderstanding.

The guys saw that the emotional strain of his professional and personal life was beginning to get to him. He no longer had a vibrant personality, and little things that never would've been noticed before were becoming big issues. Tarron was even beginning to lose his confidence in the face of all the accusations and allegations.

This prompted Ray to plan a boy's night out. He figured a night out on the town was the best thing to get Tarron back into the swing of things. He told all the guys to meet him at The Lion's Den at ten o'clock that evening, and be prepared for fun. The guys knew they had to do something huge for Tarron, since he was usually the one they all leaned on. Now it was their turn to repay him for all his kindness.

Tarron hopped in the shower to get ready for the much deserved male bonding. He wasn't sure what was in store, so he decided to exercise his hanging muscle just in case. Using the bar of soap, he stroked his manhood until his body tensed, then squirted out with a sense of relief. He hadn't had sex in a while, and jerking off was becoming a regular habit.

When Tarron entered the bedroom, he found a black garment bag on his bed. He knew Ray had left it while he was in the shower. Tarron was touched that his friend would go to such extremes to cheer him up. *All you have are your friends and family,* he thought, as he took the new tan colored linen suit out the bag.

Tarron admired his new gear for a few minutes and tossed it back on the bed. As he looked around his room, he noticed that his clothes were scattered every where. He wasn't in the mood to hear Ray bitch on this special night, so he walked around the room and picked up the clothes he wore earlier that day. As he folded his jeans, Ray's commandments fell from his pocket.

Tarron sat on the bed, as he looked over his friend's rules and regulations for the third time.

1.   Don't touch the thermostat.

2.   Put all dirty dishes into the dishwasher.
3.   No shoes are allowed on the white carpet at anytime.
4.   Eat only in the kitchen or dining room.
5.   Overnight guest must bring a cute friend for Ray.

"This dude has more rules than Secret did. I might as well move back home," Tarron said, as he tossed the note on his bed. "I even had the nerve to sign that stupid shit."

Tarron ignored Ray's pickiness, dressed quickly and sprayed his favorite Bvlgari cologne all over his body. Thirty-five minutes later, he emerged from his bedroom dressed from head to toe, meeting Ray in the hallway.

"That's a bad suit," Ray said, bowing with one hand behind his back, and the other hand stretched out in front.

"It's not the suit. It's the man in the suit," Tarron remarked.

"Damn, my tailor did an outstanding job with the pants. The jacket looks a little big, but I'll have him fix that tomorrow," Ray said, as he continued his inspection.

"It's fine. Thanks for the suit, Ray. You've come a long way in a short time, and I'm extremely proud of you." Tarron walked into the kitchen, and got a Heineken out the refrigerator. "I mean, you went from a man who couldn't keep a job and was just getting by, to now being the owner of the hottest night club in the Metro area."

"I owe it all to you, Dawg," Ray replied, as he grabbed the beer from Tarron's hand. "But don't get it twisted. This is my beer, and you should at least pass me one before you help yourself."

Tarron laughed. "It's like that."

Ray turned the beer upside down and emptied the bottle in seconds. He held out the empty bottle and let out a loud belch. "Yeah, it's like that."

Tarron smiled as he reached into the refrigerator and pulled out another beer. He twisted the cap and turned the beer upside down, finishing his cold one even faster.

"You just remember, you're only a puppy when standing next to the big dog." Tarron took a deep breath and bellowed out an even louder belch.

They were still laughing and talking shit to each other when they reached the club and walked past the long line of patrons waiting to get in. Ray was like a mini celebrity to the people in line. Everyone wanted to shake his hand or give him a pound, girls were screaming out to him, begging to be on the V.I.P list. People in cars constantly honked their horns at the sight of Ray.

One woman even took it a step further and yelled from her car, "Damn, you look good tonight, Ray. Don't forget to leave my name at the door!" Ray snickered and walked past security, headed towards the V.I.P. Lounge.

The guys arrived shortly after, one by one. Tweet was the first to enter the V.I.P Lounge and Kurt stumbled in shortly after. He had already been out drinking to celebrate one of his employee's birthday.

"Looks like the gangs all here. Give us a round of Remy Martin shots!" Tweet yelled to the bartender.

They touched their glasses together and threw back their heads at the same time. Ray immediately ordered the bartender to keep their drinks filled. Every half an hour, she would put a round of shots in front of them, which would be gone in a matter of seconds. The night was off to a good start.

The guys were in the middle of another toast when Jay walked into the lounge. One by one the laughter died as all eyes fell on Jay. Tarron was busy talking shit to everyone when he noticed the blank stares on their faces. He turned toward the door to see what was going on, when his eyes locked on Jay. *This idiot has really lost his mind,* Tarron thought. He immediately noticed that Jay was wearing another one of his expensive Ralph Lauren suits. *It doesn't even fit his ass right.* The other guys lowered their drinks and watched Tarron's body language closely.

Jay walked over to the private table. "So, a dawg can't get invited to a boy's night out anymore."

Tarron slowly rose from his seat. "You must be high," he said, raising his voice over the loud music.

"Man, not tonight," Ray said, stepping between Tarron and Jay.

"You guys are brothers. Don't let that bitch come between blood. Remember, blood is thicker than water," Kurt added, stumbling to his feet.

"Bitch? You better watch who you're calling a bitch, nigga," Jay advised, with his finger in Kurt's face.

"You better get your finger out my face. Shit, Victoria is a bitch. She fucked Tarron, and now she's fucking you. If that ain't a bitch and a ho, I guess I don't know the meaning," Kurt responded, falling back into a table.

Jay let out a little laugh. "Listen, I'm not trying to cause a beef. I was sitting at home when I remembered Tweet telling me that you guys were having a boy's night out."

Everybody looked at Tweet at the same time, who instantly looked the other way.

"I wasn't going to come, but Victoria reminded me that you guys are my friends too. Just because Tarron and I have problems, shouldn't mean I lose all my friends. I just came to see..."

"See what?" Tarron asked, cutting Jay off. "We're still here. We all look the same. We've been the same way since you were locked up, released, and now trying your best to be me."

"I ain't trying to be you, nigga. Who the hell are you?" Jay asked, now pointing at Tarron.

"The one you've wanted to be ever since we were kids. Your dick just wasn't big enough to compete. And now, you want to be father of the year. Terrance will never see you in that way."

"Ah, shit, he gotcha dawg," Kurt blurted out.

"You'd be doing the same thing if you were in my position," Jay replied, giving Kurt a nasty look.

All the guys became silent as they gave thought to Jay's words. They seemed to be thinking really hard about what they'd do if it was their situation. It's really hard to connect with a foul deed, if you've never tried to see yourself in the other person's shoes.

Kurt broke the silence. "My family would never come second to a fucking ho."

Jay moved in Kurt's direction, but Tarron pushed him back, causing Jay to stumble backwards. As he regained his balance, he tried to attack Tarron, but a bouncer rushed over and restrained him.

"Fuck all four of you. All y'all were bitches growing up, and y'all still bitches now," Jay said, in the arms of the biggest bouncer in the room.

Suddenly the V.I.P door opened, and Victoria walked in wearing a sheer black dress that exposed her bright silver thong. All the guys stared as her beautiful toned legs strutted across the room.

"Hello gentlemen," Victoria said, as she blew everyone a kiss. "I'm sorry I took so long, Jay, the line for the ladies room was unbelievable." She walked over to Jay liked she owned the place. "Ray, you really need to do something about that, because when I come up in here, everybody needs to make a path."

Ray didn't respond, but his jaw hung low. He was too busy looking at the tight fitted dress that hugged Victoria's body with perfection.

"It's okay Sweetheart, I'm done here anyway. Apparently these gentlemen don't want me part of the crew anymore." Jay jerked his arm away from the bouncer. "Can you call off your dog, Ray?"

Ray gave the bouncer a nod, indicating that everything was cool. Besides, he needed more time to look at Victoria.

"I told you these clowns weren't your real friends. I'm the only one who has your back," Victoria remarked, just before lick ing the perimeter of Jay's lips in a circular motion. "Let's go home and make love, while they stay here and jerk each other off," she said, rubbing Jay's ass.

Tarron gripped his glass as the anger rushed through his body. "Nigga, I don't know who you think you are. So just always remember you got my leftovers. I'm sure my dick print is still embedded in Victoria's pussy!" Tarron shouted.

"Oh, like my print is in Secret's! Motherfucker, do you remember that I fucked your wife first!" Jay replied.

At that moment, the room seemed to separate because everyone knew those were fighting words. Tarron instantly threw his shot glass toward Jay's head. Luckily Jay knew shit was about to go down, so he managed to duck out the way.

Ray grabbed Tarron, and the bouncer immediately escorted Jay and Victoria out the V.I.P Lounge. Jay put out his hand to hold the door open, making sure his last comment was heard.

He looked back at Tarron and smiled, "I think you really need to talk to your wife. I do believe you got the dick size mixed up. My dick was large enough to please both of your women."

Tarron didn't even try to think of a response. His eyes were angrily fixed on Victoria. *That bitch has got to pay. She's the reason for all this shit,* he thought.

Ray decided to diffuse the tension that had built up in the room. "Get us another round of drinks," he ordered. The bartender sat the shots in front of the men. "Now let's have a toast." All the guys raised their glasses, with the exception of Kurt. He had passed out in a corner and missed all the action.

Tweet decided to honor them with words. "We've been boys every since elementary school. Let's promise not to let any more drama come between our friendship, especially a bitch."

"I second that!" Ray shouted, as they clicked their glasses together. "The party had a brief interruption, but now it was time for the main event."

The guys decided to roll out of the V.I.P. Lounge to mingle

with the ladies in general population. Tweet looked back at Kurt, who had his mouth wide open. He shook his head and continued to follow his crew. Tarron noticed Monica dancing on the floor with her girlfriends when he scanned the crowd. Seconds later, the D.J. announced that it was the last call for alcohol, so he decided to make his move.

He approached Monica from behind and whispered in her ear, "Excuse me, can I get another massage?"

Monica turned and recognized Tarron from their encounter several weeks earlier. "I'm sorry, it's after work hours for me," she replied.

"Well, what about a drink? The DJ just issued a last call." His glassy eyed expression told her that he had already had a little too much to drink already.

"No, I'll pass right now, but maybe we can have a cup of coffee after the club closes," she proposed.

"Cool, I'll be in V.I.P. when you're ready to leave," he accepted.

Damn, I wonder why Ray didn't put me on the V.I.P. list, Monica thought, walking away.

Tarron spent the last hour of the boy's night out sipping his Long Island Ice Tea in his private booth. Tweet had hooked up with an ugly girl with a bangin' body, and Ray was on the phone, making arrangements for someone to take Kurt home.

"Yeah, please hurry up because I have a special appointment in about ten minutes," Ray said, to the person on the phone. A hot new bartender was waiting for him in his office, so he didn't want to waste time fooling around with Kurt.

Monica was able to slip pass the guy at the V.I.P. door to look for Tarron. When she entered the room, she headed straight toward his table. She stood in front of him with her hands on her hips,

"I'm ready to leave," Monica's soft voice announced.

Tarron smiled and stood up. He dropped a few bills on the bar and yelled to Ray that he was leaving.

They found a small all-night diner several blocks from the club. Tarron ordered an omelet with coffee, while Monica ordered water. *Damn, I hope she's not one of those anorexic girls,* he thought. They sat at the table and talked, as Tarron ate his breakfast. He was so glad to be in the presence of another woman that he couldn't stop smiling.

"How are you feeling?" Monica asked.

"Much better now that I have some food in my stomach," he replied.

"Good. Let's go to my place so I can fuck the shit out of you," she ordered.

Tarron eyes widened. "Excuse me."

"You heard me. No need to be shy. I've already seen you naked, felt your body in my hands, so now I want to feel your dick inside my pussy."

"Check please," Tarron said, to the waitress.

Within minutes, he was following Monica to her apartment on Pennsylvania Avenue. Tarron parked his car in the visitor's area at the rear of the building, and jetted around front to meet his new friend. A light drizzle began falling as they entered the front door. They rode the elevator to the eighth floor in silence. It was difficult for Tarron to tell whether he felt anticipation or tension, but neither of them said a word until they were inside Monica's apartment.

"Nice place you have here," Tarron commented.

"No need for small talk. Take your clothes off. We're losing the night," Monica replied.

Tarron snatched his shirt over his head with excitement, and removed his pants in three seconds flat. It had been months since he felt a woman's body, so he could barely control himself. Monica disappeared into a back bedroom, as Tarron stood naked in the middle of living room. Suddenly, she walked out wearing an open silk robe, carrying a black leather bag.

Tarron watched as her stiff nipples popped in and out of her robe with each step. Monica sat the bag on the coffee table, grabbed Tarron's head, and slammed his face into her breasts. He licked her nipples with long strokes as he squeezed her fat round ass with both hands. His dick poked her belly button as it stood at attention.

Monica reached into the bag, pulled out a cock ring, and slipped it onto his penis. He thought she was rolling on a condom until she clicked the button and the vibrating ring sent sensations through his body.

"What's this?" he asked.

"My favorite little sex toy. It's made to keep your dick from going soft on me," she said seductively. Tarron put his head down to see what she had slipped on his dick. He was speechless as he watched Monica pull out a two-sided glass dildo. "Have you ever used one of these before?" she asked.

Tarron cleared his throat. "No."

"Well, let me show you how to use this in a sixty-nine position. The blue tip is for my pussy, and the red tip is for my ass."

Shit, I thought Victoria was a freak, he thought.

She pulled Tarron into her bedroom, and slowly laid on the bed. Tarron followed by placing his legs over her face. Monica didn't waste any time inserting his dick into her mouth, while Tarron teased the lips of her pussy with the tip of the nine inch dildo. *She's already wet.* Tarron began to suck on her hanging lips, sliding the dildo fully into her ass at the same time. He felt her body clinch from the deep penetration. To his surprise, Monica pressed another button and the cock ring sped up, causing him to moan with excitement. She moved her mouth further and further down his shaft, until her lips were touching the cock ring. She made her tongue wiggle around his dick as her jaw muscles pulled back and forth.

Tarron made long slow strokes with the dildo. *I don't understand why they have the different color tips. Her pussy is about to swallow the whole thing,* he thought, as the glass dick continued its decent into the eye of her personal storm.

"Give me more! Push it in!" she shouted.

Tarron slid his hand to the blue tip and pushed it further inside. Her head rocked from side to side, as she devoured his dick again. Both of them screamed, coming closer to a climax.

Monica reached down with full force and clamped Tarron's balls together. The sharp pain rushed in, causing a tremendous explosion. The longer she held his balls tightly in her hand, the more cum shot from his dick.

Surprisingly, Tarron wasn't the only one able to shoot cum. As Monica felt her body reaching an orgasm, she pushed Tarron's hand away and pulled the dildo out. Using her deepest muscles, she squirted out her own large amount of cum.

Tarron instantly became upset. He thought she was pissing on his face. He had never met a woman that could shoot cum like a man. He tried to release himself from under her little waterfall, but couldn't. Monica still held a tight grip on his balls.

"I know you didn't just piss in my face," Tarron said angrily, as she released his jewels.

"Relax. That ain't piss, but if you're in to that, I think I can make it happen," she responded. "It's just cum."

"Wow! That was a lot of cum," he said, wiping his face.

"I know you're not talking. My face and chest aren't sticky for nothing," she replied. "Are you ready for round two?"

"With your favorite toy, I'll be ready for anything."

Tarron regretted saying those words, as Monica reached inside her bag and pulled out a Karma Sutra position chart. "I want to do each position twice."

What in the hell is wrong with this chick? Maybe she's on ecstasy pills, he thought. They completed each position twice, some three times. Monica and Tarron went through every room of the apartment, including the balcony in the rain. When the sun came up, Tarron's dick was still sunk in her deep ocean like the

Titanic. They even used every item in her black leather bag, but he enjoyed using the bullet vibrator the most. At the end of the sex marathon, they both slept with their backs to one another with the cock ring still humming.

The loud sound of Tarron's cell phone ringing woke him up from a wonderful dream. Tarron knew exactly why his friend was calling as he looked at the number.

"What's up, Ray?" Tarron asked.

"I hope you enjoyed Monica," Ray replied.

"How did you know I was with her?"

"Some things happen by chance. Other things happen because your boy make them happen," he replied.

Tarron turned his head to look at Monica. "Please don't tell me she's a prostitute."

"Naw, she's a stripper turned massage therapist, that wanted to help cheer you up."

"She definitely cheered me up. I'll tell you all about it when I see you," Tarron confirmed.

Monica rolled over and looked at him with a smile. "Let Pretty Boy Ray know the next time he can come and watch. Tell him you have to hang up and finish the last round. I love a stiff one in the morning."

Chapter 12

Jay was tired of working his toll-booth job in the Baltimore section of I-95. He and Victoria had lied about his mailroom job, to impress the judge during the custody hearing. He didn't want the judge to know that he took change for a living. Lately, he was starting to worry about Victoria. She was becoming distant, and he wasn't quite sure of her loyalty. He had been working every Friday and Saturday night over the past few weeks, so it was hard for him to keep tabs on her. Jay knew that Victoria was like a dog in heat, and needed to be on a short leash. Anybody with a dick could get between her legs, and that bothered him the most.

Victoria had been hanging out with her girlfriends at the Lion's Den every chance she got. Jay made it a point to call her every ten minutes during her nights out, because he was always afraid she would bump into Tarron and rekindle their romance. But it didn't matter, because Victoria never answered his calls.

She even put Jay on a two night a week schedule, so she could have more free time. During his visits, they spent most of the time arguing about her whereabouts. He knew two nights a week wasn't enough for a highly sexual woman like Victoria, so he had to find out what was going on. Jay began to think about all the times she was with Tarron one day, and him the next, and sometimes the same day. He hated giving Victoria the room to fuck around on him. *She better hope I don't catch her ass if she's up to something,* he thought. Jay wasn't about to let Victoria hurt him, as she did his brother. He'd kill her first!

As the cars passed by, he reminisced about the time he found out that Tarron and Victoria were having an affair. It was during a boy's night out at the Billiard Room in D.C. Tarron had been bragging all day about his secret little friend, and the fact that she was a dime. Normally, Jay didn't pay his brother any attention when he talked about other women, because most of the time, he seemed to be lying. However, when Victoria walked through the door, Jay almost choked on the Corona he was drinking. He couldn't believe that she was the same girl that he'd met a few weeks ago.

He smiled as he remembered the gold low cut shirt, and Baby Phat jeans she wore that showed every curve. Jay remembered looking at her long black hair that hung over her shoulders, and the bright red lipstick that made her lips shimmer. Needless to say Victoria, was just as shocked. During the course of the night, Jay and Victoria both excused themselves and went to the bathroom at the same time. He clearly remembered Victoria begging him not to tell Tarron, which he agreed to do.

Jay was fresh out of jail, and wasn't looking for anything serious. As long as Victoria continued to fuck him at the same time, he was cool. He often wondered if he should tell Tarron that after she had sex with him in his bathroom at Terrance's birthday party, they also fucked in his car the same night.

Understanding that Victoria had an insatiable appetite for sex, Jay worried constantly when she was out of his sight. Lately, every time he was at her condo he found strange phone numbers on the back of napkins. Victoria's answers were always the same when he confronted her.

"Men talk to me and buy me drinks. They give me their numbers, but that's all. Stop being so jealous, I'm here with you, so that's all that matters."

At that moment, Jay's co-worker, Barron, entered the booth to take over the next shift breaking his trance. "What's up, Jenkins? Are you fanaticizing about that fine ass woman of yours?"

Damn, how did he know that? "Is the new schedule posted yet?" Jay asked, ignoring his question.

"Yeah, I think so."

Jay walked into the office with his fingers crossed. He really wanted to take Victoria on a nice romantic getaway to Annapolis that upcoming weekend. His smile could be seen from across the room as he saw the words OFF written under Saturday and Sunday. He did a little two step in front of the coffee machine, as he grabbed his cell phone to call Victoria.

"Hey, what's going on, baby?" he asked.

"Nothing, just doing my nails," Victoria replied, without enthusiasm.

"Listen, I'm not scheduled to work this weekend. How would you like to go to Annapolis? I know about this great hotel with romantic views of the water."

Victoria made a long heavy sigh. She never liked being smothered, and Jay was becoming a real pest. She couldn't understand why he wanted to spend all his free time with her. *Doesn't he have a life outside of me?* she asked herself.

The bootleg tracking device he tried to put on her wasn't going to work. That was one of the main things she loved about Tarron. Since he was married, he didn't have a lot of time to spend with her. They would meet each other, do their thing, and go their separate ways. Victoria recalled that it was after Tarron moved out the house he shared with Secret that their relationship began to dwindle. She went from sharing one or two secret rendezvous a week with Tarron, to spending almost every night with him, which was a complete turn off. Victoria began to feel closed in, like she couldn't breathe. Jay was causing her to get that feeling all over again.

"Hello, Victoria, did you hear me?" Jay asked.

There was a long pause. "This is not a good weekend for me. I've made plans," she finally responded.

"You can't break your plans for me?" he asked.

"Your brother would never have asked me to do that. He understood that my personal space was important to me, and he respected that."

"I know you didn't just compare me with my brother. That's fucked up!" Jay exploded.

"I wasn't trying to compare you with your brother." *It wouldn't be much to compare even if I did,* she thought.

"Then what are you saying?" Jay responded, with an attitude.

"Look, Jay, I need to get ready. I'm going out with my girls tonight. We can have this conversation another time."

"Tonight? Did you forget that we have court tomorrow? Don't we need to prepare?" Jay asked, sounding confused.

"I didn't forget. Besides, I'm a grown woman. I don't need you to question my every damn move!"

He looked at the phone, as if he was talking to a stranger. Victoria was starting to remind him of someone who was bi-polar. A few months ago she couldn't get enough of him, but now things were different.

"Look, just leave the spare key in the spot. I'll be waiting for you when you come home," he ordered, before hanging up.

Of all the things he could have said, that wasn't one of them. "That motherfucker must be crazy if he thinks he's going to mess up my plans!" Victoria jumped up off the couch and headed toward the bedroom. She looked at her nails, to see if they were dry, before pulling out her Louis Vuitton duffle bag from the closet. *I got a trick for his ass. I'll leave him the key, but he'll be here alone, because I'm not coming back,* she thought, as she put her favorite perfume inside the bag. At that moment, Victoria thought that maybe it was time to kick Jay to the curb. He was starting to cock block her style, and she couldn't have that.

When Jay arrived at Victoria's house, he found the key inside the mouth of the ceramic frog like he requested. He went inside and made himself at home as usual. He kicked off his shoes, made himself a turkey and cheese sandwich, and flipped through the channels of the television. Minutes must have turned into hours as Jay looked at his watch that read 5:30 a.m. He had fallen asleep watching an old Clint Eastwood movie.

"Where the fuck is she?" Jay said out loud, as he dialed Victoria's cell number.

"You have reached the Sprint PCS voicemail of Voluptuous Victoria, to leave a message press one now," Jay heard the automatic response say.

"Victoria, do you realize what time it is? Get your ass in the house now!" Jay screamed into the phone.

As he walked around the house, he immediately began to search for clues. He wasn't sure what to look for, but it didn't matter. Jay started in her bedroom. He decided to search the nightstand first, because that was where she kept all her sex toys. As he pushed the numerous dildos and anal beads aside, he stumbled upon more napkins with phone numbers on the back. *Just buying you a drink, I don't think so.* He balled the napkins up, and threw them into the wastebasket. Next, Jay went through her dresser, but couldn't find anything except her numerous pairs of thongs. He picked up a red diamond studded pair, and inhaled deeply. The sweet aroma of her wet treasure still lingered over the scent of the detergent she used.

Jay went downstairs to her office, after leaving the bedroom. He searched through the mail on her desk, and found her latest cell phone bill. Jay felt his heart stop when he noticed Tarron's work and cell phone numbers on the bill. He counted fifteen to twenty calls a day. *She calls that nigga more than she calls me.* Jay could feel the rage building inside of him. He paced back and forth, before taking a seat in the plush leather chair at her desk. He needed to catch his breath.

Jay threw the phone bill back on her desk, pushing the mouse to the computer. Instantly her beach screensaver appeared. Jay tried his best to gain access, but it was password protected. He began typing in all sorts of keywords, but twenty minutes had passed with no success. Finally, in a moment of frustration and desperation, he typed the letters T A R R O N.

When Jay saw the computer loading, he freaked out. Without thinking, both his fist slammed the innocent keyboard, smashing it to pieces.

"Oh, shit, what have I done," he said. Now I can't check her e-mail." He had to think of something else. He'd come too far to turn back now.

His rage was now bubbling at the surface. Thoughts of him hurting Victoria flashed before his eyes. He needed to talk to someone before he made a big mistake. Jay knew he couldn't call any of the guys, so he picked up the phone and dialed the only person he could talk to. The phone seemed to ring fifty times before he remembered that Motherdear had moved in with Secret and the kids temporarily. Jay didn't want to call Secret's house at that time of morning, so he decided to wait.

He continued to search Victoria's desk until he found a small box in one of the drawers. As Jay opened the box, his curiosity was in overdrive. He couldn't wait to see what other secrets Victoria had. The box contained several letters from Tarron and even a few poems. Jay opened one and began reading.

Dear Victoria,

There was a time when I was in love with my wife. I loved her deeply. Then I woke one morning, and I felt different. I watched her as she slept and knew that something had changed. It wasn't because of you. It's very difficult to identify a particular thing as the reason. The longer we tried to make our marriage work, the further we drifted apart.

I've found a new strength in being with you, a desire to become a better man. We seem to be on the same page in every aspect of our lives. Even when you are not around, I feel your touch. I smell your scent. I hear your voice in the passing wind. When I look at others, it's your face I see. I taste your sweet peach on my lips.

My wish is that we make a life together, a life that completes us both. One day, we'll be able to share our love before the world, and be the envy of everyone. Until that day, remember that even though you're not my past, you are my present and, most importantly, my future.

Tarron

Jay placed the letter back in the box and picked up another one.

Dear Sweetness,

I want to stop at the grocery store and buy packs of different types of candy bars. Then meet you in your bedroom and take off all our clothes. I would begin by making a happy face out of Skittles on your naked chest, and eat them off one by one until only your nipples are left for me to suck.

I would use a king size Snicker bar to tease your pussy, until it was covered with the thick liquid you produce naturally. I would rub it around, my lips and take a huge bite. I would then use a candle to melt a Twix on your moist thighs. My tongue will twirl around licking the dripping chocolate and caramel. Once all the chocolate is gone, I would use my dick to fuck you like you've never been fucked before.

Love,
Tarron

More Secrets More Lies

My brother is such a fag, Jay thought, deciding not to read anymore of the high school letters. He was certain that each one would contain the same bullshit. He carefully put the box back, and spent the rest of the night making sure that nothing was out of place. He even emptied the wastebasket with the balled up napkins. He wanted to see what lies she would come up with once he asked her about everything. Hopefully Victoria wouldn't realize that he'd played Inspector Gadget while she was gone.

Jay grabbed a vase off the shelf behind the computer and dropped it onto the keyboard. That would be his excuse for the broken plastic, a simple accident. He looked at the clock on the office wall, and wondered where the time had gone. 7:00 a.m. and Victoria was still not home. Jay began rubbing his temples when he noticed the yellow envelope they were given in court. As Jay looked at the documents, a huge smile appeared on his face. *How should I use this against my brother,* he thought.

Chapter 13

Victoria rolled over and rubbed her hand up and down the empty side of the bed next to her. *Where the hell is he,* Victoria thought, as she opened her eyes and sat up. She tried to find a reason why he would leave without saying anything. Victoria looked at the nightstand to see if he'd at least left a note, but the only thing she noticed was the alarm clock that read 8:14 a.m.

"Shit, I'm going to be late!"

Victoria jumped out of bed and ran to the bathroom to throw a few splashes of water on her face. As she looked in the mirror, a big purple bruise on her neck stuck out like a sore thumb. *Is that a hickey,* she thought. Whatever it was, it had to come off. Victoria little out a little giggle, as she thought about her night of wild passionate sex. She hadn't seen that many orgasms in one night since they first met. After washing her face, she grabbed her purse to search for some makeup. She needed to cover the evidence before meeting Jay at the courthouse. At that moment, she wished a turtle neck or a scarf was somewhere in reach. Victoria knew she would have to explain her whereabouts to Jay the minute they made eye contact, so this added drama wasn't needed. After glancing at the clock for the second time, Victoria panicked. She only had fifteen minutes to make it across town.

Damn, maybe we should've gotten a room closer to the court building, she thought, as she put on the same wrinkled clothes from the night before. Taking a shower was out of the question. She grabbed her Vera Wang perfume and sprayed it in every direction to cover up the scent of sex that clung to her body. She didn't even apologize to the small Spanish housekeeper, who she almost knocked over on her way out the door.

*   *   *

Tarron noticed a woman staring at him as he walked toward the court building. He smiled thinking, *today is an important day, baby. I had to put on my Sunday's best to impress the judge.* He remembered staring at his clothes that morning, trying to decide which suit would be a winner. When Ray saw Tarron's dilemma, he told him to go with his dark gray striped Armani suit. Ray told him that the suit represented class, something that Jay nor Victoria possessed. It didn't take him long to find the right tie to set the outfit off. Tarron shinned his black Bruno Magli's, and did a once over in the mirror before leaving.

Before Tarron could enter the building, his cell phone vibrated. It was Motherdear.

"Good morning, Mother," Tarron said.

"Boy, you better be on your way to court. If you're late again..."

Tarron cut her off. "I'm already at the courthouse. Where are you?"

"Me and the kids are in a cab. We should be there in five minutes."

"In a cab? Where's Secret?" Tarron asked.

"She left the house really early this morning. When I went downstairs to fix the kids some breakfast, a note was on the refrigerator, saying that she had something to do. It doesn't sound like she's even coming," Motherdear answered hesitantly. "You know she needs a shrink, right?" She laughed slightly at her comment.

"What! How could she run out at a time like this? We have a better chance standing in front of Judge Willis as a family."

"Calm down, Son, don't get yourself all worked up. Everything will work out."

Tarron wondered what Secret was up to as he hung up the phone and waited outside for his family. When they arrived, Terrence and Tika ran to him with open arms. They all walked to the courtroom holding hands. Tarron could see his lawyer, Steven, reviewing some paperwork as they approached the door.

"Good morning, Jenkins family," Steven said. "Where's your wife?"

"We don't know," Tarron responded, shaking his head.

"What do you mean, you don't know? I told you that we really need Secret here, because the Judge may ask her to testify. Besides, she wasn't here the last time," Steven replied. "Tarron, you're not the biological parent of Terrance. The Judge will give custody to the biological parent over anyone else filing, unless there's a serious reason why he shouldn't. You know, like a drug addict or a child molester."

Before Tarron could respond, the elevator doors opened and Jay stepped into the corridor. He was accompanied by one of the best child custody lawyers in the Washington area. Tarron's stomach began to turn. "We may have a battle on our hands," Steven whispered to Tarron, as they passed by. "He's one of the best lawyers in the city." Tarron watched as his lawyer straightened his tie before entering the courtroom.

The bailiff asked everyone to rise as Judge Willis entered the room. He fumbled with several papers before beginning. "Good morning, are all parties ready to proceed?"

"Yes, Your Honor," the lawyers responded.

"I see you found legal representation, Mr. Jenkins," Judge Willis said, looking over his glasses.

"Yes, I have Your Honor," Jay answered.

At that moment, Victoria entered the courtroom, breathing as if she had just ran up twenty flights of stairs. Jay had the look of death on his face when he turned around and saw her coming toward him. Tarron let out a little chuckle, as she tripped going to the empty chair behind his brother.

"Where the hell have you been?" Jay whispered.

"Not now," she responded, patting his shoulder like a little puppy.

"It's nice to have you in my courtroom today, Mr. Washburn," Judge Willis said, gaining Jay's attention.

His lawyer stood. "The pleasure is mine, sir. I wish we weren't here for this sad turn of events, but nevertheless."

"Well, this is what happens when adults can't make responsible decisions."

The Judge had the clerk remove Terrance from the courtroom until he was ready to ask him questions. At that point, the lawyers began their presentations of the case. Each called several witnesses on behalf of their client. Tarron's witness painted him as a model citizen with impeccable character. Jay's witnesses talked about how much he had turned his life around, and all the wonderful things he did for the community. *All lies.*

After several testimonies, the case seemed to be leaning in Jay's favor. Almost everyone in the courtroom was certain that the Judge would award custody of Terrance to his biological father. When Mr. Washburn rose to give his closing statement, the courtroom doors flew open. All eyes in the courtroom turned to see Secret walking down the aisle, followed by five men dressed in thousand dollar suits. Tarron's eyes widened when he recognized three of the lawyers from VIAX. A smile replaced the sinking feeling in his stomach. *I don't know how Secret pulled this off, but thank God she did,* he thought. One of the lawyers walked to the front of the courtroom, and immediately asked the Judge if he could approach the bench. Even though Judge Willis didn't have the slightest idea what was going on, he told them to proceed. The lawyer walked through the swinging gate and handed Judge Willis a motion for dismissal.

"What's your name, son?" Judge Willis asked, in a low tone.

"Your Honor, my name is Daniel Thomas, and I represent the VIAX-Shin Investment Firm. The men behind me are the rest of the legal team."

"Yeah, it looks like you guys brought the entire firm. This is not the O.J. Simpson case you know," the judge responded, with a slight grin.

"Yes, we know, but we're here to prove that Mr. Jay Jenkins should not be awarded full custody of the child."

"Who's the young lady?" Judge Willis demanded.

"Secret Jenkins. She's the mother of Terrence."

Judge Willis looked at Secret. "Well, I'm glad she finally decided to show up. Mr. Thomas, I can't grant a dismissal without hearing more of this case. You and Mrs. Jenkins can have a seat next to the defendant, if his current attorney doesn't disagree. The rest of your team will have to sit behind you," he ended, with a stroke of the gavel. "Let's continue ladies and gentlemen."

Secret smiled at Motherdear and touched her hand, before taking her seat next to Tarron. He took her hand and shook it lightly. Secret knew Tarron well, and could see the tension on his face. It was clear they both wouldn't be able to deal with the loss of their son. Secret looked over and gave Victoria and Jay a hateful look. Victoria stared back at her with equal animosity, but Jay didn't even make eye contact.

Tarron shook the hands of each lawyer as they walked to the front row. His eyes followed the last lawyer and halted when he recognized David standing in the back of the courtroom. *What the hell is he doing? Why is he here?* Tarron wondered.

The Judge instructed Mr. Washburn to take his seat so that Secret's lawyer could present her case. Daniel was also one of the best child custody lawyers in the country. VIAX kept him on retainer to handle difficult custody cases when their executives were involved in messy, or complicated divorces. He had to be the best, because he charged two thousand dollars an hour for consultations.

Mr. Thomas called in expert after expert, to testify on Secret's behalf. The presentation alone was worth the fee. He was able to mix complicated legal jargon and common sense into an exhibition of perfection. Every now and then, one of the other lawyers would pass him a sticky note. The sticky notes contained questions to ask, cases to note, or motions to press.

"This lawyer is good. I've heard about some of his cases around the office, but never really paid much attention. How did you manage to hire him?" Tarron whispered to Secret.

"David put the team together for us. We need to talk after this is over, Tarron," she whispered back. He turned to face her with questions in his eyes.

Tarron looked back at David, and gave him a small nod. David stood frozen, showing no expression. At that moment, Tarron felt that David was looking through him, not at him.

Motherdear could feel the momentum changing in the court. The new lawyer was doing such a wonderful job, that Steven didn't have to say another word. Motherdear silently thanked the Lord for having these young men come into their lives. It felt as though everything would work out like she promised. She had a smile on her face that glowed, and said screw you to Jay and Victoria.

Finally, Mr. Thomas concluded, and the Judge called for a ten-minute recess while he reviewed his notes on the additional information. Everyone stood as he left the courtroom, and whispered amongst themselves the moment he disappeared.

Tarron and Secret's lawyers talked silently about the case, while Motherdear and Tika went to check on Terrance. During the recess, Secret and Tarron walked out into the hallway to have a private conversation. Before they could begin, Jay and Victoria walked out of the courtroom. Victoria winked at Secret as she passed by.

"I know that bitch didn't just wink at me," Secret snarled.

"Let it go. We've got more important issues right now," Tarron suggested.

Victoria kept walking, holding on to Jay's arm. She looked back, stuck her tongue out, and laughed.

"Do something else and I've got something for your silly ass," Secret said, loud enough for Victoria to hear.

Victoria stopped and turned. "No, baby. I've got something for the both of you!" she yelled back.

Secret looked at Tarron. "What the hell is she talking about now?"

Tarron shrugged his shoulders. "How should I know? Secret, I'm sorry. It never even crossed my mind for me to hire Daniel Thomas. I just never thought it would go this far, or this way." Tarron looked from left to right. "Have you seen David Jordan from my job? I saw him in the back of the courtroom earlier. Someone is trying to set me up at work, so I need to talk to him."

"I haven't seen him since we met downstairs with all the lawyers. But Tarron, we need to talk," Secret replied urgently.

The light came on outside the courtroom, acknowledging that the Judge was ready to continue. When all the parties returned, Judge Willis entered.

"I'll now hear the closing remarks by the plaintiff," Judge Willis said, adjusting his seat.

"Before I give my closing statement, I would like to present new evidence relevant to this case," Mr. Washburn said. He opened a folder and pulled out the yellow envelope. All attention was on him as he twirled the little red string.

"These are pictures of a sexual and financial nature. I enter them into evidence, to counter the sweet perfect home life the defendant's lawyer painted."

Tarron immediately recognized the pictures as Mr. Washburn held each one in the air. There were pictures of Tarron and the guys having threesomes with strippers, and even some of Secret's girlfriends were photographed. *That's a low blow,* Tarron thought.

Next, Mr. Washburn pulled out financial statements, showing that Tarron had been suspended from his job, and was on the verge of being fired, pending the embezzlement and fraud charges. He had signed letters from David that alleged Tarron had been stealing money from clients and the company for years.

Tarron wanted to throw his chair across the room. He shook his head and listened as Mr. Washburn continued. However, nothing could prepare him for what Jay's lawyer pulled out next.

Tarron gasped, as pictures of Secret and another man were shown to the courtroom. He moved his head slightly to the left, trying to get a closer glimpse. Unfortunately, even with a squint he still couldn't identify the guy. One by one, pictures of Secret and her lover were shown, with each one sending a sharp pain through Tarron's heart. He thought he was going to pass out as the picture of them entering a hotel was revealed.

Tarron experienced a wealth of emotions within a few seconds, from anger to jealousy. He didn't even know that he was capable of feeling that much anger towards another person. The fact that another man touched his wife the way he used to, caused his eyes to well up. He couldn't trust himself to remain seated next to Secret, so he stood, and walked quietly out the courtroom.

Secret dropped her head as tears fell on the table. Victoria's laugh was low, but could be heard, as her face expressed a deep hatred of the woman seated across the aisle. Her smile was only a hint of the victory she felt was hers. Secret looked over and saw Victoria smiling from ear to ear. Her temper exploded when she watched Victoria's lips move into a pucker motion. Suddenly, Secret lunged over Mr. Washburn, in an attempt to get her hands on her enemy, but Jay grabbed her before she got the chance.

"Judge Willis, the husband is obviously going to jail and the mother is too emotionally unbalanced to get custody of Terrance Jenkins!" Mr. Washburn shouted, over the commotion.

"Order, Order, Order in the Court," Judge Willis demanded, banging his gavel. "Bailiff, please take Mrs. Jenkins to her seat immediately, or remove her from my courtroom."

Motherdear moved over quickly to console Secret. "I know you're mad child, but this is not the way to keep your children. Calm down," she whispered soothingly.

Judge Willis continued banging his gavel. As the courtroom calmed down, he continued. "This is a strange case, to say the least. We've heard testimony and received evidence from several sources. Someone will be hurt, no matter what decision I render. But first I'm going to allow Terrence Jenkins to take the stand. I would like to hear from him before I make my final ruling in this case. I believe everyone involved has issues, and should seek counseling to rectify their issues." Judge Willis instructed the bailiff to bring Terrence into the courtroom.

Terrence walked timidly as he entered the room. He sat in the witness chair, scooted up to the edge, and adjusted the microphone so that he could speak. Judge Willis addressed him.

"Terrence, we have a difficult decision to make regarding your welfare. I believe you are familiar with some of the issues surrounding your parents. I guess by now you know that Mr. Jay Jenkins is your biological father. Do you understand what that means?"

"Yes sir. My mom and my dad have explained it to me. It means that my mother had sexual intercourse with Uncle Jay before she met my dad, and that's how I was formed," Terrence explained maturely. "But Uncle Jay is still only my uncle, and I love him, but Tarron is my father, no matter what."

"Will you tell us with whom you would prefer to live," the Judge continued.

"Well, I want to live with my mommy, my daddy, and Tika. But if I can't live with them, then I want to be with my mommy and Tika. Daddy says he will always take care of us no matter what happens, and I believe him." Terrence stopped and cleared his throat. Tears flooded his eyes, and his voice began to tremble. "Please, Mr. Judge, can I go home with my mommy and daddy?"

Sniffs could be heard throughout the courtroom as Judge Willis banged his gavel. "It's final. Secret and Tarron Jenkins will retain full custody of Terrence. Mr. Jayson Jenkins, I believe that it is in the best interest of the child, and that the relationships remain the same. I cannot, in good conscience, award you any custodial rights. I hope that you and your brother are able to reconcile your differences and continue as a family. I can only suggest that all parties involved seek family counseling, as we are removing this case from our supervision. Thank you, and I wish the best for all of you."

Secret burst into tears when Judge Willis banged his gavel and walked out the courtroom. She stood, raised both hands to the sky and shouted, "Thank You!"

Instantly, the legal team got up and gave each other hugs. They even included Steven.

Terrance ran off the stand, and jumped into his mother's arms. It was a joyous occasion for everyone involved. Motherdear watched as Victoria stormed out the courtroom, followed by Jayson and their defeated lawyer. She prayed that her son would get himself together. A mother knows when her child is hurting.

Jay shook Mr. Washburn's hand, before watching him disappear down the hallway. He had done a hell of job, and Jay would definitely refer his services to someone else. *Maybe I'll hire him when I kill Victoria.* Instantly he turned to her with an evil look.

"Can we leave now?" Victoria asked, obviously irritated.

"No, I want to talk to my mother when she comes out," Jay responded, looking at her up and down.

"We're not going to sit here and wait for your mother, so she can rub that shit in our faces! Let's go!"

"First of all, who are you talking to? I'm not your child. Secondly, where the fuck did you stay at last night? You show up late this morning looking like shit…on one of the most important days of my life, and now you want to call the shots…I don't think so."

Here we go, Victoria thought, as she tried to turn on the charm. She was already pissed that Secret and Tarron had won the custody case, so she wasn't in the mood to argue. "I'm sorry, baby. I fell asleep over my friend, Alisha's house last night after we went out. I know I should have called, but my cell phone battery went dead."

"Cut the bullshit, Victoria. Do you think I'm that stupid? I know you were with somebody. "Jay stopped to take a good look at his woman. He grabbed her chin, and lifted it in the air, to get a closer look at her neck. "Is that a fucking hickey?"

"What are you talking about?" Victoria looked around at the audience of people they had acquired. "Can we talk about this at home?"

"Fuck you, Victoria! Do you think you're the only one who can play games?" Jay said, as he walked towards the elevator. *I got something for her ass. It's time for me to bring out the old Jay.*

✳   ✳   ✳

Tarron was on his third Hennessy and Coke when Ray got home from the club. He could tell that something had gone wrong in court today. *Shit, they must have given custody of Terrence to Jay,* he thought. Ray didn't say anything. He went into the kitchen, took a glass from the shelf, dropped in several ice-cubes, and took a seat next to Tarron. He made himself a Remy and Coke, and leaned back on the couch, to relax with his friend. They had several more drinks in silence before Tarron had the energy to talk.

Tarron filled Ray in on all the details about his day. He even broke down and cried when he told his friend about seeing Secret embraced with another man in the photos. It was a pain that he couldn't describe, and a memory that he never wanted to relive. Tarron's heart felt as if it had been taken out of his chest and stomped on multiple times. He began to wonder if this was how Secret felt when she found out about Victoria. As Tarron prepared another drink, his phone began to vibrate. After ignoring the call, he looked at his phone and saw *20 Missed Calls* on the little screen.

"Who was the dude?" Ray asked quietly.

"I don't know. I couldn't see his face, and after seeing that, I was too fucked up to ask Secret anything. I might have physically hurt her if I had said anything at that moment," Tarron replied.

"Well, what are you going to do?"

"I don't know. I haven't had a rational thought since I walked out of that courtroom. I can't think clearly yet. I have so much going on in my head right now. Losing Terrence may be more than I can take," Tarron said softly.

Tarron's phone vibrated again. Ray decided to answer. "Hello."

"Where in God's name are you?"

"This is not Tarron. This is Ray, Motherdear," he answered.

"Where's that boy? Tell him to get on this phone right now!"

she commanded.

"Hey, Tarron, it's your mother on the phone!" Ray shouted, pretending that Tarron was in another room.

Tarron took the phone. "Yeah, Mom."

"Yeah, Mom? I know you're not over there drinking and feeling sorry for yourself."

"Yes, I'm drinking, but I'm not feeling sorry for myself. I'm mad. I'm mad as hell," he responded.

What do you mean you're mad as hell? Who you mad with? Did you forget you left your wife and family for another woman, a woman who is, by the way, sleeping with your brother?"

"But still," Tarron complained.

"But still what? I do believe you had sex with that woman in the house where your wife and kids sleep. You had some nerve trying to get an attitude today. Leaving your wife again, when she needed you the most. Finding out that your mate is with somebody else hurts, don't it? You shouldn't have played the game if you can't handle the score, Tarron. You have no idea what you've done to Secret. You ought to have your sorry behind over here, thanking her for having the foresight to get that lawyer from your firm to fight for Terrence. She knew you couldn't stand to lose that boy. And you need to find out what Terrence did in court," Motherdear scolded.

"What happened after I left?" Tarron inquired.

"The Judge gave full custody to you and Secret. Jay has no custodial rights. The Judge suggested all of you attend family counseling."

"That's good, I guess."

Motherdear let out a loud sigh. "Are you drunk? All you can say is that's good. I hate it when you drink. You're never the strong black man I raised when you drink that stuff. You're a totally different person."

"I really don't need this right now. If you called to yell and scream at me, you can do that anytime. I just want to be alone. I don't want to talk, or see anyone for a little while," he replied.

"Fine. If you want to act like some cry baby, then go right ahead. I won't stop you. But remember, everything was fine when it was just your little dick around Secret. Now that your dick has competition, you can't handle it. You need to be a man, Tarron," Motherdear said, just before slamming the phone down in his ear.

Chapter 14

Several weeks had gone by since Jay had lost the court case. He was actually glad that it was over. He knew that he could never take Terrence away from Secret. He wasn't even sure if he could've taken him away from Tarron. Victoria was the major fuel behind the custody suit.

He remembered the day when she told him they needed Terrance to complete their family. She also told him that once he gained full custody, they would get married, but Jay knew that was another one of Victoria's many lies.

Terrence was where he belonged. Jay knew he could never be half the father Tarron was, he could barely take care of himself. Things between him and Victoria seemed to be fading away by the minute. He often wondered why she let the loss of the case affect her so much. It wasn't like Terrence was her son. Jay had never even seen the two of them having a conversation.

Victoria took advantage of their distance, by hanging out to the wee hours of the morning, and sometimes deciding not to come home at all. She would rush Jay off the phone, by telling him she had a headache and needed some rest. Then pack her overnight bag and head out the door. Little did Victoria know that Jay was on to her little games, and began sitting outside her house. He would then follow her to the same Hyatt hotel in downtown D.C. Like clockwork, he would always lose her once she went upstairs, and he never saw who she was there to meet.

Even though Jay knew Victoria was seeing somebody else, he played along. Besides, she'd been fucking two people simultaneously ever since he met her, so what difference did it make now? Victoria would never belong to just one man. The only thing that would get under Jay's skin was when she would compare him to Tarron during their arguments. Victoria knew that when she said things like, "your brother would do that", it would send Jay into a rage. But she never seemed to care.

Victoria had her own battles. She hated the fact that Secret had won the custody suit, even though she knew being a stepmother to Terrance was out of the question. Victoria hated kids. She only wanted the satisfaction of knowing how much pain Secret and Tarron would be in by losing their son. That's why she only found joy in the memory of Tarron storming out the courtroom. Victoria would smile at the beginning of the replay, but by the end, she would be in tears. *Something must be wrong with me,* she thought. Victoria was dealing with so many different emotions. *Maybe I'm coming down with something?* She would have a few good days, but the bad ones outweighed everything. In her heart, she believed that Jay was the reason for many of the bad days. They argued constantly.

Jay walked silently to the bedroom door and found Victoria sitting on her bed. She wasn't aware of his presence, so he watched her every move. Her saddened eyes gave her face a worried expression, as she stared toward the window in deep thought. Victoria's fingers tapped anxiously on the magazine that laid beside her. She wore a sheer lavender gown with thin spaghetti straps that revealed her large breasts. Jay was mesmerized by the sight of Victoria. She had been putting on a little weight lately, but it was going in all the right places. He often asked himself how someone so beautiful could be so devious. *I wonder if she's waiting for that nigga to call,* he thought, walking into the room.

Annoyed by the disturbance, she looked up and pointed "How did you get in?"

"I used my key," he replied.

"I didn't put the key in the frog, and the extra key is in my purse."

"I had a key made a long time ago," he informed her.

"Why didn't you ask me if I wanted you to have a key? What made you do something like that?" Victoria shouted.

"What the hell is the big deal? Let me guess, are you tired of me now? What happened to all that talk about us getting married?"

Victoria didn't reply. She walked over to the dresser and began organizing her makeup and nail polish. Jay walked up behind her and began to kiss the back of her neck. He wrapped his hands around her body and caressed her breasts with both hands. His erect dick began to press against her ass, as his fingers moved under her skimpy gown. He smiled as he felt the wet lips of her pussy. As usual, she wasn't wearing any underwear.

Victoria closed her eyes, as the feeling of warmth took over her body. Her head moved from side to side as Jay's finger tickled her clitoris. Victoria's breathing increased. She opened her eyes and saw the man she loved in the mirror. It was Tarron standing behind her.

"Oh, Tarron," she moaned.

"What the fuck did you say?" Jay asked, quickly pulling his hand away.

"Nothing. I didn't say anything," she replied.

Jay snatched Victoria around by her hair. "Bitch, you called me Tarron! You must've lost your fucking mind." His nostrils flared. "Let's see if we fuck the same," Jay snarled, pushing her against the wall.

"Stop! Get off of me!" Victoria yelled.

Jay ignored her cries. He snatched her gown off with one hand, as he held her neck tightly with the other. Within seconds, Victoria was naked, as she pleaded with Jay to stop.

He threw her on the bed, and firmly began to take his pants off. Victoria tried to get up, but was stopped by Jay's fist landing on her face. She screamed as he crawled on top of her, and used his knees to pry her legs open. Suddenly, Jay rammed his dick deep inside of her. Victoria cried out in pain. She tried desperately to bite his arm, but couldn't seem to reach it. He continued to beat against her inner walls, tearing her vagina tissue. She stared at the ceiling as Jay continuously pushed with forceful strokes.

"Do I look like Tarron? Go ahead, call me Tarron now!" he yelled at her.

Tears ran down Victoria's face. She closed her eyes and began to think about the deep dark secrets of her childhood. Flashbacks of her Uncle John raping her at the age of nine raced through her mind. She had promised herself to never revisit those memories again, but now things had changed. She knew at that point her painful past was the reason she could never trust, or be faithful to any man. They were all worthless, and deserved to be treated like shit.

Jay lowered his body as he felt an orgasm closing in. Victoria grabbed a large portion of his chest and bit with all her might. He screamed in pain, causing the orgasm to quickly disappear. His eyes watered. He punched her in the face with a blow that would make a 200 pound man cry.

"Oh, you wanna get rough?" he yelled, pinning her arms down.

Jay slid his dick out her pussy and snatched her off the bed. He spun her around, and gave Victoria a hard slap on her back. She went face down onto the bed. He grabbed a handful of hair, and rammed his dick into her dry ass. Victoria screamed in pain as his dick tore her tissues to shreds. He continued to pound deep inside her, ignoring the blood running down her leg.

Excited by the blood, Jay sped up his long thrusts. He pulled her head further back, causing her neck to strain. It felt as if her head was about to detach from the rest of her body.

"You still wanna call me Tarron? My brother has nothing on me. You'll never confuse me with him again after this!" Jay shouted.

The strain on her neck caused her screams to cease. Tears continued to run down her cheeks like a waterfall, as he forced his thick dick inside the small space. Jay stopped his thrusts once he heard Victoria whispering softly.

"What did you say?" Jay asked, releasing her hair.

"You'll never be the man your brother is."

"What?"

Victoria let out a little laugh. "You heard me. Tarron is more man than you'll ever be. All you did was prove it to me even more. I'm gonna make you pay for this."

Jay's eyes clinched and his nostrils were breathing out fire. He wrapped his hands around her neck and began to squeeze with all his strength. Victoria tried to spit on him, but her swollen lips didn't allow a long distance, so it landed on her stomach. Jay leaned back, smacking her with an open hand across her face.

"Bitch, I'm going to kill you for saying that!" Jay shouted, as he caught the other side of her face with a back hand. Jay smacked her repeatedly, until her body went limp.

As reality finally hit Jay, he was stunned to see the injury he had inflicted on Victoria. Blood covered his upper body, the sheets, and even the floor. It looked like a crime scene. He looked down at his knuckles that were raw and also covered in blood. He stood in disbelief as he stared at Victoria, whose limp body was barely conscious. *Shit, what did I do,* he thought.

Jay grabbed his pants and pulled out his cell phone. He had to call Motherdear. He could hear his heart beating faster with each ring.

"Hello."

"I'm in trouble, Mom," Jay mumbled.

"What is it, Jay? What have you done now?" she asked.

He paced back and forth in Victoria's bedroom with one hand on his head. Thoughts of him leaving town entered his mind. He couldn't go back to jail. Jay walked into the bathroom to look for some towels. He had to clean everything up.

"Hello, Jay did you hear me?" Motherdear asked, in a concerned tone.

"Me and Victoria."

"You and Victoria what, Son?" Motherdear coaxed.

"We were having rough sex, and I think I went too far," he lied.

"What happened? Where is she?"

"I left her in the bedroom. I...I think I knocked her out. She's bleeding. There's a lot of blood."

"Dial 911, boy. Go see if she's breathing. I'm on my way over there right now." Motherdear paused for a second. "Shit, where are you?"

"I don't want to go back to jail," Jay said, sounding like a child.

"You're not going back to jail. I'm sure everything is okay. Go check on that child."

Before Motherdear could hang up, she heard a lot of commotion in the background. "Jay, what's going on?"

The police had entered the house with their guns drawn. Apparently Victoria had managed to call them from her cell phone while Jay was in the bathroom.

"Freeze, show me your hands!" one police officer ordered, while the others searched the house.

Jay stood on the cold tile and lifted his hands, dropping the phone. His body was covered with blood.

"Turn around!" a burly officer yelled, resembling Sylvester Stallone. "Down on your knees! Put your hands on your head."

Everyone looked on the floor as Motherdear screamed through the phone, "What's happening? Somebody pick up this phone!"

Jay never got the chance to answer. The phone went dead. A police officer grabbed the towel that was meant for Victoria's blood, and wrapped it around Jay's body as other officers pulled him off the floor. The sound of the metal handcuffs being placed around his wrists was all too familiar. They rushed Jay out the house before he could get another look at Victoria.

Motherdear quickly dialed Tarron's cell phone, but he didn't answer. She tried several more times before leaving a frantic message on his voice mail. "Tarron, this is your mother. Your brother is in real trouble. He and that woman were doing something and Jay hurt her somehow. He just got locked up, and I don't know what to do. Please call me as soon as you get this message."

The police searched each room with their weapons drawn. They finally saw Victoria in her guest bedroom curled up in a corner, holding her cell phone. She raised her hand to shield herself as the police flashed their lights in her face.

"Are you okay?" an officer shouted.

"Please, no more," Victoria whispered.

"We need an ambulance at 9910 Connecticut Avenue. There's a black female with evidence of physical and sexual abuse," the officer said, into his shoulder radio.

A female officer grabbed a blanket from the bed to cover her. Victoria began to wave her hands as the officer got closer. "I'm not going to hurt you, Miss. I just need to put this over you. You're safe now," the female officer said, as gently as she could.

Victoria burst into tears, as the warmth of the blanket did little to soothe her pain.

Chapter 15

Victoria's nosey neighbors looked out their windows as the police put Jay into the back of the squad car. They knew it was only a matter of time before something went down. Listening to Jay and Victoria arguing through the walls of her condo was nothing new. For the neighbors with no lives on their own, it was pure entertainment. But what they didn't expect to see was Victoria being taken out of her house on a stretcher. Their eyes became glued to the glass as paramedics placed her in the ambulance.

They raced out of the neighborhood, and made it to the Georgetown Medical Center in record time. Victoria eyes squinted as the bright emergency room lights blinded her vision. She pulled the blanket closer together to get some comfort from the freezing temperature of the hospital. A nurse walked over to check the damage, and gave Victoria a once over.

"What's her status?" the nurse asked.

"Her vital signs are strong and normal, but her face seems to be swelling at a rapid pace," the lead EMT said. "She called the police after being raped by someone, who we assumed is her boyfriend. So it looks like you guys need to prepare a rape kit as soon as possible."

The nurse began searching Victoria's arm for the perfect vein to insert an IV. "Don't worry, Ms. Smiles, we're going to take real good care of you, Sweetie."

Within minutes, Victoria was being pulled in every direction and poked in several locations. One nurse swabbed beneath Victoria's nails with a thin Q-tip, to gather evidence, while another one drew her blood and took a sperm specimen. Victoria watched as all the evidence was placed in a large plastic bag.

After receiving fifteen stitches for her busted lip, Victoria was given a sedative, and taken to a private room to relax. She hadn't stopped shaking since her arrival.

✳   ✳   ✳

A police officer held Jay's head as he got out the back of the squad car in front of the First District police station, still covered by the tiny towel. Jay could hear several people laughing as he entered the station.

"Damn, it looks like we got some sort of pervert," a female officer said, looking Jay up and down.

"No, this motherfucker decided to rape his girlfriend tonight," the arresting officer responded.

"If it's one thing I hate, it's a fucking rapist," the female officer shot back.

After several hours of asking for something to wear, Jay was finally given an orange jumpsuit, after being processed and placed in a small cell. He was paced in the six-by-six feet room, while flashbacks of him raping Victoria ran through his mind. *What in the hell is wrong with me,* he asked himself. *This has to be a dream.*

Jay stopped and stared at himself in the small dirty mirror over the toilet. At that moment, he hated the face that looked back at him. He made no attempt to clean the small spots of dried blood that were still on his face. Instead, he laid on the metal bed and began to cry silently. Jay was overwhelmed with grief because he knew this incident would cause Motherdear a great deal of pain. *This is my third strike, so I know they're going to put me away for life this time. My mother doesn't deserve to go through this again.* Surprisingly, Jay didn't feel bad for what he had done to Victoria. In his heart, he truly felt that she deserved it for destroying every life that crossed her path.

He began to reflect on his relationship with Tarron over the years. Finally, Jay admitted to himself that he was the root to all their problems. He made a mental confession. *Tarron made the right decision to back Pretty Boy Ray's venture. He knew I wasn't responsible enough to handle it.*

His thoughts drifted further as he laid on the thin mattress. Jay had wanted to be just like Tarron when they were growing up. Ever since he could remember, Tarron was Marchelle Jenkins' handsome little boy and star athlete of the neighborhood. Many of the older people would tease Jay, because he wasn't as talented or as good looking as Tarron. He often heard his own mother say from time to time, that he was nothing like his brother, and those words still affected him today.

A part of him started hating Tarron as they grew older, causing their relationship to take a turn for the worse. It was hard being the little brother of the perfect sibling. The sibling who was the captain of the football team, dated all the fly cheerleaders or aspiring models, and got everything he wanted. Jay, on the other hand, got all Tarron's leftovers, and had to beg for everything he got. The irony of it all was that in spite of the cool persona he tried to project, he still chased Tarron's leftovers.

At first, he found triumph in knowing that he'd been with Secret before Tarron. But even that turned to bitterness, because just like all the rest, she chose Tarron over him. Now he and

More Secrets More Lies

Victoria were probably seeing each other again. Jay just couldn't catch a break.

After years of life on the street and frequent trips to jail, Jay had turned into a walking block of concrete. His feelings were buried so deep, that he barely knew how to find them. The tears he shed had washed away some of the dirt and grim from his soul, and allowed him a moment of insight. A new outlook took shape within his mind, *Somehow he would step out of Tarron's shadow, no matter what it took.*

138

Chapter 16

Victoria flipped the channels on the small television in her room just as her doctor walked in. Embarrassed, she turned her head slightly to hide the bruises with the pillow. She hated to look bad in front of any man.

"Good morning, Ms. Smiles."

"Morning, Doctor Edwards. I don't know how good it is."

The doctor let out a slight laugh. He had seen patients like Victoria many times throughout his career. "All of your tests are back, and I have some good news and some bad news for you. Which do you want to hear first?" he asked, sitting in the chair beside the bed.

"You should start with the bad," she replied. Victoria didn't think things could get any worse.

Doctor Edwards reached over and grabbed her hand. "You'll have to be placed on bed rest for the next few days."

"Why? What's wrong with me?" Victoria inquired, as she sat up looking frightened.

"Well, that's the good news. Luckily your baby wasn't harmed."

"What baby?" Victoria asked, with a confused look on her face.

"Oh, I thought you knew, Ms. Smiles. You're eight weeks."

"Eight weeks what? Pregnant?"

"Yes, you're entering your second month," the doctor said, with a confused look on his face.

Victoria fell back on the bed. Her eyes stared at the ceiling. At that moment the doctor knew it wasn't good news after all. Neither of them spoke as he patted her hand and left the room. Victoria laid on the bed motionless. The words, *eight weeks pregnant,* pounded continuously in her head. *I can't be pregnant. I had my period last ...* Instantly she remembered not having a period last month and probably not the month before that. Victoria slumped down in the bed. *If I'm two months pregnant, then who's the father?*

Victoria quickly began to reconstruct her sexual activities over the last two months. She had fucked Jay, and...*no, it couldn't be his because we always used a condom. Damn, maybe one of them broke.* Victoria shook her head as she tried to make sense of everything. *What a minute, I did fuck Jay and Tarron on the same day several weeks ago, maybe its Tarron's.* That thought instantly took her back to the Jenkins family reunion.

Victoria and Jay snuck away when Tarron had gone to the store to get more ice. Jay told her to walk around the pond in the backyard and follow the dirt path to the elementary school playground. Victoria felt the warm country air blowing across her face as she followed the instructions of her other lover. The sounds of humming birds and crickets sung in her ear. It was peaceful and picturesque. When she reached the playground, there was no one in sight. Victoria walked over to the swing set, and sat in the familiar seat. It had been years since she felt like a kid. Suddenly Jay emerged from behind the school building, walking in his slow gangsta strut. The strut that turned her on with each step. He wore a long black T-shirt and baggy Sean John jeans. His gold chain sparkled from reflections of the sun.

His baldhead and black camouflage bandanna set off his thuggish, look reminding her of Tupac. Victoria licked her lips as he slowly approached her.

"We don't have long," he whispered into her ear.

They walked behind the school building, looking in both directions like two sneaky students. As they turned the corner, Jay threw Victoria against the warm brick building and licked her neck with his thick tongue.

As he unbuttoned his pants, his long erect dick was immediately exposed from the gray boxers he wore. He pushed up Victoria's jean mini skirt and ripped her white thong, taking position between her legs.

As Jay lifted Victoria in the air, she grabbed his neck and wrapped her legs around his back. The wall provided the perfect position for them, as Jay pushed his dick deep inside Victoria's pussy and moved his hips back and fourth. He kept a steady pace for ten minutes, before telling Victoria he was about to explode. She clinched her legs tightly around his waist, as an indication that she wanted more. Victoria buried her face in Jay's chest as she felt his warm juices gushing into her soaking pussy.

Victoria smiled as she thought, *I fucked Tarron the exact same way that night across the hall from his wife and children.* Within seconds, Victoria's smile disappeared as she recalculated the time of the family reunion. *Shit, that was almost four months ago, so Tarron can't be the father.*

"Excuse me, Ms. Smiles. It's time for your medication and lunch," a voice said in the distance, bringing Victoria back from her trance. It was her nurse.

Victoria blinked a couple of times before responding, "This can't be happening. I'm not ready."

"I'm sorry, Ms. Smiles, but it's 11:45. It's time for you to take your medicine," the nurse replied.

"I wasn't talking to you," Victoria snapped. "I was talking out loud. My entire life has changed with an eight letter word."

"What eight letter word could change a person's whole life?" the nurse asked.

"P-r-e-g-n-a-n-t, pregnant!" Victoria shouted.

"Honey, that word will change a person's life, but changes like that are blessings from God," the nurse said, trying to comfort Victoria, as she handed her a little plastic cup with two pills.

I wish I could get out this bed and smack you dead across the face for even thinking this is a blessing from God, Victoria thought, reaching out to take the pills.

"Do you want your lunch now or later?" the nurse asked.

"I'll take it now. Hell, I'm eating for two, and the little bastard might be hungry," Victoria answered sarcastically.

The nurse turned around abruptly when she realized what Victoria had said. The look on her face changed drastically. The nurse dropped the tray on the table, and rolled her eyes before walking out of the room.

I know that bitch doesn't think she's better than me because I don't want this thing, Victoria thought, staring at the nurse as she exited her room.

Victoria lifted the lid on the entrée and realized it just wasn't her day. The vegetables were hard, the salad looked like grass from her backyard, and the dried up Salisbury steak made her nauseous. Victoria nibbled on the wheat roll, when she was struck by an epiphany like lightening hitting water.

I need to make this pregnancy work in my favor. Until I figure out who the father is, I have to convince both of the men I love that they have a child coming in a few months. Somehow one of them has got to be the father of this baby, no matter what. I refuse to let that bitch ass nigga, Jay, be a part of this. If they want blood tests, then I have to find a way to make one of the tests positive. I don't have pussy power for nothing. There's got to be somebody I can seduce to make this happen, even if it's a woman, she thought. Victoria knew the chances of Tarron being the sperm donor were zero, but she could care less. *Let the games begin.*

Victoria reached for the phone and began dialing. She tapped her fork against the food tray as she waited for someone to answer. Her face displayed a sinister smile.

"Hello," the woman's voice said on the other end.

"Yes, I would like to speak with Mrs. Marchelle Jenkins," Victoria announced, using her professional voice.

"This is she."

Victoria took a deep breath, "Motherdear, this is Victoria."

"Victoria who?" Motherdear asked, in disbelief.

"It's Victoria, the mother of your next grandchild."

"Well, Victoria, that would truly be a tragedy. No child deserves a mother like you," Motherdear said, sounding frustrated.

"Too bad you feel that way, because like I said, the doctor just gave me the wonderful news that I'm four months pregnant," she lied. "In six months or less, we'll be family for the rest of our lives. Isn't that great?"

"No, it wouldn't. Please understand me when I say this, Victoria. You may be pregnant, and my son may be the father, but you'll never, understand me, never be a part of this family. You really do have some nerve, calling to tell me that you're pregnant with my grandson, after you had his father locked up for rape. You know this will be Jay's third strike and he may be locked up for the rest of his life. And for what, a little tramp like you," Motherdear said, with contempt.

Victoria closed her eyes as anger filled her body. *Does she think I asked her son to rape me? Nobody deserves to experience that pain. I can't believe she's taking up for his sorry ass.*

Victoria saw this opportunity to inflict more pain on Motherdear. "Slow down, old lady. You shouldn't refer to your grandson's mother as a tramp. Besides, who said that Jay was the father?" Victoria laughed victoriously.

"I know you don't think Tarron is the father?" Motherdear said, in disbelief.

"Maybe…maybe not, who's to say. Listen, my dear mother in law, I didn't call to argue with you. I just need to tell Tarron about the good news, but I don't have his new cell number. Do you think you can give it to me?"

"Absolutely not, you little slut!" Motherdear responded

Victoria was about to hang up her phone when she heard another voice in the background. "Motherdear, did you say something? Speak up, old lady!"

"Bitch, you better pray to God that Tarron isn't the father of your devil seed," Secret said, with so much hatred, Victoria could feel it at the other end of the line.

"Well, if it isn't Secret Jenkins. I guess you heard the wonderful news by now. Who knows? I might be the lucky one and give Tarron a boy he can really call son."

Secret took a deep breath to calm herself down. "You will never deliver a child for Tarron. I'm going to…"

"You're gonna do what?" Victoria asked, in a low tone. "You ain't gonna do nothing but try and kill yourself again like you did the last time things didn't work out for you. That's the only way your dumb ass can get attention from Tarron. Now me, on the other hand, I'm going to use this baby to get Tarron back. Trust me on that. Can you just tell him I called?" Victoria didn't even give Secret a chance to respond. She softly hung up the phone and the line went dead. *I'll find a way to get his phone number.*

Victoria smiled when the nurse came back to retrieve the plate of untouched food. "You're right. This child is a blessing from God."

The nurse gave her another strange look. *Thirty minutes ago, you didn't even want the baby,* she thought, as she picked up the tray and left the room.

Secret held the phone against her chest, when it began making that loud irritating buzzing sound. She gently placed the phone back into the cradle. Secret sat on the bed and stared at a picture of she and Tarron on their trip to Barbados. They both looked so happy.

Motherdear abruptly walked into the room. She could see the collection of tears in Secret's eyes. "Why were you listening on the phone?"

"It wasn't intentional. We answered the phone at the same time. When I recognized her voice, I decided to see why she felt the need to call my house," Secret whispered.

"Baby, don't let that woman keep hurting you. Believe it or not, my son loves you. I can see it in his eyes. Tarron regrets hurting you and the children to be with that bitch. I know he has plans for getting his family back," Motherdear said, comforting her.

Secret's eyes widened. She began to think about all the wonderful times she and Tarron shared in the past. All the hot Saturdays they spent in the sun, watching Terrance play in pee-wee football games, the two and three day track meets, and the countless dance recitals for Tika.

"We had a good life. Do you think we can ever get it back?" Secret asked.

"Baby, anything is possible. I think the two of you can have that and much more," Motherdear replied.

"Which hospital do you think she's in?" Secret asked.

"I don't know, child. Why do you need to know? Listen, this family is already in enough trouble. Don't go and do something you'll regret," Motherdear ordered.

"I wouldn't jeopardize my children's happiness again. I just wanted to know so I can send her some flowers," Secret said, w with a grin.

"Yeah, right," Motherdear said laughing.

The phone rang. Secret and Motherdear looked at each other with concern. It rang again. Motherdear reached over and picked up the receiver.

"Look here you little tramp!" she began, in a harsh tone.

"Excuse me! I'm trying to reach Tarron Jenkins," the woman's voice sounded confused on the other end.

"Oh, please excuse me. Tarron's not home right now. Can I take a message?" Motherdear asked.

"Yes, this is his secretary, Shanice, from the firm. Tell him that it's very important that he returns my call."

"I'll have him call you as soon as possible," Motherdear assured, as she hung up the phone.

"Who was that?" Secret questioned.

Motherdear turned with a puzzled look on her face. "That was Tarron's secretary, Shanice, looking for him. She said she had some important information for Tarron, and that he needs to contact her immediately."

"Motherdear, whatever you do, please don't tell Tarron about Victoria's call or her claim to be pregnant." Secret walked over and hugged her mother-in-law. "I don't think he can handle any more drama, especially if Shanice has bad news for him from the firm."

"I think it's better that he finds out right away. If he hears about it from someone else, and finds out that we knew, and didn't tell him, it'll make things worse."

"In that case, I'll tell him myself. But I'm going to wait until after he talks to Shanice," Secret replied.

"I don't like this one bit, but if you really believe it's for the best, I won't say a word. Handle it your way," Motherdear said, before leaving the room.

Secret grabbed the phone and scanned the incoming calls on

the caller ID. She had to know what hospital Victoria called from. When she reached the second number, the letters GEORTWN MED CTR popped up on the screen. *So that's where she's at,* Secret thought, as she dialed the number with anticipation. As the phone rang, Secret pulled a pen and a small notepad from the nightstand.

The receptionist who answered the phone seemed a bit irritated. "Georgetown," she said.

"Do you have a Victoria Smiles registered there, and if so, can you tell me which floor she's on? This is her mother. I need to speak to a nurse on this shift." she said, trying to sound older.

After a brief pause, the receptionist responded. "She's on the fourth floor. Let me transfer you to the nurse's station."

Damn, that was easy. I don't even know if she was supposed to give out that information, Secret thought.

"4 West, can I help you?" a young lady asked.

"Yes, this is Victoria Smiles' mother. Can you give me the nurse's name who is taking care of my baby on this shift. I want to give her some information about Vicky's allergies," she lied.

"Her nurse is Darlene," the young lady said. "Hold on, I'll let you speak to her."

Secret noted the information on the paper and hung up without waiting for the nurse to get on the phone. She got her coat from the closet, ripped the piece of paper from the notepad, and headed out the house.

❋   ❋   ❋

Secret entered the hospital and headed straight for the fourth floor. Once she reached the nurse's station, she asked for Darlene.

"Darlene's in the bathroom," an older nurse said, pointing to the ladies room.

Without thanking the lady for the information, Secret turned around and quickly walked to the bathroom. Her hand shook as she pushed the wooden door. *I can't believe I'm doing this,* she thought, as she looked under each stall. Luckily there was only one person in the bathroom, and it had to be Darlene. Secret looked in the mirror and played with her hair, as the stall door opened, and a woman wearing Garfield scrubs came out and walked to the sink.

"Is your name Darlene?" Secret asked.

"Yes, it is, but who wants to know?" Darlene said, with a concerned look. She reached for the paper towel, after washing her hands.

"I'm here to make you an offer, so I'll get straight to the point. You have a patient by the name of Victoria Smiles, who just found out she's pregnant, and I need to find out two things. One, if she's really pregnant, and two, once she has the baby, I need to know who the father is. So I was hoping that you could help."

"How am I supposed to do that?" Darlene asked.

"Well, the first part is easy. Just look in her file, and tell me if she's really pregnant, and if so, how far along. The second part will take some time, but I'm sure you can figure out how to get those results as well."

"Listen Miss, I'd love to help you out, but I can't do that. It's against patient confidentiality. I could lose my job if someone finds out. If you know Ms. Smiles personally, then you just need to ask her yourself," Darlene responded.

At that moment, Secret pulled out a stack of money and waved it in Darlene's face. "Here's two thousand dollars to get me the first piece of information. I'll pay you an extra three thousand to get me the second part," Secret said, with a look of desperation. "Trust me, no one will ever know." Secret had taken all the money David had given her over the past few months to make this happen.

Darlene looked back and forth between the money and Secret for several minutes. "Okay listen, I'll do the first part, but I can't guarantee the second. I'm almost finished my shift, so meet me in front of the hospital in thirty minutes. I'll have your information." She walked toward the door, before looking back. "Lady, if anyone finds out about this, me and my son will track your ass down. Don't let these scrubs fool you, because I'm straight from the hood! I'm only doing this because me and my kids really need the money. Besides, Ms. Smiles appears to be a bitch anyway. By the way, put that damn money in a bag or something!"

As Secret paced back and forth in front of the hospital, thoughts of her hiring someone to kill Victoria's baby entered her mind, but quickly disappeared. *I'm tripping...what if the baby doesn't even belong to Tarron. The father could really be Jay. Having a baby might do his ass some good.* Secret continued to pace until she saw Darlene walking out of the building.

"Let's make this real smooth. Hand me the money, and I'm going to hand you this slip of paper," Darlene said, like she'd done this sort of thing before.

Secret had gone to the gift shop and purchased a bag with balloons attached. She handed the bag, with fresh green stacks of bills inside to Darlene, as she handed the paper to Secret. Darlene turned around instantly, walked to her car with the bag held tightly under her arm and never looked back. When Secret got in her car, she unfolded the paper,

Positive- 8 Weeks.

Chapter 17

The inmate shackled to Jay was having trouble walking with chains around his ankles. *This must be his first time in the joint, a new fish,* Jay thought. He, on the other hand, had worn the familiar metal objects so much that he could run a 100 yard dash if he needed to. Even his famous gangsta walk could still be seen.

Jay and the other inmates had arrived at D.C. Superior Court earlier than usual for their arraignments. The officer transporting them from the D.C. jail seemed to be in a rush for some reason. As Jay walked in the court building, he began to sweat when he thought about his charges. *First degree rape, second degree felony assault, and second degree sexual assault. Damn, I'm going down!*

On top of all of that, he had to go in front of the most feared Judge in the district; Ronald Martin. Jay instantly remembered standing in front of him eight years earlier for his drug distribution charge. He also remembered when Judge Martin sentenced him to Lorton Penitentiary for seven years. When Judge Martin gave his little speech, he reminded Jay that this was his second strike, and the third would have him locked down for life. Those words stuck with him throughout his years behind bars. Luckily, Jay's lawyer was able to get him out earlier, even though the remainder of his sentence had to be spent in a halfway house.

More Secrets More Lies

Jay walked through the swinging gate and took position next to his court appointed lawyer. He looked at the small Caucasian man with thick glasses as Judge Martin received his case folder.

"Well, well, well, Mr. Jenkins, you're back again. But I do believe we have you at the plate swinging for the last time. I told you that your next offense would be strike three, so you may be out for the rest of the game this time," Judge Martin said, shaking his head. "Counselor, how does your client plead?"

"Not guilty, Your Honor," Jay's lawyer stated boldly.

"I see here that you've moved up to some different charges this time, Mr. Jenkins. First drugs, now sexual assault. If you're going out, I guess you decided to swing out of the ballpark with a home run," the Judge commented.

Jay looked at the Judge but, didn't say a word. He was getting irritated at his baseball analogies. His court appointed lawyer had advised him to remain silent. Jay watched as the Judge organized his folder and wrote down a few numbers on a piece of paper.

"I'm going to set bail at fifty thousand dollars," Judge Martin said

"Your Honor, my client has just acquired his own place of residence, and never missed a meeting with his parole officer. Mr. Jenkins also has a good job, where he works hard, and has shown his commitment to getting his life on track. He's a man of limited finances. All of his family resides in this area, so he's not a flight risk."

"Counselor, Mr. Jenkins has been in my courtroom several times before, and I've noticed that the levels of his crimes escalate each time he is brought in front of me. If he wants to be back in society, he will have to pay," Judge Martin replied.

Jay looked around the courtroom and dropped his head. There wasn't a familiar face in sight for support, not even Motherdear. The reality of just how many bridges he'd burned was clearly evident to him as he was taken back to D.C. jail in the blue fifteen seat passenger van.

During the ride, Jay began to notice things that he would've ignored on a normal day. As the van stopped at a light, he saw an elderly couple walking their dogs with huge grins on their faces. He also watched a father teaching his
daughter how to drive. Jay smiled as the car jerked every few seconds from the inexperienced driver. He began to think that there was a strong possibility that all of these things would soon become a memory to him.

Jay went through the gates of the jail, feeling very depressed. He had to get out and needed someone to call for the bail money. None of his dawgs on the street had that kind of cash, and after the episode at the club, they probably wouldn't give it to him anyway. His brother was definitely out the question, and Motherdear probably wouldn't have that kind of money to give a bail bondsman. *Maybe she could take out a loan against her house for the money,* he thought. Jay would use this plea as a last resort, but in the meantime, he had one very shaky possibility. He walked down the corridor of his cell block to the recreation room and made a collect call to Secret.

Secret had second thoughts when she heard the recorded message say, "You have a collect call from Jay Jenkins. Will you accept the charges?"

She took a couple of deep breaths and responded, "Yes."

"Why are you calling my house?" Secret asked.

"Secret, I need some help. I've really fucked up."

"Tell me about it. You've fucked up big this time. Why, Jay? Why would you go after custody of Terrance? You're tearing this family apart."

Jay gave a brief sigh before responding. "Things were happening so fast. You were on your death bed, and Tarron was being an arrogant asshole. I don't know, Secret. I'm sorry for taking you through that," Jay said.

Secret grunted a few times. "I see you didn't mention that no good tramp. You mentioned everybody's name except Victoria's. Please help me understand what's so special about that woman? What does she have that makes you Jenkins men lose your minds? Oh, but I guess she can't be that special since you raped her!"

The line went silent. Jay used the next few seconds to try and think of a good response to Secret's low blow.

"Victoria is you," he blurted out.

"What! I know you've lost your mind now," Secret responded.

"No, I'm serious. Victoria is like the younger version of you. Think about it. You two have so many similar physical features. The major difference is that Victoria is still the wild woman you used to be."

"How can you compare me to that bitch? I'm nothing like that..."

Jay cut Secret off mid-sentence. "You had sex with me on a dare from your girlfriends the first time you laid eyes on me. I could have easily been a married man with loving kids at home, but that didn't stop you."

"That was different," she responded.

"Really, well what about your limousine rides?" Jay asked.

"What are you talking about?"

"You know, Secret, that's the one good thing about being raised in the streets. You meet all sorts of people. And these people can't wait to run their mouths about things they see. I've had several people tell me that they saw you in Georgetown with another man. They also saw you and this dude get into a long black limousine with INVEST 1 on the license plate. I doubt it if you were going to the prom." Jay knew the guy was David, but wanted to see if she would confess.

Secret became silent. Jay had hit a nerve. *Can there be any truth in what he's saying,* she thought. Secret began to compare their backgrounds. *Victoria had slept with both of the Jenkins brothers. She had done the same thing. Victoria had an affair behind Tarron's back. Secret was also guilty of that. They both had explosive sexual appetites, and now Victoria was going to have a baby, and probably wasn't sure which brother is the father. Damn, maybe we are just alike.*

"You might be right, Jay. I just got off the phone with my so-called twin and guess what?"

"What?"

"She's pregnant, and you or your brother is the father of her child," Secret said.

"You're lying. Please tell me you're lying," he begged.

"I wish I was, because that truly only means one thing. No matter which one of you is the father, one of my children will have a half sibling by a woman I fucking detest."

"You have to help me get out of here," Jay pleaded.

"Jay, I have no idea how to help you. I don't have any money," she replied.

A correctional officer walked up to Jay as he continued to beg for Secret's help. "You have a visitor."

"Secret I have to go. Do whatever you can to get me out of here," Jay said, as he hung up the phone.

The correctional officer escorted Jay down the dull grey hallway to the visitors' room. The loud metal doors opening and closing caused his face to cringe. He didn't want to go back to hearing the familiar sounds. Jay looked around once he stepped into the room, but didn't notice anyone familiar. As he gave the room another scan, a face caught his eye.

The man gestured for Jay to come over. Thoughts raced through his mind as he slowly walked to the metal table. He wondered what the man wanted.

"I know you," Jay asked, as he sat down across from the man.

"I hope so, my name is David Jordan."

"Yeah, I know who you are. You're my brother's boss at that big firm," Jay replied. "How did you know I was in here?" Jay scanned David like an x-ray machine, paying close attention to his Armani suit and diamond bezel Rolex.

"I was in your brother's office looking for some important documents when I saw an urgent note from your mother. When I called to inform her that Tarron wasn't in the office this week, she told me about your little dilemma. I immediately contacted Tarron, but he quickly told me that he wasn't going to help you, and he raced to the hospital to see a girl named Victoria." He lied with a straight face.

Jay slammed his fist on the table. The correctional officers in the room quickly looked in their direction. "That nigga ain't shit!" Jay shouted. "I gotta get out of here."

"Well, that's why I'm here. Your mother is a wonderful woman and I've always adored her. I hate to see her upset, so I'm going to get you out of here. My lawyers are working on bail reduction and I'll take care of the bill."

"Why are you doing all this?" Jay asked suspiciously, remembering the pictures of him and Secret in the courtroom.

"Your brother only cares about himself. Your mother is going through more than her share of problems. I don't want her to suffer any longer. I'm in a position to help you, and at the same time, maybe you can help me," David replied.

Jay stared straight into his eyes. "What type of help can I be to you?"

"Tarron is hurting a lot of people. I've watched him manipulate and dominate so many others in the past. Tarron has talked about you as if you're meaningless, so I thought this would be a way to get him back. Jay, you must've heard the saying, keep your friends close and your enemies even closer."

"I'm not following you. How can I be any help to you when you get me out of here?" Jay asked, sitting up on the metal chair.

"I hope I'm not out of line when I say this, but Tarro
to be taught a lesson. It's time he learns that you can't have what
doesn't belong to you," David said, with eyes that were cold as
water. He crossed his legs, giving Jay a glimpse of his thousand
dollar crocks.

"What do you have in mind?" Jay asked enthusiastically.

David cracked his knuckles and let out a deep sigh. "Well,
I've been working on his finance issues at work, so I'm hoping
that you can help me with a plan outside of work."

Jay used both hands and pushed himself to his feet. He paced
back and forth thinking of ways to hurt Tarron. The guard sent
Jay a warning look. He quickly sat back down. Jay knew Tarron
was on the border of depression because he was starting to lose
control of every aspect of his life.

"I know how to get to Tarron," Jay said, to David.

"How?"

"You rich guys hate to lose money, women, and expensive
possessions. Tarron is a different kind of rich guy. He grew up
without money, we shared several women in the past and possessions don't mean that much to him. But Tarron has always been
a control freak. Every since we were young, he had to be in control, or he was lost. Take away his control and you've got him,"
Jay said.

"His control? Control over what? How will we take his control away?" David asked, looking at Jay skeptically.

"You just get me out of here, and I'll handle that," Jay replied.

Chapter 18

Tarron was on his fourth Heineken and second *Good Times* episode when his cell phone rang. *Damn, why did someone call me in the middle of this Janet Jackson episode,* he thought. Without looking at the caller ID, he answered.

"Yeah," Tarron said, sounding annoyed.

"Is that anyway to greet the love of your life?" Victoria asked seductively.

Tarron looked at the phone like it had a disease. He couldn't believe Victoria was on the other line. "What in the hell do you want Victoria, and how did you get my number?"

"Tarron, Tarron, Tarron, I thought you knew me better than that. You know I always find a way to get what I want."

"Oh yeah, so I guess you really wanted my brother, huh? For some reason, in the back of my mind, I always thought he was the one who went after you."

This conversation is going the wrong way, Victoria thought, as she tried to lighten the mood. "Listen, Tarron, I didn't call to exchange blows with you. I called because I have some really good news to share. You're going to be so happy." She waited for his response.

"What could you possibly have to tell me that's good news Victoria?" Tarron asked.

Without hesitation, Victoria blurted out, "I'm pregnant."

Surprisingly to her, Tarron roared with laughter. He laughed so hard, Victoria immediately caught an attitude.

"What the fuck is so funny?" she asked.

"Because you called me with that bullshit ass story. You play so many fucking games, who's to say that you're really pregnant? And, even if you are, do you really think that I care about you and Jay's baby?" he responded, as anger filled his body.

"What makes you think Jay is the father?"

"Isn't he the one you're fucking? Besides, you said you had good news, so if somebody else is the father, why would you call me?"

"You're the father, Tarron!" Victoria shouted. "You're the one I've always wanted. And now we're finally going to be a family."

Tarron's loud laugh pierced Victoria's ears, as her eyes filled with tears. Normally his reaction wouldn't have bothered her, but today was different. *Damn, this baby is making me soft.*

Tarron stopped when he heard Victoria sniffling. "Listen, there's no need to pull out your crying card now, because that shit isn't going to work. How in the hell could I be the father? We haven't fucked in months!"

"I'm four months pregnant," Victoria said, hoping her lie would change his attitude.

Tarron's expression of anger turned to concern. He immediately thought back to the last time they had sex. *Shit, if she's telling the truth, then I could be the father. Lord, why me,* he thought, as he tried to act as if he wasn't affected by her last statement. "Well, I'm pretty sure you were fucking several other niggas at the same time you were fucking me, so that still doesn't prove anything."

"Tarron, you know I only had sex with you back then. Please trust me, this is our baby," Victoria responded.

He let out another huge laugh. "Trust you, are you serious? Victoria, the more you talk, the more I'm convinced that you need to go lay on somebody's couch. Listen, tell Jay I said congratulations, and please stop calling my phone!"

Victoria went into a rage. "Jay is not the fucking father of this baby! As a matter of fact, the next time you talk to your rapist ass brother, tell that motherfucker to watch his back!" All Tarron heard next was a dial tone.

He wasn't sure what kind of game Victoria was trying to play, but he wasn't falling for it. A few minutes later his phone rang again. This time he checked the caller ID. It was Motherdear.

"Yeah, Mom," Tarron said, when he answered.

"Where have you been? I've been calling your ass for days."

"I've had a lot of my mind, and needed some space, Ma. Is everything alright?" Tarron asked, with concern.

"Hell no, everything is not alright! Your brother got locked up again!" she shouted.

"When?" Tarron could tell Motherdear was starting to cry.

"A few days ago. That little slut, Victoria, accused him of rape," Motherdear said, speaking slowly.

"So that's what she was talking about," he said.

"What are you talking about, son?" Motherdear asked, as she blew her nose.

"I just got off the phone with Victoria, and she made a comment about Jay being a rapist, but I didn't pick up on it."

Motherdear instantly started to worry. "What else did she say?"

"Nothing, Mom, stop crying. I'll take care of this. I promise."

"Please, baby, I couldn't take it if your brother was locked up again," Motherdear said. As they got off the phone, she couldn't help but wonder if Victoria had told him about the baby.

Tarron jumped up to put on his black loafers, causing his beer to spill on the coffee table. Even though he knew how anal Pretty Boy was about his house, he never looked back. At that moment, his brother took priority over cleaning.

Tarron drove across town to 19th Street in Northeast like a mad man. For some reason, he thought the sooner he arrived at the jail, the sooner his brother could get out. He pulled his car into the visitor's parking lot outside of the D.C. Jail within minutes. Tarron walked through the parking lot making angry strides. As he approached the last row of cars, he dropped his keys. While he looked on the ground, a long black limousine rolled out the parking lot.

When Tarron stood up, the limo had quickly turned the corner. He continued to the front door of the jail. When he arrived in the visitor's section, he immediately removed the metal items in his pocket to walk through the detector. He knew this procedure all too well. He had been there several times to visit Jay during his run in with the law. This time however, Tarron knew it was a mistake. There was no way his brother would rape Victoria, or any woman, for that matter. Tarron grabbed his belongings out of the little blue tray, showed his driver's license, and hurried to the inmate visitor's room.

"How can I help you?" a chubby policeman behind the desk asked.

"I would like to see Jayson Jenkins," Tarron said, putting his watch back on his wrist.

The police officer began to flip the pages in the brown notebook on the desk. "I'm sorry, Jayson Jenkins has already had a visitor for today. Due to the number of inmates, only one visit per day is permitted."

Tarron was disappointed. He knew Jay needed him at a time like this. "Can I leave him a note so he'll know I was here?" Tarron asked.

"Sure."

J. Tremble

The officer handed Tarron a pen and a piece of paper.

Jay,
What happened to us? We used to be so tight growing up.
Sometimes it felt that it was us against the world. If there was
one thing I knew, I knew you had my back, and I thought you
understood I would always have yours. That fact is still true.
I'll get you out of here. Trust me, brother, when I say that blood
is thicker then water. Keep your head up.
Brothers forever,
Tarron

Tarron folded the paper and handed it to the officer. He
walked out the jail doors with even more anger than before. He
turned and banged his right fist on the brick wall. "When will
this shit stop?" Tarron shouted, looking up into the sky.

At that moment, several police officers getting off duty came
out the door. "Main man, you alright?" one officer said.

"Just when I think everything's alright, shit like this happens
and life shows me something different," Tarron replied.

The officers looked at one another. No one was really sure
how to respond. "Life could always be worse," one finally said.

Tarron looked over his shoulder at the police officers. He
quickly fixed his clothes and walked through the parking lot. "If
things get any worse, I'll be in here, too," he whispered to himself.

Tarron got into his car and drove straight to the Lion's Den.
The closed sign ignited in the window caught his attention. He
was about to drive off, when he noticed Pretty Boy Ray's car on
the side of the building. He parked his car, and rang the buzzer
on the side door.

"Who is it?" Ray yelled, from inside the club.

"Open up, Ray!" Tarron shouted back.

It took a few seconds for Ray to unlock all the dead bolts. He could immediately tell that Tarron had not had a good day when he stepped through the entry way.

"Jay was arrested for raping Victoria," Tarron said, as he shoved his way past Ray.

"Get the fuck out of here!" Ray responded, in disbelief.

As they walked up the steps to the office, Ray scurried ahead of Tarron, and pulled the door shut.

"What are you doing?" Tarron asked.

"I forgot. A couple of my friends are inside," Ray replied.

"So?"

"Two of my special friends that do special things. You know, special friends to each other," Ray said.

"Oh, yeah," Tarron replied. He finally got it.

Ray asked Tarron to give him a minute. Before Tarron could respond, Ray went inside the office and closed the door. Tarron tried to sneak a peak, but was unsuccessful. Minutes later, Ray called him inside.

Tarron opened the door to find a woman lying on the pullout sofa bed underneath a tan silk sheet. With a huge grin, Tarron walked over to the bar to watch the show. Instantly, the bathroom door opened, and a beautiful caramel colored woman walked out. She reminded Tarron of Chili from TLC, but her hair was cut very short and dyed blonde.

Tarron blushed a little as she walked over to the bed wearing only a pair of red stilettos. He noticed a dragon tattoo at the top of her ass when she bent over to pick up her thong. The other woman kicked off the sheet to expose that she too was naked.

She got up off the bed and gave her blond headed friend a playful smack on her voluptuous ass. Tarron stared as her ass jiggled. He never took his eyes off them as he fixed himself a drink. Both of their bodies were gorgeous. *Ray always knows where to find a bangin' honey,* Tarron thought, as he watched the two women enter the bathroom. A few seconds later, the sound of running water could be heard. *Wish I could join them.*

"Tarron, fix me one too," Ray said, interrupting his small fantasy.

As Tarron dropped the ice cubes into the glass, the women emerged from the bathroom. His eyes quickly locked on the blond headed girl's huge breast. *A D Cup at least,* he thought. When she felt Tarron's eyes staring at her, she made her ass shake with each step.

"Can I get my drink?" Ray asked loudly.

The other woman walked over and took the glass from Tarron's hand. She looked at her friend. "Hey, Peaches, I think you have an admirer."

"You know, Diamond, you might be right," Peaches replied.

Tarron was speechless. He sat on the black leather bar stool watching Peaches' every motion. Her subtle but meaningful movements reminded him of someone. At first, he didn't know who she reminded him of, but then like a flash of lightening, Secret's face became clearly focused in his mind.

It was the little things about Secret that captured his heart. The way she never let a day go by without doing something to acknowledge her love. She would do things like put a piece of chocolate on his pillow, place a love note in his briefcase, or have flowers sent to his job.

Tarron realized that he didn't love her because of the great sex they once shared or her great body. Their love was so much more. It was becoming clear that sex with Victoria was never better, it was just a change. *Why did I blame Secret for the decline in our sex life, when it was me who stopped giving my all?*

"Here you go, Ray," Diamond said, handing him his drink. "Is your friend alright?"

"He has a lot on his mind right now," Ray replied.

"Hey, Cutie, is there anything that we can do for you or to you?" Diamond giggled.

Tarron sat frozen with a strange content look on his face. Diamond and Peaches assumed he was thinking of different positions he could put them in, but he wasn't. Tarron was in the midst of an epiphany. A weight was lifted from his heart.

Tarron jumped off the stool screaming, "I love Secret!"

"Oooh, me too," Peaches echoed, putting on her bra. "Especially when it's a juicy secret about someone with a lot of money."

Tarron looked over at Ray. They both had puzzled expressions on their faces.

Ray got up and sat next to Tarron at the bar, as Diamond and Peaches continued to put on their clothes. Tarron downed his Hennessey and Coke.

"Do you need me to make you another before we leave?" Peaches asked.

"Another what?" Tarron replied.

"Long Island Iced Tea with a long stem cherry."

Tarron turned his glass upside down. "I wasn't drinking that, but no thanks, maybe next time."

The ladies grabbed their bags and headed for the door. Before they left, Diamond looked back. "Next time, you won't need a Long Island or anything else. Just the whip cream," she said, as she used her right hand to lift her skirt and expose her shaved pussy.

Ray laughed. "I'll make sure he calls you after we make that trip to the grocery store."

They waved goodbye to Tarron, and gave Ray a kiss on the cheek. He gave Diamond a light smack on the ass just before the door closed.

"I need to get my shit together. I can't win Secret back living like this. I need to find a job," Tarron said, with his head down.

"Why don't you work here with me at the club? You're already the General Manager. We can split the responsibilities up between us," Ray replied. "Hell, I could use a partner I can trust."

Tarron looked at Ray and smiled. "If we become partners, you better not try to get your rocks off by bossing me around in front of your tricks."

"You know me. If the girl is fine enough, I'll boss my mother around if it might get me some."

They both laughed.

"Oh, by the way, did I tell you I saw Victoria at the Grand Hyatt downtown last week."

"Man, I don't care about where you saw Victoria," Tarron said, fixing himself another drink.

"Oh yeah, well guess who I saw her with?" Before Tarron could ask, Ray gave him the answer. "I saw her kissing that boss of yours. You know that bitch is a real ho," Ray said laughing.

Tarron's eyes almost popped out of his head. "You saw Victoria kissing David. Are you sure?"

"Of course, I'm sure. I was there taking one of my waitresses on a lunch date, when I saw David checking in. A few seconds later, Victoria's hot ass walks in and kisses that nigga right in the mouth. Trust me when I say they weren't having a business meeting. Not the way he had his hand clutched onto her fat ass on the way to the elevator."

Tarron couldn't believe what he was hearing. Victoria had just called him, talking about how she was pregnant with his baby. She was up to the same bullshit.

Ray continued. "If that had of been any other nigga, I probably would've tried to skunk their grove, but David is the reason why I got this place. I don't want to lose the first thing that I've ever done right."

"That bitch!" Tarron shouted.

＊　　　　　＊　　　　　＊

"Let's go, Inmate Jenkins. Get all your belongings and follow me," the guard announced. Jay rolled over on his cot to see C.O.

167

Bell standing outside his bars. "What?" Grab my stuff?"

"Yeah, and whatever you leave is going in the trash. Your lawyer is here. You made bail," C.O. Bell replied.

Jay popped up. He couldn't believe he was getting out. *Did David really bail me out,* he thought. Jay snatched the plastic trash bag C.O. Bell hung on the bar before finally looking around.

"I'm tripping. My ass didn't come in here with anything, but a bloody towel," he said out loud. He pulled out his dick and paid the water bill one last time. "I'm so glad I don't have to see this nasty ass cell anymore," Jay said, as he flushed the metal toilet. A large smile raced across his face as he put on the flip flops he was given.

Out of all the times he had been locked up, Jay was extremely happy to leave this time. He had no idea what procedures they'd put him through before actually allowing him to leave the jail. It could take twenty minutes or two hours. Everything was at their pace and the releasing officer's mood, but he could care less. Jay was waiting at the door of the cell, like a child waiting for the ice cream truck, when C.O. Bell returned.

"Oh yeah, I forgot to give you this letter. A guy came to visit you the other day, but we couldn't let him in, so he asked me to give you this note," C.O. Bell said, as they walked down the cell block.

Jay opened the note and read it. He displayed no emotions. His face remained hard as stone. When he entered the release room, he noticed David standing next to his lawyer. Jay folded the paper and stuck it into his back pocket.

"Good news, Jay. Mr. Jordan has put up the bail money," his lawyer said. "Also Mr. Jordan may be able to pull a few strings to get the charges dropped. I don't know how, but if he does, that will help you out tremendously, Mr. Jenkins."

"Good looking out, Dave," Jay replied. He extended his fist, and David hesitantly returned the pound.

The three men exited the jail and walked up the west side gates that led to the far parking lot. Jay's lawyer showed two guards Jay's release papers and a loud click was heard as the automatic gate swung open. After the guys walked through, David grabbed Jay's arm.

"We'll meet you at the car," David said to Jay's lawyer. "I need to talk privately with your client."

The lawyer nodded his head and continued to walk.

He gave Jay direct eye contact. "First, my name is David. Don't ever call me Dave again. Now, I need to know if you have a plan." Their eyes locked on one another. "If not, I've thought of something to get Tarron, and get him good."

As Jay listened to David's plan, his attention was diverted when he noticed David's long black limousine with INVEST 1 on the license plate. *There's that fucking black limo. This low-life is trying to get at Tarron because he wants Secret. I guess he's trying to live up to his biblical namesake,* Jay thought.

"So, what you think?" David asked.

Jay turned his attention to David and gave him a blank stare. "I think we might have to tweak it a little."

"Tarron is never going to see it coming," David said, with a loud laugh.

"You can bet money on it. That fool will be so surprised. He'll never see this in his wildest dreams," Jay replied, as he too began to laugh.

Chapter 19

Victoria sat on her king sized bed, thinking of how she got caught in her love triangle. Even though she loved Tarron, deep down inside Victoria knew she didn't want to be with him. She had always been able to manipulate and lie to him, which was a complete turn off to her. Besides, he was weak and could use help with his pussy eating skills too. But more importantly, Tarron had a family, which meant less time and money spent on her. David, however, was a different kind of breed. He was strong, demanding, and most of all, controlling, which made her pussy wet every time she thought about it. They shared the same qualities, so Victoria always knew they would make a great couple. Thoughts of the day she and David met began to dance in her head.

Victoria had only been working in the strip club for a week when she met him years ago. She was performing a lap dance on a nerdy looking white guy when David walked in. She watched closely as the owner escorted him to the V.I.P section of the club. Instantly, Victoria was attracted to his tall frame and his money. Somehow she had the nose of a blood hound when it came to cash. Besides, his expensive tailor made suit and diamond studded watch were dead giveaways. David turned all the other strippers away, as they tried to offer him private dances and God knows what else.

Before she could finish her dance with Pong Dexter, the owner came over and ordered her to entertain David. Once she gave him the best head job of his life in the V.I.P room, he quickly became one of her regulars. The more he came around, the closer their relationship got. Despite what the other strippers thought, on many occasions, all they did was go to the V.I.P room and talk. No fucking or sucking, just innocent conversations.

They seemed to really enjoy each other's company. Before long, they began dating on her days off. David spoiled Victoria with expensive gifts, and often exposed her to many new things. Being with him quickly showed her how money could make life a lot better. They flew in private jets around the world for lunch, took cruises on yachts for fun, and most importantly, made love in the most fabulous places on earth. Everything was going perfect until David approached her one day with a proposition.

What Victoria didn't understand was how a simple business transaction could turn her life into a real life soap opera. But despite the drama, she knew if David asked her to do the same thing all over again, she would because she was in love, unconditionally.

Victoria snapped out of her trance and walked into the bathroom. She rubbed her stomach and thought about how life would be if David were the father of her child. The more Victoria rubbed her stomach and fantasized about being with David, the more she realized how much she loved him. It was time for Victoria to confess her love for her man, and give him the opportunity to accept the fact that no one would ever love him like she did.

Victoria searched through her closet until she found the perfect outfit. She decided to wear her sexy black off the shoulder dress, that showed every curve on her body. Especially the front, which had a low cut that displayed her perfect round breast. Victoria got in the shower, and applied David's favorite vanilla scented body wash. He loved it when she smelled like a scoop of ice cream. It took several more hours to get her hair and make-up right, and when she was done, she looked in the mirror with a smile.

"Damn, I look good," Victoria said, as she grabbed her purse and overnight bag. She had no plans on coming back home.

Victoria smiled all the way to David's house. She couldn't believe how happy and content she felt at that very moment. She had finally found true love. She walked to the front door and rang the bell. *I wonder why the gate was open*, Victoria thought.

"Secret is that you," David said, through the intercom. He had called Secret several times that day and asked her to come over.

Victoria let out a huge sigh. "Hell no, it's not Secret, it's me."

David's frustration could be heard over the intercom as he buzzed her in. Victoria stomped through the house with her six inch heels, looking for David in every room. When she finally found him in the basement, he was sitting at his bar with a drink in one hand and a picture of Secret in the other. Victoria had rehearsed all the things she was going to say on the ride to his house, but watching him stare at Secret's picture made her speechless.

"I love you," Victoria shouted out. "I've loved you since the day we met, and now I know that more than ever. Do you want to know why?"

"Why, Victoria?"

"Because normally I would be ready to cut your dick off for staring at a picture of a woman who I despise, but for some reason, I don't care. As long as you love me, then we'll be fine."

David put Secret's picture down on the bar and looked over at Victoria. "I don't love you. There's only one woman in this world for me."

Victoria's heart must have fell in her shoes. She lowered her head, as tears fell on the plush tan carpet. "That woman is right here. I love you so much that I've compromised everything about myself to prove my undying love for you."

"No, Victoria, that woman is Secret. Don't play dumb here. You know I hired you to get that fucking Tarron out of my way. You know I've always wanted Secret. Why are you playing games?"

"I'm not playing games, David. I knew you wanted me to fuck Tarron, to get him to leave his wife, but I always thought that in the end we would be together. Honestly, I thought you just wanted to fuck Secret, and then when you were done, you would come back to me."

David looked at Victoria and laughed. "Are you serious? What would make you think that I wanted to be with a stripper? I mean come on, you're fantastic in bed, but that's as far as I ever intended for us to go. Besides, I paid you to fuck Tarron, not his brother. That wasn't a part of the deal, you slut! Now look what happened, he raped your ass!"

Victoria was shocked. She couldn't believe David was talking to her that way. He had always been so nice to her before.

"Jay was one of my regulars from the club, but having a relationship with him was an accident. I never meant for it to go that far. Please David, don't shut me out of your life. I need you!" she yelled.

"How can fucking somebody be an accident? Did his dick accidentally land in your pussy? You don't need me. All you need is a fresh dick and some money. So now that my dick is old, and you've probably fucked up my chances to be with Secret, I think you should leave." As David stood up to walk away, Victoria spoke slowly, and as strong as she could.

"You know you're the one who I've always wanted. And now we're finally going to be a family!" Victoria felt stupid for repeating the same line she'd told Tarron days ago.

"What are you talking about crazy woman?" David asked, in an irritated tone.

Victoria screamed, "I'm pregnant! Please say you love us!" She held her stomach tightly. "I can't live without you!"

David stared at Victoria as she fell to the floor, and cried like a baby. He couldn't believe she was putting on this type of performance. He'd been with a lot of women like Victoria in his lifetime, but none of them had ever gone this far. He was expecting the normal slap on his face, but she deserved an Oscar for this.

"Get up!" he shouted.

Victoria didn't move. She was balled up in fetal position.

As he pulled her off the floor, Victoria started swinging wildly. "Didn't you hear what I just said? I'm pregnant with your child, David!"

He blocked several swings from her fist, and grabbed her wrists to take control of the situation.

"Look, Victoria, you and I both know that I used a condom every time we had sex, so there's no way in hell that child belongs to me. You need to try this shit with someone else."

"What makes you think the condom didn't break?" she asked, as the running mascara burned her eyes.

"Because I always used two condoms with your nasty ass. Do you think I'm stupid? I know how many men you've fucked," David responded.

Victoria looked at David with the coldest set of eyes that he'd ever seen. Her raccoon appearance was starting to look a little scary.

"You inconsiderate son of a bitch! I gave myself to two men like a whore. I broke up a perfectly happy family, and now you're telling me that I did all that for nothing."

"You're a grown woman. I didn't make you do anything that you weren't already doing down at that strip club," David said, letting her wrists go. He walked back to the bar and picked up

Secret's picture. "She would have never done any of that shit."

"You made me believe that we were going to be together. Every time we made love, you made it clear that you loved me. What the fuck was that all about?" Victoria asked, moving closer to David.

David jumped off the stool. "Don't you get it? You were just a piece of ass! I love fucking you, but there's more to life than just fucking someone. If your dumb ass didn't think with your pussy all the time, you might know that."

"I can't believe you're saying this to me. I was expecting to spend the rest of my life with you. I bet you'll change your mind when that bitch, Secret, is out the picture," Victoria said.

David grabbed Victoria by her neck. "If anything happens to Secret, I'll kill you myself, bitch. Now take your bastard ass baby and get the fuck out of my house."

Flashbacks of Jay raping her quickly entered Victoria's mind, as she gave David a sharp knee to the groin, and jetted up the stairs to the front door. Victoria never looked back.

Chapter 20

The Lion's Den was having its first year anniversary celebration. It didn't take long for the club to fill up with pretty ladies and every baller in the city. Tarron and Pretty Boy Ray spared no expenses for the event. Tarron had hired the Smith Marketing Company to advertise in all the local media markets, and rented emergency flood lights with decals of lions covering the lamps. It appeared that the great beasts were in a heated battle in the black sky when the lights finally came on. Several waiters and waitresses dressed in safari attire, served cold drinks to people as they waited in the extremely long line.

As patrons walked into the club, they passed through a tunnel decorated with all sorts of vines and trees, while the sounds of a jungle echoed through the speakers. The number one was shaped from huge blocks of ice, and placed on each bar, as Ray's beautiful waitresses served the guests in skimpy Lion costumes. Tarron and Ray were pleased at how the club had turned out.

Tarron had invited Mr. Shin and Mr. Lee, two of his former clients from the Marki Corporation to the event, who were also blown away by the décor. They were immediately escorted to the V.I.P. Lounge by Tarron, as Ray played bartender and poured the first round of Veuve Clicquot champagne. Each man grabbed a glass, and found a seat at the large circular black and chrome table.

"Here's to a great year," Mr. Shin said, holding up his glass.

"It's only going to get bigger and better," Tarron replied.

The men clanked their glasses, and the night was officially started. The dancers had prepared new routines, which they performed flawlessly. Ray renamed many of the drinks with words or phrases to coincide with the first anniversary - Alpha Martini, Uno Ice Tea, and Top Dog Margarita, just to name a few.

Tarron's clients were having a wonderful time. They danced, did their own personal karaoke, and downed numerous drinks. The guys had just finished another toast when Mr. Shin pulled Tarron to the side.

"Tarron, I heard through the grapevine that VIAX is looking to sell off some of its shares."

"What?" Tarron asked, in disbelief. He slammed his glass on the table, attracting Mr. Lee's attention.

"That's right," Mr. Lee chimed in.

Mr. Shin placed both hands on the table. "We're very interested in purchasing the investment firm. However, we're not sure if we have enough knowledge or connections with the right person to run the company."

"What about Jordan?" Tarron asked.

"Every since we caught serious billing errors and other questionable mistakes when he was over our account several years ago, we're not very confident that Mr. Jordan has our best interest in mind. Why do you think you became the primary investor of our accounts?" Mr. Lee asked.

"David told me that he had too many accounts, and that's why he was giving your account to me. He also said your business was seasoned, and that it would be a simple account to manage for a new guy," Tarron replied.

"No, Tarron. We researched you and watched your track record. David had no choice but to either put you over our account, or we would leave the firm. Plus, I believe he's only selling the shares for the money. David has been in financial trouble for years. We've been his personal bank for a long time. How do you think he got the money to invest in this club?" Tarron was speechless. "Don't you think it's kind of weird for his company to be named Viax-Shin?" Mr. Shin asked, as he smacked Tarron on his back, like they had been friends for a long time.

Tarron shook his head in amazement. This was too much information for one night. "Do you already own the company?" he asked.

"No, not legally, but with all the money he owes us we should own it. So we made him change the name. We wanted to see how desperate he was, and to our surprise he did it," Mr. Shin said laughing.

It's a good thing Shanice is sending me some of my old files because something is about to go down, Tarron thought. He threw back his shot of V.S.O.P. and chased it with his glass of champagne. Just as he was about to share his idea, Jay walked into V.I.P toward Tarron, with his fist clinched tightly.

Ray tried to get around the table and block for Tarron, but was too slow. Jay raised both his hands. Tarron lifted his arms to protect his face, as a sign that he was ready to battle, but Jay's fist opened and he grabbed Tarron's shoulders. He pulled Tarron into a strong embrace.

Tarron's eyes widened in surprise when he heard Jay shout above the music, "I'm sorry, bro. Please forgive me."

Tarron put his arms around the back of Jay, and squeezed him tightly. "I'm sorry, too."

Kurt and Tweet were shocked when they entered the V.I.P., and saw Jay and Tarron embracing. Ray walked over and threw his arms around both the brothers. He was so glad that all the nonsense was over. Kurt and Tweet ran over and joined in on the moment of affection. Not to be left out, the Marki Corporation executives also rushed over and connected to the circle.

"Tarron, why are we doing this?" Mr. Lee asked.

"My brother, Jay, is out of jail," Tarron replied.

"If I was locked up and released from jail, I'd rather have women hugging me, instead of six men with rock hard dicks pressed against my hip," Mr. Shin said, with laughter.

"Ugh, get off me," Tweet shouted. "I thought that was your belt buckle." They all laughed.

"I'm not wearing a belt," Mr. Shin said, laughing even harder. He lifted his shirt to expose his waist. He was obviously drunk. All the men laughed again as Tweet brushed off his hip.

Ray put Jay in a head lock, "Come on, jailbird, I know you can use a drink."

Pulling his head from Ray's embrace, Jay walked toward his brother. "In a minute, I need to talk to Tarron." Jay looked at his older brother. "I really need to talk with you about something important."

"Come on, we can use Ray's office," Tarron said. "How did you get out?" Tarron asked, as they walked toward the office.

"Your boss, David Jordan, footed the bill," Jay said.

Tarron paused and gave Jay a long stare. *Why in the fuck would David bail Jay out of jail?* Tarron thought. Jay continued past Tarron and walked in the office first. The smell of fresh sex filled the air, as Tarron shut the door.

"Damn, is this an office or the strip club? It smells just like pussy in here," Jay said laughing.

Tarron ignored Jay's question, and as eyed his brother from head to toe, he was still confused. But several things were beginning to make sense to Tarron. It was David who changed the numbers on his accounts, and David was also behind the investigation and his dismissal from the firm. David was the reason his life was turned upside down. *But why? What had he ever done to him?*

Tarron was skeptical about everything. He wasn't sure who

could be trusted. Even Jay showing up out the blue all apologetic was suspect.

"Tarron, your precious Secret is having an affair with David," Jay said, as he sat down on the couch.

Nothing made sense to Tarron. "I don't believe you."

"A while ago, I had so many of my boys on the streets telling me about seeing Secret getting into a long black limousine with INVEST 1 on the license plate. Now the only nigga I know riding around in a limousine as his personal car is David. Remember what mom always said, one person tells you - it's a rumor. But when five or more tell you - it's a fact."

"Why would Secret cheat on me with David?" Tarron asked, sitting down behind the desk.

"Maybe for the same reason you cheated on her. Besides, didn't you see him in the pictures in court that day?"

"No, for some reason I couldn't see who the dude was." Tarron paused for several minutes, but surprisingly wasn't upset about finding out the new information about his wife. "To be honest, I don't even know why I cheated. I thought Victoria had something that Secret couldn't give me, but I was wrong."

"And what was that?" Jay asked, as he looked at Tarron.

"I let the sex convince me that Victoria was my soul mate. She was supposed to make me complete."

Jay let out a little laugh. "You thought the day time ho and night time stripper was going to make you complete?"

"Night time stripper!" Tarron's astonishment couldn't be hidden.

"Yeah, how do you think we met?"

"I thought you guys met at Terrance's birthday party."

"Tarron, you can be so naïve at times. Have you ever asked yourself how she even found out about Terrance's party? Do you remember that day we were all at the pool hall?"

Tarron shook his head.

"Well that was the day I found out that we were fucking the same woman once again. She begged me
that day not to tell you about her night time occupation, or the fact that we were fucking. Victoria and I actually met that first night I was released from prison. Some of the hustler's from the old neighborhood took me to Club 55, and Victoria was the first girl that caught my eye. Shit, you know how bangin' her body is."

"Yeah, I do. That's one of the things that had me hooked too. I remember that night you got out of jail, because Motherdear kept calling, asking if I'd seen you yet," Tarron said.

"The guys treated me to a few lap dances, then a trip to a private room upstairs. I was lying on the black massage table when Victoria came in. Her hands were so soft. She quickly rubbed all those years of being locked up right out my body. We talked a little about this and that, and before I knew it, she had my punk ass screaming like a bitch. It was if she had me in some sort of trance. Victoria fucked me like she was the man." Jay chuckled before continuing. "Can you believe her stripper name was Sweet Honey? There's nothing sweet about that woman."

"That bitch got more shit with her than all the ho's we fucked from back in the day combined." Tarron got up and went to the bar. "I can't believe I messed up my family over a piece of ass."

Jay walked over to the bar to join him. He made himself a Remy and Coke on the rocks. "I was thinking the same thing. I can't believe I let Victoria play me like that."

"Why didn't you tell me about your rendezvous with Secret and Victoria? When we were young, we never kept secrets from one another. I thought we had a better bond," Tarron said.

"You were married to Secret before she even knew my connection with you, so don't blame her. It was one stupid mistake she made on one stupid night. I wanted to tell you, but Secret begged me not to. You two seemed so happy. I knew deep down that you would never forgive her if I told you, so I thought it was better if she told you."

Tarron took a long sip from his glass. "But when she never told me, you should've stepped up."

"Why? It might've changed what the two of you had. I never really wanted to be the one to cause you or Secret any pain. I was just pissed off at you for helping Ray with this club. I was only tripping because I couldn't admit to myself that I needed to get my shit together." Jay slowly shook his head, with his eyes closed. "As time went by, I thought she would tell you, because she made a promise to me, especially when I got out, but I guess things didn't go according to plan."

"What about Victoria?" Tarron asked.

"What about that cunt?"

"Did you rape her?" Tarron asked, with a concerned look. "Please don't lie to me, bro. I'm not the enemy."

Jay sat in silence as he tried to gather his thoughts. He wanted to lie, because letting his family down again was something he didn't want. He didn't want to be labeled a loser all his life.

"Jay, did you rape her?" Tarron asked again.

"Yes," Jay responded, as he downed his drink.

"Listen, man, I'm not here to judge you. I just want to help. We'll get through this."

"Well, since I'm sitting here spilling my guts, I might as well tell you how it started."

Tarron was all ears.

"In the beginning, I was fucking Victoria twice a week. Sometimes she would tell me about this married man she was seeing, but I didn't know it was you."

"So again, why didn't you tell me?"

Jay played with the ice cubes in his glass, and leaned his head back on the couch. "I was mad at you then. When you backed this club with Ray, I wanted her to grind you up like dog food. I was so mad, that I told Motherdear all about Secret, Victoria, and anything else I could think of that would hurt you. I just knew Motherdear would run and tell you."

"Motherdear thought it would be better to tell me in emails from an anonymous person," Tarron said.

Jay began to laugh. "I wonder who taught her old ass how to email."

Tarron thought about it for a second, then let out an even louder laugh. But suddenly he stopped, and his face turned cold and lifeless.

"It's only right if I'm honest with you right now as well." Before Jay could respond, he continued. "I wanted to fuck you up when I found out about you and Victoria, especially when you all started sending me those torturing ass emails."

"Yeah, I have to admit, that was fucked up. I know that was hard to deal with."

"You have no idea how hard it was for me to see you and her together. My plan was to find a way to get you back, but I never got the chance," Tarron said.

A feather falling on the ground could be heard from the silence in the room, that seemed to last forever. The tension was starting to make Jay uncomfortable.

"So who do you think is the father of Victoria's baby?" Jay asked.

"Hopefully it's you, because I don't want anything to do with that home wrecker. Maybe we should push her ass down a flight of steps or something," Tarron said, as he used his hands to show Jay how he'd do it.

Jay laughed and reached into his back pocket to pull out a piece of paper. "I was about to make another stupid mistake until a guard gave me your note." Jay threw the folded paper at Tarron.

Tarron opened and gave it a quick read. "What mistake?"

"David is out to get you. He wants Secret badly, and there's nothing he won't do to get her. His sole purpose for getting me out of jail is so I can help him destroy you," Jay said.

Tarron stared at Jay long and hard. "So, what's his plan?"

More Secrets More Lies

Chapter 21

Tarron woke up the next morning with a tremendous hangover. He and Jay had spent way too much time at the bar drinking shots and talking shit. Tarron rubbed his temples, as his head pounded with every move he made. Even blinking was becoming an unbearable task. He hadn't felt the wrath of alcohol in years, but it was worth it, because he and his baby brother had finally gotten over their differences.

Tarron eased his way out of bed, and stumbled all the way to the bathroom. *I'm still fucked up,* he thought, as he turned on the water in the shower. Tarron took off his boxers and stared at his manhood in the mirror. He was glad that Motherdear had blessed him with a big dick. He couldn't imagine going through life with anything less than his eight inches.

"Damn, I feel sorry for white dudes," he said out loud. Tarron started to impersonate body builders before stepping into the shower. The hot water felt good on his throbbing muscles, but did little for his urge to throw up. He needed to sober up quickly, so he turned on the cold water. *That's more like it.*

Tarron felt better after being in his personal spa for over an hour. He put on his favorite Redskin shorts, a wife beater, and headed to the kitchen. Food was the next destination. As entered the living room, he saw Ray sitting on the couch with his dick in one hand, and Tarron's cell phone in the other.

"Are you in this motherfucker jerking off? And who are you talking to on my phone?" Tarron asked, looking at Ray like he had three heads.

"I'm on the phone with your secretary Shanice. She's been calling here all morning while you were sleep, so I finally decided to answer. Now we're just having a nice little conversation."

"Why do you have your dick out?" Tarron asked.

"Sshh, she doesn't know that!" Ray said, with his hand over the phone.

"Give me that," Tarron said, grabbing his cell. "Shanice, please don't tell me you were having phone sex with him?"

"No, Mr. Jenkins. We were having a normal conversation. But…" Shanice stopped.

"But what Shanice?" Tarron was curious.

"I should've known something wasn't right when he asked me what size panties I wore."

Tarron looked at Ray, who displayed a huge grin. Tarron shook his head and walked back to his room.

"What's going on?" he said, closing the door.

"Well, I emailed you something important earlier, so I was calling to see if you received it," Shanice responded.

"No, I haven't checked my e-mails yet. Let me get online and I'll call you back," Tarron said, as he turned on his laptop.

"Please call me back, because I need to know how you want me to proceed."

He hung up the phone and sat at his small desk. As soon as he logged on, the familiar voice called out, YOU GOT MAIL.

<Click>

Tarron,
I'm glad that you finally woke up. I've been watching David go in and out of your office for weeks. At first I didn't think

anything of it, but the more he went in, the more curious I became. So I asked my boyfriend to install a small camcorder on your book shelf. I go in your office to change the tape every day, so we can make sure we get everything. I guess meeting that guy who was into electronics wasn't bad after all. Please don't get upset with me for not talking to you first. I tried calling you a couple of times, but I couldn't find you.

If you open the attached files, you'll see a couple of his searches. I've also been collecting all the documents that you wanted. I'll ask you later on how you knew where these files were hidden. There should be enough on them to send David away for the rest of his life.

When you view the video, give me a call. I have Melissa in human resources doing a few favors for me. I think David is getting a little suspicious. We need to hurry up.

Shanice

At the moment, Ray walked in his room. "Don't you know how to knock?" Tarron asked angrily.

"I thought you might be in here talking to my future wife too long," Ray responded with a smile.

"Man, Shanice isn't thinking about you. Besides, she's too young."

"Shit, I don't discriminate. Anyway, I'm headed to the club," Ray said, as he shut the door.

Tarron turned his attention back to his computer. He needed to send a response to Shanice on how to find more important files.

When he finished, he returned back to his inbox and saw an important e-mail from a former client.

<Click>

Tarron,

We heard about your dismissal from the firm. This news made us hesitate to continue to do business with the company. Please let us know if we can assist you in any way.

Damon Green,
CEO Green Industries

The message made Tarron feel at ease. He was happy to know that somebody had valued his hard work and dedication. His new feeling of confidence prompted him to write an e-mail of his own. He had to get his old life back, and this is where he was going to start.

Dear Mr. Shin,

It's time for you to put the future of expanding your company's dynasty in my hands. You know my background, experience, and knowledge are strong enough to bring you the leadership that you require.

You told me last night that you all might be interested in purchasing a controlling interest in the VIAX-Shin Investment Firm, but you didn't have a person in mind that could oversee this ven-

ture. Well, I believe that I'm the right
person for this job. I have inside knowledge of all the contracts, the influence to
bring in new bigger deals,and a reliable
and proven track record that will
make the clients want to remain with us.

I'm sure you know by now that I'm
going through personal problems with VIAX,
but I can prove to you that someone is trying to set me up. The company was wrong for
trying to tarnish my name and destroy my
career. However, the truth will surface
soon enough.

I believe your attempt to purchase the
VIAX-Shin Investment Firm is an outstanding
business opportunity, and hopefully you
will succeed in doing so. I look forward to
hearing from you soon.

Sincerely,
Tarron Jenkins

<Send>

*   *   *

Secret sat in the mirror applying her makeup. For some reason, she was extremely nervous. *I need to make this right,* Secret
thought repeatedly. She was applying several layers of eye
shadow, when she noticed Motherdear standing behind her.

"Why are you getting all made up? I thought you said that you weren't going to be long," Motherdear said, folding her arms.

"I won't be out late. I have to finish…," Secret turned around and looked into Motherdear's eyes.

"Finish what child?"

"Something that I should've done a long time ago." Secret quickly changed the subject. "How do I look?"

Motherdear reached down and grabbed both of Secret's hands. She immediately turned over her wrists to reveal the scars from the past. "Baby, you look beautiful. I hope you remember all the things that got you to this point, and not be stupid enough to do them again."

Secret looked down at the marks, and shook her head up and down. Those scars would be painful memories for the rest of her life. "Nothing will ever get me to that point again. I promise." She kissed Motherdear on the cheek, fluffed her hair, and headed out the door.

"Please make the right decision," Motherdear said, as she turned the corner.

Secret leaned back in the door and looked at Motherdear. "Don't worry. For the first time in a long time, I know I'm doing the right thing."

Secret stopped long enough to kiss the children. She gathered her purse, grabbed her keys, and headed to the garage. She could see Motherdear standing in the upstairs window as she pulled out the driveway.

Chapter 22

Secret drove slowly past the expensive homes in Potomac, Maryland, admiring the beautiful landscaped lawns. David's house sat at the top of a hill on a semi-private road, and appeared to be the best looking house in the development. Chills ran through her body as she approached the large black cast iron gate in front of his home. Her nerves were a wreck. Thoughts of what she was going to say to her former lover raced in her mind as she pushed the little white button on the intercom box.

"Is that you, baby?" a voice said, through the speaker.

His response made her even more uncomfortable. "Yes, it's me. Are you going to open the gates?" Secret asked.

She watched the gates close in her rear view mirror as her car crept up the long driveway. Driving slower gave her more time to think. Secret checked her makeup one last time before getting out the car, and walking slowly toward the front of the house. David was standing inside the open door waiting, as Secret strolled up the wide steps. She paused long enough for him to kiss her on the cheek.

"You look incredible," David said, as he closed the door. Secret's DKNY jeans looked as if they had been painted on.

"Thank you," she said blushing.

"I'm so glad you finally accepted my invitation to come over. Why don't we have a drink in the living room?" David asked, as he closed the door.

Secret sat on the couch and kicked her heels off, making herself at home. The new shoes were already killing her feet. David hurried to the kitchen and came back with a bottle of Dom Perignon and two glasses. *Maybe that will calm my nerves,* she thought. Secret watched as David filled her crystal glass with the expensive beverage, it quickly over flowed with bubbles.

"I hope you aren't planning to get me tipsy and have your way with me. I should've told you that I'm here for a purpose and nothing else," Secret explained.

"I have everything in place to calm you down. You seem to be a little on edge tonight. So just relax and let me cater to all your needs."

"David, I just came over to talk to you about our situation," Secret said.

He gave her a seductive look. "We have plenty of time to talk about our situation after we eat. I can smell the broccoli stuffed chicken breasts I made," he said, running into the kitchen.

This might be a long night. Secret grabbed the remote for the radio and nestled in the oversized recliner. She began clicking through the many stations until a song caught her attention. Secret closed her eyes and rocked her head to Heather Hadley's, *I'll Always Be Your Lady.*

David peeked through the swinging kitchen door and smiled. "Is that song dedicated to me, Boo?" he asked.

Secret shook her head up and down, as she listened to the words. "Of all the damn songs, why did I have to stop on this one," she whispered to herself. She took a sip of her champagne and ignored his question.

David rushed back into the kitchen with love in his eyes. It amazed him how beautiful Secret looked. At the moment, he couldn't believe how stupid Tarron was for cheating on her. He put the chicken breasts, along with some wild rice, on his best china and carried the plates above his shoulders like a waiter in a five star restaurant.

The delicious aroma quickly filled Secret's nostrils. She stood up and followed her nose to the dining room. Her eyes widened when she saw how well David had organized dinner. The lights were dim, and an eight candle candelabra glowed in the middle of the table. The closer she got, the more she noticed the steam rising from the buttered rolls.

David entered the dining room with a platter of baby back ribs lightly covered with honey bar-b-que sauce, and a bowl of green beans.

"I sure hope you're hungry."

"How many people are joining us tonight?" Secret asked.

David let out a small laugh. "It's just the two of us. As you can see, I got carried away. Trust me, I don't want to share you with anybody else on my night."

"Your night?" Secret repeated.

"Yes, my night," David said. He put a tiny portion of each dish on her plate. "I want you to taste everything. Then you can decide what you like best."

"It's a good thing you said something. I was about to go off. I thought you were trying to say I was fat or something by giving me all that food," Secret responded.

"Baby, you're the most attractive woman I've ever seen. Even if I had the power to change you, I wouldn't. You're perfect from head to toe."

Secret began to blush. She realized that what she came to do might be more difficult than she expected. She grabbed a glass of red wine off the table and took a sip. *This has got to end. I love my husband too much to continue with this. Right after dinner I'll tell him.*

David stared at Secret throughout the meal, and continued to refill her wine glass. "The dinner was delicious," she said, trying to break his trance. She was ready to have the discussion. "Can we take this into the living room?" Secret asked.

"Sure, I'm right behind you." He watched her ass with every

step as she walked into the living room and sat on the couch. David slid next to her and put his arm around her shoulders.

"I really need to talk to you," she said, taking his arm away.

"We have plenty of time for that." David began to rub Secret's shoulders.

She pushed his hands off. "I'm serious, David, this has to stop."

David leaned over and kissed the side of her neck. "What has to stop?"

Without hesitation, she looked him in the eyes. "David, I love Tarron. We're going to work out our problems, but we have to get rid of the distractions."

He sat straight up. His facial expression went hard. "Is that what I am to you, a distraction? If I'm such a fucking distraction, then why are you here? You could've told me all of this over the phone. There was no need for you to get all dressed up, and spend this time with me if you really wanted to end everything."

"You're right. I shouldn't be here. I just thought…"

"You just thought what?" David blurted out.

"You deserve more than a phone call. You should at least get this face to face," Secret said.

David grabbed Secret's arms. "I deserve you. Tarron can't love you like I do." She tried to pull away, but David held her tighter. "Tarron will never be enough man for you. You have to under-stand that," David said, squeezing her shoulders.

"You're hurting me!" Secret yelled.

David released his grip. "I'm sorry."

"Coming here was a mistake. I've gotta go," Secret said. As she turned to leave, David ran over and blocked her path. "Don't try to stop me, David. It's over!" she shouted.

"Can we end this on a kiss? I would like to taste your sweet lips one last time," David asked.

Secret knew better deep down inside, "No, David, let's just forget the kiss and say good bye."

Instantly a vase flew past her head, and smashed against the door. Secret quickly turned and noticed David breathing hard. "I can't live without you, and I won't let you live without me."

"What are you saying, David?" Secret asked nervously.

"I'll kill us both before I allow you to leave me for that no good husband of yours," David said, walking closer.

Even though Secret was afraid, she had to take a stand. "You'll just have to kill me then, because I still love Tarron, and nothing you do will ever stop the way I feel," she replied.

"How in the fuck can you love somebody who left you and your children for a stripper?" David asked. He hoped the comment would hit a nerve.

"I don't except you or anybody else to understand my feelings for Tarron. Now I'm going to leave. Please do me a favor and stop calling me, because I'm not going to answer." Secret grabbed her purse and looked at David one last time. "Take care of yourself."

David watched as she walked down the walkway. "You must be crazy if you think you're getting away that easy. This will never be over! I'm your man, and no one else will have you, especially Tarron. I love you more than life itself," David said out loud.

When Secret made it to her car safely, thoughts of what David said made her very uneasy.

A stripper, she thought, stepping on the gas.

Chapter 23

Secret drove around the beltway for hours. She should have gone home to check on Motherdear and the kids, but an urgent need to see Tarron had her driving past the exit to her home. Instead, she headed straight to The Lion's Den. If Tarron wasn't there, Ray would know where to find him.

The line to get into the club was around the corner when Secret arrived. The media hype was pushing the club to a new level. Secret parked her car and strolled to the V.I.P. entrance. Ray's best employee, Ryan, was working the door when she entered.

"I need to see some ID miss," Ryan stated.

"Listen, I'm Tarron's wife, Secret. Can you go find Ray for me because I'm really not in the mood for this?"

Ryan looked at Secret up and down. The tight fitting jeans she wore were easy to look at. "Sure, I'll be right back. Derrick, cover the door," he said, to another employee.

Ryan ran upstairs to the office. "Ray, where's Tarron?" he asked, without knocking.

"Boy, didn't I tell you to always knock on my door before entering. I don't know where Tarron is," Ray responded.

"Sorry, but his wife, Secret, is downstairs, and she's got that *I'm going to fuck somebody up look.*"

Ray knew exactly what that meant. Secret had a history of

losing her control. He remembered when she found out that Tarron had slept with his friend Pinkey. She went berserk. He smiled when he thought about Tarron's swollen left eye and busted lip.

"You look in the V.I.P. Lounge and the main area. I'll check the kitchen and storage room downstairs. If you find him before I do, have him meet me back here. Don't tell him Secret is in the club," Ray ordered.

Ray walked around every inch of the club, but could not find Tarron. When he returned to his office, Tarron was sitting at his desk. "Where were you?" he asked.

"Ryan told me to meet you up here. I was in the V.I.P Lounge working the bar. "What's up?" Tarron asked.

"Secret's in the club."

"Is that it? Why are you tripping?" Tarron asked.

"Because Ryan told me she had that crazy look when she got here. Plus, I just saw Victoria sitting at the general population bar, so you might have a problem. I just wanted you to be totally prepared if something kicked off," Ray explained.

Tarron went to the far wall and hit a button. Suddenly, a section of the wall slid open and Tarron looked through the two way mirror over the main area. His eyes scanned the bar, the sitting area, and finally the dance floor. Finally he noticed Victoria talking to an older guy near the restrooms.

"I guess it's going to be one of those nights."

Ray and Tarron began walking around the club. Every five steps someone stopped them to share a story or shake their hands. They were halfway around the club, when Victoria stepped out from one of the ladies' rooms.

"Tarron, just the guy I was hoping to find," Victoria said, as she grabbed his arm.

"Is he all you see?" Ray asked.

Victoria rolled her eyes. "What's up, Ray?" Her eyes scanned Ray's body, then focused back on Tarron. "So, Tarron, can I get a second?"

"You've got to be crazy if you think I'm going to give you any of my time. You need your fucking head examined. Besides, I thought you were supposed to be pregnant. What are you doing here?" Tarron responded. "Looking for the daddy?"

Ray looked as if he had seen a ghost. "Pregnant...who's the father?"

"Fuck you, Ray!" Victoria yelled.

"What are you getting mad at him for? Do you know who the father is?" Tarron asked.

"This is your baby, Tarron. I told you that the other day. That's what I came to talk to you about," Victoria responded.

"Victoria, let me explain this to you, since you obviously did-n't understand me the first time. I seriously doubt if the child you're carrying belongs to me, and even if it does, I will never claim it. Call me whatever you want, but I already have two children by a woman I love unconditionally. So you can go ahead and roll out on that note."

Ray covered his mouth to hide his laughter. Victoria rolled her eyes again, and watched Tarron disappear into the crowd.

"I'll be the father," Ray propositioned her. He laughed hysteri-cally as he waited for Victoria's response.

"I don't need you to do shit for me," Victoria said with an atti-tude as she hurried to catch up with Tarron.

"I don't know why not. You don't know who the father is any-way. The little bastard is going to need a role model, or at least a play uncle!" Ray shouted, still laughing. "Maybe you need to go on the Maury Povich show!"

Tarron continued to look for Secret, when Victoria caught up with him. He tried to ignore her, but she kept jumping in front of him trying to get his attention.

"What the hell do you want, Victoria?" Tarron asked, sound-ing frustrated. He tried not to cause a scene.

"We need to talk," she replied.

"We don't have anything to talk about. Go find David if you need to talk." Victoria stopped suddenly and looked at Tarron with a guilty conscience. "That's right. You didn't think anybody would find out about your little secret, did you?"

She tried to play it off. "I don't know what you're talking about."

"You never stop lying, do you? Let's put it this way, does the Hyatt Hotel downtown ring any bells?" Tarron asked.

Victoria's rendezvous had been revealed, but she still wasn't trying to admit it. "Again, I don't know what you're talking about. Maybe you have me confused with someone else. Seriously, Tarron, we need to talk about the baby, our baby."

"Bitch, there is no our when it comes to your bastard child."

Secret screamed, stepping from behind the wall. She pushed Victoria and she stumbled back into a waitress, who was carrying a tray of drinks. Beer bottles and glass splattered all over the floor.

"Watch what you're doing!" the waitress yelled.

"Pregnant or not, I'm gonna fuck you up for that," Victoria said, rushing back toward Secret.

Tarron jumped in her path and grabbed Victoria by her wrists.

"Get out the way, Tarron! I'm going to beat this bitch's ass!" Secret yelled.

"You wish you could beat my ass." Victoria tried to push Tarron's hands off her. "Let me go, Tarron. She shouldn't have put her hands on me."

"Both of you need to cut this shit out," Tarron said, as he walked Victoria backwards. "This is my place of business."

Half the onlookers in the main area were watching the entire episode. Ray walked up with two bouncers, who began to disperse the small crowd.

"I'm going to let you go, Victoria. Are you calm?" Tarron asked.

"I'm cool, let me go," Victoria responded.

"If you try anything, I'm going to make Big Moe put your ass out," Tarron said.

Victoria pointed at Secret. "This is not over. You better watch your back."

"What did I just tell you!" Tarron shouted at Victoria. He made a hand gesture, and Big Moe came over and stood next to Tarron.

Victoria pushed Tarron in the chest. She bumped into several people as she stormed away. Tarron watched as she strutted to the bar in the next room, sat on the stool and just stared.

"Tarron, I need to talk with you," Secret said.

"Let's take a drive. I think we need to get out of here," Tarron replied.

Victoria watched as Tarron and Secret walked toward the door. She slowly followed at a distance. As they stopped at the coat check to retrieve their jackets, a hand was smashed against the left side of Secret's face.

As Secret fell back into the counter, Victoria threw two quick punches to her body. Tarron reached over and pushed Victoria back. When Secret gained her balance, she squeezed her fist so tight the veins popped out the back of her hands.

"Bitch!" Secret screamed. "I'll kill you!"

"I'm right here," Victoria answered, pointing her finger toward the ground.

Secret tried to take Victoria's head off, but Tarron was still in the way. She swung her fists wildly over Tarron's shoulders. "Move, Tarron!"

"How you like being smacked?" Victoria said, laughing behind Tarron.

At that point, Tarron had heard enough. It was obvious that Victoria wanted to get her ass beat, so he moved out the way. Secret immediately started throwing punches. Victoria responded with a flurry of haymakers and short hooks. When a crowd circled the fight, both women had a hand full of each others hair.

The red lights on all the bars blinked, as an indication that a fight had broken out. Within seconds, bouncers were running into the crowd. It took several minutes to pry the tight grip both women had of each others hair.

"Get your wife out of here, Tarron," Big Moe said.

When they got outside, Secret tried to pull herself away. "Get off me, Tarron! I can't believe you!" she screamed.

"I know you're not talking. That sure is the pot calling the kettle black."

"Kettle, pot, what the hell are you talking about? Tarron, you started all of this bullshit. You were the only who compromised our marriage with a fucking stripper."

Damn, how did she found that out? I guess everything else needs come out tonight too, he thought. "Be careful, Secret. Do you really want to compare affairs? If you want to compare David to Victoria, we can."

Secret couldn't believe what she'd just heard. She was speechless. *How did he find out?* Tarron walked over and grabbed her. At first she resisted. She already had one death threat for the night, so she wasn't taking any chances. He tried again. This time she gave in.

"I love you, Secret," Tarron shouted, as he wrapped his arms around her. "I'm so sorry for hurting you. Please forgive me. I don't want to lose what we had."

Secret's eyes filled with tears. She pressed her face into Tarron's chest. "I love you too. You don't know how glad I am to hear you say all of that. I'm sorry for hurting you as well."

Tarron lifted Secret's head. He slowly rubbed away the tears running down her face and pressed his lips against hers. They both felt the passion being transferred from one another. Visions of the very beginning flashed and replayed like an old movie.

Chapter 24

Tarron followed Secret down the long, empty streets. He watched her from behind continuously wipe her eyes in the rear view mirror. Tarron was somewhat surprised as she made a left into the Grand Hyatt Hotel. *Does everybody come here?*

They parked their cars in the lower level of the garage. He noticed several used pieces of tissue in the passenger seat of her car as he rushed to open her door.

"What are we doing here?" Tarron asked.

Secret exited the car and looked deeply into Tarron's eyes. "I want to make love to you. Now! I want to spend the entire night making love to you over and over again."

Tarron was speechless. He hadn't heard her talk like that in so long. He reached out his hand and pulled his wife close. A soft smile spread over his face, as they entered the elevator in the far corner of the garage.

As Tarron checked into the hotel, Secret used her cell phone to call Motherdear.

"Baby, it's late. Where are you?" Motherdear asked.

"I'm standing in the lobby of the Grand Hyatt downtown," Secret replied.

"No, child!" Motherdear shouted. "Just come home. Don't do anything you'll regret."

"I won't regret anything tonight. I need for you to stay with the children. Tarron and I will not be home until late tomorrow."

"Did you say Tarron?" Motherdear asked, with a high pitched voice.

"Yes, Ma'am. Tarron and I need some time to work things out."

"Remember child, sex will only go so far. Eventually, both your hearts will have to heal and take it the rest of the way."

"Do you think my heart will heal first?" Secret asked.

"I don't know, baby. Hopefully, both of your hearts will mend at the same pace. Go ahead, child. The children are in good hands. You two stay until you've worked everything out," Motherdear ended.

Secret was closing her cell phone, just as the clerk gave Tarron their room key. She walked over and grabbed the back loop on Tarron's slacks, something she used to do all the time. Secret rested her head on Tarron's back, as they waited by the elevators.   She was surprised when Tarron opened the door to the beautiful suite.

"You didn't have to go all out, baby," Secret said, dropping her purse on the floor.

"Yes, I did. We haven't been together in a very long time, so this night is special." He walked over to his wife and gave her a long deep kiss. "Meet me in the bathroom in five minutes," he whispered.

The kiss instantly made the insides of Secret's panties soaking wet. She couldn't get undressed fast enough. As she sat on the bed to take of her jeans, she spoke to herself. *Tarron was just doing him and I was just doing me. I have no right to be mad, or even think about it anymore at this point. I'm going to let everything die from the past and start living for today.*

At that moment, Tarron walked out the bathroom completely naked. His rock hard dick swung from left to right. Secret's eyes followed as he walked to the nightstand. He turned the small radio to 93.9 and the sounds of *Knocking the Boots* by H-Town blasted through the speakers. Tarron slowly began moving his hips in a circular motion. Secret set up on the edge of the bed, like a child waiting for a gift. He spun around and pumped his hips, causing his dick to bounce up and down. Secret smiled and licked her lips, ready for a tasty treat.

Suddenly he remembered the running water and ran to the bathroom.

"Is the show over?" Secret asked, playfully.

"Not at all, get in here," he demanded.

When she entered the bathroom, Tarron was waiting for her in the tub. He watched closely as Secret walked to him in her birthday suit. *I was a fool to leave all of that,* he thought.

"You look so beautiful," Tarron said, as she gently positioned herself in the tub.

"Stand up," Secret ordered, ignoring his compliment.

Following her commands, Tarron stood in position, while the soap suds ran down his thighs. Secret grabbed his throbbing dick with her hand, and began stroking it before inserting it into her mouth. Her lips were so soft and moist. His eyes immediately rolled up into his head, as tiny goose bumps appeared on his arms.

Secret sucked his dick like she'd taken a class, forcing a tingling feeling from the base of his hips to his circumcised head. He loved it when she made circular motions with her long tongue around the tip. It caused Tarron's dick to flick up and down inside her mouth.

Tarron pressed both of his hands against the back wall over the tub. He was starting to become lightheaded. His head rocked back and fourth with pure pleasure. Suddenly, Secret released his dick and pulled Tarron down into the tub by his hand.

He softly kissed her forehead and slid his tongue down her face until he reached her lips. They both kissed each other forcefully.

Tarron eased his pulsating dick between Secret's thighs and tickled her clit. She let out a loud moan. The position of her body caused his dick to press against her inner wall. The force caused little pains to shoot up her thighs, past her chest, and up to her neck.

Secret lifted her legs and rested them on the outer edge of the tub, to allow Tarron's thick dick to tap her deepest zones. He slowly began to speed up the motion of his strokes. The faster he dug, the louder she moaned.

Secret began squeezing his dick with the muscles of her pussy. Tarron knew what this meant. She was about to have an orgasm. He quickly reached under the water and grabbed her ass with both hands. He pinched her cheeks, as the inner walls opened and closed around him.

Tarron had a blueprint to Secret's pussy. His dick always hit the right spot that other partners from the past probably missed. Tarron smiled when Secret's head shook frantically from left to right.

"Fuck me harder!" she yelled.

Her kinky demands made Tarron make rougher and deeper thrusts with every stroke. "Is this how you want it?" he asked, between heavy breaths.

"Yes, just like that, baby!"

The more he continued to pound, the closer he was to exploding. "I'm about to cum…I'm about to cum!" he roared.

The warm cum sent chills throughout his entire body as he began to shake. Secret sunk her teeth deep into his chest, causing Tarron to moan.

Tarron collapsed into the water. He hadn't had an orgasm like that in a while.

"Your dick felt so good," Secret said, as she grabbed a washcloth off the side of the tub. Tarron gave her a head nod, which meant he agreed. She put the cloth inside the water, and slid it across his chest. His nipples got hard as Secret rubbed them with soft strokes.

"This reminds me of our wedding night," Tarron said.

"It really does. We were so happy that night. Hopefully we can get back to the way things were," she replied.

Secret washed Tarron's entire body, and he returned the favor. They stayed in the tub until their hands resembled prunes. They patted each other dry with the large white fluffy hotel towels. Tarron kissed Secret as he lifted her into his arms and carried her back into the other room, placing her on the bed.

Tarron kneeled down next to her and began to lick her toes. He knew that always drove her crazy. He sucked on every toe, and made his tongue wiggle between each one, until his dick stood at attention.

Tarron stood up and crawled on the bed. Her dripping vagina stared at him. Tarron used his fingers to open her lips. His tongue worked mini laps around her clit. He then dove his entire face between her pussy. Secret's eyes widened and closed with pleasure. She couldn't focus. The pleasure he gave Secret sent her into convulsions. She reached down and grabbed his hair as he worked his magic between her thighs.

Secret became flooded with orgasm after orgasm. She jammed her nails into his back and almost drew blood. Her thighs shook from the mighty spasms. Suddenly, she locked her legs behind his head like a wild woman. He couldn't breath. Tarron pulled with all his might, but couldn't pry her legs open. He had to bite her clit just to get her off.

"Ouch! What the hell you do that for?" Secret yelled, releasing her lock around his head.

Tarron coughed as he gulped for air, "You almost killed me!" he yelled back.

Secret sat up and pushed Tarron onto his back. He looked at her as if she'd gone crazy. She bent forward, arched her back and slid her wet pussy down his body leaving a trail of pussy juice behind. Secret placed her body on top of Tarron's hard dick, and started to pop her pussy up and down. Tarron watched her closely as her vagina worked his dick perfectly. Tarron began to smack Secret's ass with his right hand. He could no longer control the urge, so he stuck his thumb into her bouncing asshole.

"Is this the type of pussy you want? Did you cheat on me because this pussy wasn't freaky anymore?" she whispered.

"No, I love this pussy. I love you."

He made his body move with Secret's strokes. They bounced to the foot of the bed, where Tarron was able to place his feet on the floor. He grabbed Secret's legs and stood up. Tarron pounded deeper with every inch of his erect dick.

"Let my legs go, and put me down!" she shouted.

Tarron quickly obliged. Secret got on top of the bed and arched her back. *Now she's in my favorite position,* he thought, as he rammed his throbbing dick in her juicy pussy. Tarron held her waist tightly and made barking sounds as he rotated his hips. Secret found her own little groove, and backed her ass up on his dick, his favorite position.

"I want you to fuck this pussy like you never fucked anyone else in you life. You'll never leave this pussy again!" Secret shouted.

Tarron took deep jerks, to allow his dick to hit and rub against Secret's erogenous spots, but knew he wasn't going to last much longer. He worked the ugly faces, trying to fight back the next orgasm. Tarron pushed harder and harder, until Secret's head hit the headboard. He grabbed her thighs and used them to get even more leverage to pound deeper. Seconds later, he finally exploded.

They both collapsed on the bed at the same time. The term exhausted would have been an understatement at this point. As they looked up at the ceiling, Tarron thought back to the cheating comment Secret made. In his mind this was the start of a new marriage for them, so he wanted to start off the right way. Honesty.

"Baby, from here on out, I want us to be completely honest with each other," Tarron said.

Secret hoped he wasn't going to ask her about David. "I agree," she responded, trying to catch her breath.

"Let's also agree not to talk about the past. What's done is done. We can't move on like that."

She was relieved. "I agree with that as well."

"So, with all that being said, I have something to tell you because I don't want you to find out from someone else." Tarron paused. He wasn't sure how Secret was going to react, but he had to get it off his chest. "I know you heard Victoria talk about her pregnancy at the club tonight." He paused again. "And even though I don't think I'm the father, she's four months pregnant, so there's a slight possibility that I could be. How does that make you feel? "

Secret turned her head and looked at her husband. "I'm not going to sit here and lie to you. If you're the father, then I'm going to be hurt," she said.

Their eyes met. He didn't want to hurt Secret anymore, so he had to find a way to make this work. "Would you leave me?" he asked.

"I really can't answer…" Secret sat straight up in the bed.

"What's wrong?" Tarron questioned.

Suddenly Secret got off the bed, and searched for her purse. When she found it she dumped everything on the bed. Tarron wasn't sure what was going on, so he remained quiet. Secret opened up a small piece of paper and displayed a huge grin.

"What about if she's only two months?"

"What are you talking about?" he asked.

"Victoria is a liar! She's only two months pregnant," she said, showing him the note from the nurse at the hospital.

Tarron looked at the paper, and then back at Secret. "Is this a joke?"

"No, it's not. I'm not going to say how I found out, but trust me when I tell you that she's only eight weeks. So what are your chances of being the father now?"

Tarron grabbed Secret and kissed her all over her face. "The chances are zero. Victoria and I weren't together eight weeks ago."

It had been a really long time since Tarron and Secret made love for hours. They were tangled around one another when the alarm clock sounded. She rolled over and tried to find the button to shut it off.

"Who would set the alarm clock for this time in the morning?" Secret asked, still fumbling with the clock.

"That would be my wake up call I set for myself," he replied.

"Why do you need a wake up call? Are you going somewhere?

Tarron didn't reply. He rolled over to get his mouth in position to kiss her nipple. Tarron began sucking on Secret's left breast and massaging the right.

"Oh my, you set the alarm to wake yourself up to start all over again?" Secret questioned.

Tarron looked up and smiled. He rolled Secret onto her stomach and slid between her legs. Once again, he positioned himself to make passionate love for the next two hours.

Chapter 25

Jay listened for hours as David talked about changing claim forms to make it look as if Tarron was embezzling money from the firm. They'd been having phone conversations over the last few days, but this time, David wanted Jay to come to his house. He also discussed little things that Jay could do like sending anonymous e-mails, and finding out more details about Tarron's personal life. Jay shook his head as he thought about how sick David was.

David even bragged about how he'd been watching Secret's every move since she broke it off with him a week ago. He told Jay that he'd been sitting outside her house for days, but hadn't seen her coming or going.

"Do you know where she might be staying?" David asked.

"She's been staying with Tarron at his apartment in D.C.," Jay replied.

David started to crack his knuckles. "I can't believe she would go back to that man, after all he's done," he said.

"Don't worry, Tarron's gonna get what's coming to him," Jay responded.

David looked sadly out his living room window, as if he were lost in his own home. *Loving this woman is killing me,* he thought.

"Is this meeting over with? I have another appointment?" Jay questioned.

"Yeah, we're all done here."

Jay finished his Corona and headed for the door. He turned around as David called his name.

"When this is over, I'm going to back you with a club of your own. Your brother might not believe in you, but I do." David thought he knew just what to do to make sure Jay was on his side, and he figured *a club* would do the trick.

Jay listened to David intensely as he continued to talk. The moment he was done, he gave him a long stare, followed by a head nod. *This nigga is crazy. He must think I'm a fool. When all this is over, the only thing he's going to back -is his ass against a wall - so his cellmate can wax that ass,* Jay thought.

"Look man, I've got a few errands to run. I'll get up with you later," he said, headed to the door.

Moments after leaving the meeting, Jay rushed to see Motherdear. He hadn't seen his mother since he'd gotten out of jail, and needed to hear her voice. He drove to Tarron's old house in complete silence, as he thought about Victoria. He knew she never wanted to see him again, but he had to know if the baby was his. When he approached Tarron's house, he saw an old friend of his walking her dog. He parked his car, and walked across the street.

"Hey, Leslie. How's the little mutt?" he asked, trying to get a quick look at her body. He hadn't seen her in a while and wanted to know if she'd maintained her sexy, petite, shape.

"That's not funny," she replied, catching his stare. "What are you doing around here?"

"I'm here to visit my mother. Listen, I was wondering, do you have a second?" Jay asked.

"Sure," she replied. "Let's go inside."

Jay's eyes remained glued to Leslie's ass as she walked into her house. They had been having sex off and on for a couple of years, so he wasn't sure if she wanted to do more than talk. He'd love to hit that ass, but knew other things were more important at the moment.

As soon as they reached the living room, Leslie plopped down on the sofa, "So, what do you want to talk about?" she asked.

"Well, I need you to do me a big favor. There's this crazy ass nigga who's been sneaking around my brother's house lately. I need for you to keep an eye out for him," he said, with a more serious look than usual. "If you see anybody creeping around, or sitting in a black limousine, please give me a call."

Leslie shook her head up and down. "No problem, Jay." She knew he was concerned, but she was also very interested in Jay staying a while. "Now, are you going to stay a while and do me a favor?" she asked, with a slight grin.

Even though he wanted to take her up on the offer, he decided to decline. "Maybe later," he said. Jay kissed Leslie on the forehead and left. He saw Motherdear taking groceries from the trunk of her car as he walked across the street. "Can I give you a hand, pretty lady?"

Motherdear turned to see Jay holding out his hands. "How can you show your face around here and joke after all you've done?" She obviously wasn't in the joking mood.

"Things aren't what they seem," Jay replied.

Motherdear looked into Jay's eyes. Something was very different about him. "Oh really, so how are things?" Motherdear asked, with concern.

Jay grabbed the bags from her hand and headed in the house. "We can talk about everything inside."

Motherdear suddenly wondered if Tarron would freak out if he came home and found Jay inside his house. She instantly become nervous. When Motherdear got to the front door, she heard a horn. She turned and saw Tarron parking his car. *His ass hasn't been home in days, and as soon as his brother shows up, here he comes,* Motherdear thought.

"What up, Mom?" Tarron asked, kissing Motherdear on the cheek.

"Hello, Son. This is a surprise. What brings you around?" Motherdear asked nervously.

"I've got a little business to take care of." Tarron cut the conversation short, and proceeded to walk past Motherdear, but she moved her tall frame in front of him.

"Son, I need you to get something from the store for me."

Tarron was about to respond, when Jay appeared at the front door. He paused and looked at his mother strangely. Motherdear stood in between her sons, and looked at each one of them with concern.

"Tarron, honey, I can explain," Motherdear said.

"Explain what?" Tarron asked.

"Your brother was in the neighborhood and helped me bring the groceries in the house," Motherdear said.

"Don't worry, Mom. I told Jay to meet me here."

"You did?"

"Yeah, he did. Now come inside before someone sees us," Jay replied.

Motherdear's eyes widened. "Before someone sees us. What are you boys up to?"

"Don't worry, Mom, we'll explain everything when we get inside," Tarron said, walking into the house.

Motherdear closed the door and immediately drilled her sons. "Now, somebody better start talking. I want to know why you all are getting along all of a sudden, and who you two are afraid of being seen by?"

Tarron cut her off. "Alright, I've come to find out why my boss, David, is the one causing all my problems at work. He's in love with Secret, and believes that having me locked up for stealing from the firm will help him out."

"Why that no good son of a bitch!" Motherdear shouted.

Tarron looked at Jay, and they both smirked.

"Now, what happened between you two? I can't remember the last time I saw both of you together, without trying to knock each others heads off," Motherdear replied, looking at Jay with a scolding expression.

"I gave my life a real good look when I got arrested, and I realized that I needed my brother." He smiled.

"My baby did some soul searching," Motherdear said, and returned the smile.

"I guess," Jay replied. "I finally realized that I blamed every-body for all the wrong I've done, when I should've been blaming myself." Jay walked over and put his arm on Tarron's shoulder. "Just when I was about to make another dumb decision, a note put me in the right frame of mind. A simple piece of paper from my brother made me realize that blood is thicker than water."

"That's why we're working together to make everything right," Tarron added.

Motherdear's eyes filled with tears. She was so happy to see her boys getting along. "What about that Victoria girl? I heard she's pregnant, and one of you is probably the father," she point-ed. "I thought we had that talk where I told you not to screw those fast ass girls without protection. Who forgot to strap up?

Tarron laughed. "Well, I have some good news and some bad news. Which one do you want first?"

"The good news," both Jay and Motherdear said, at the same time.

"The good news is, I just found out that Victoria is only eight weeks pregnant. This clearly means that I can't be the father. The bad news is that still leaves you, bro," Tarron said.

"Thank you, Jesus!" Motherdear shouted. "One down and one to go."

"It's okay with me if I'm the father. I need a little responsibility in my life," Jay said.

"My baby really has changed," Motherdear responded.

"Well, whether you're the father or not, Victoria is going to get hers when all this mess with David is finished," Tarron said.

"Okay. What can I do to help this plan work?" Motherdear asked.

"We need you to keep an eye out for Tarron's boss. He's been talking real crazy. If you ever see anything out the ordinary around here, call us immediately," Jay responded. "I've got a hunch that he'll be sneaking around here."

"Whatever he has up his sleeve, I'll find out. I know his every move when he's at the office, because Shanice and a couple of other employees have been keeping me posted," Tarron said.

"David is losing his mind. He's been following Secret around town. When we met earlier, he told me that Secret ended everything between them because of her love for you. Needless to say he's not happy about that, and wants to get rid of you for good," Jay replied.

"Oh, hell no! You boys need to stop playing with this fool. A nut like him is unpredictable. You need to take care of him before he does something real stupid." Motherdear stood with her hands on her hips.

"Don't worry, Mom. If David tries to mess with one, he'll have to deal with the both of us," Tarron said.

"I don't like this. I really think we should notify the police or someone. But if you boys are sure, then I'll leave you all alone to talk," Motherdear replied.

"We're sure. Go make yourself comfortable," Jay said, walking over to the sofa. They watched as Motherdear disappeared into the kitchen. "So, where are Secret and the children?" Jay asked Tarron.

"The kids are on a camping trip with their school, and Secret should be at the apartment," Tarron said. He gave Jay a look that said, *why are you asking.*

J. Tremble

Jay noticed Tarron's facial expression. "Don't even trip. I was just making small talk." They both had a quick laugh before Jay continued. "Let me ask you something. bro. Why haven't you moved back in the house yet? It's obvious that you and Secret are working things out."

Tarron pulled out his cell phone to call a few of his old clients. "Because even though we're working on our relationship, we still decided to take things slow. Can you dig it?"

Before Jay could respond, Tarron started talking to someone else. He wrote down several numbers, and little abbreviations with each phone call, as Jay sat and watched him work his magic.

Jay's cell phone rung. When he looked at the caller ID it said: JORDAN. He got up and walked into the dining room.

"What's up, Dave, I mean David," Jay joked.

"Nothing much, Jay. What are you doing?"

"I'm just over this little freak's house getting ready to smash some ass," Jay replied. He laughed, until he noticed David didn't think it was funny.

"Man, I can't believe you're out trying to get some pussy when you need to be working on how to get Tarron. I got special agents hounding me about my financial books for my company, and they're not ready. I haven't changed all the files to make Tarron look like the bad guy yet," David said. "But you're not helping at all!"

"So, what do you need me to do?" Jay asked.

"You're from the streets, so be creative. Put some drugs around his house or something. You're also supposed to be finding Secret for me. You need to be working on breaking down his whole fucking life! I didn't bail your ass out of jail so you could sit around!" David shouted, then hung up.

Jay walked back into the living room full of laughter. "That was David. That nigga is freaking out. He wants me to make your house hot, and to find Secret too." Jay flopped back onto

219

the couch, unsure about how Tarron would respond to the news.

Tarron looked up at Jay and held up his pointer finger. He cracked a huge smile as he wrote another note on his notepad. "Everything is almost in place. Two weeks from now, we'll be kings," Tarron said, before hanging up the phone.

"Now what did that motherfucker say?" Tarron asked. David was really starting to piss him off.

"He wants me to plant some drugs in your crib, so we need to work fast."

Jay and Tarron sat in the living room for hours, going over the plan. When they were done, they gave each other a pound, and both kissed Motherdear goodbye. As they walked out the door, a black limousine peeled off down the street.

"I know that wasn't who I think it was," Tarron said to Jay, jumping back inside the door.

"Who else rides around in a limo," Jay responded. "I hope he didn't see me."

*   *   *

A week went had gone by, and Jay was still meeting with David, and reporting his agenda to Tarron. The plan seemed to be working like clock work. The only thing that worried Jay were the text messages from Leslie, about seeing David sitting outside Tarron's house everyday. Even though Secret, Motherdear and the kids had been ordered to stay in the house unless the kids were going to school, he was still concerned. Jay didn't want one of his family members bumping into David by any means. The guy was obviously a time bomb waiting to explode.

Tarron continued to get a lot of useful information from his contacts at work. The time was almost right for the CEOs of the

Marki Corporation to make an offer on the shares for VIAX, so he was very excited. Something told Tarron that they were going to offer him some sort of position. He was on an important phone call with Mr. Shin when Secret beeped in on the other line. Tarron put him on hold and clicked over to answer the call.

"You need to come home now!" Secret shouted into the phone.

"What's wrong?" Tarron asked.

"That bitch, Victoria, is out front, yelling she needs to see her baby's father."

"She's doing what?"

Secret took a deep breath. "I'm going to have to kill this bitch, Tarron. This shit is embarrassing. All the neighbors are looking out their windows. She won't stop screaming your name and honking her horn. What am I supposed to do?"

"I'm on my way," Tarron said, and hung up the phone. He was already at his front door, ready to leave when he realized Mr. Shin was still on the other line. Tarron ran back and picked up the receiver, but the line was dead. *I'll call him later,* he thought, as he rushed out the door.

Tarron hit the beltway going 80 mph, racing over to his house in Bethesda. When he pulled up, Victoria was pacing back and forth on the front lawn, resembling a mad woman. Tarron double parked his car in the middle of the street, and jumped out like the police rushing to the scene.

"Girl, have you lost your mind?" Tarron shouted, as he approached her with anger.

Victoria got chills when she saw Tarron walking toward her. She began to back up, and moved around to the other side of her car. "I need to talk to you," Victoria replied.

"Why are you in front of my house, acting like some ghetto ass girl? You know damn well I'm not staying here."

"Well, if you give me your new address, I wouldn't have to come here. Look, our baby is driving me crazy. I don't want to go through this alone," Victoria said.

"Victoria, let me go ahead and break this down. I just recently found out from a very reliable source that you lied about how far along you are," Tarron said.

"Oh yeah? Well, what false information do you have this time?" she asked.

"The fact that you're only eight weeks pregnant, which is only two months and not four months like you originally said. You and I both know that it's been more than two months since the last time we were together, so that means I'M NOT THE FATHER!"

Victoria felt like she was going to faint. For the life of her, she couldn't understand how Tarron found out the truth. She tried to speak, but nothing came out.

"Please take all your lies and leave my house. There is nothing more you can do or say at this point," he stated.

"I love you, Tarron. We can start all over," she said. Victoria started to walk around the car, to be near Tarron.

Tarron shook his head. *This girl will not take no for an answer,* he thought. "It can never be like before. I don't ever want to see you again!" Tarron shouted.

Victoria stopped and looked Tarron up and down. "You think I'm crazy, but I'm not. You're the crazy one. When I have our baby, I'm gonna be in your life forever."

Tarron had reached his boiling point. His face became hard as stone. He quickly stepped toward Victoria and chased her around the car.

Secret swung the front door open. "Tarron, she's not worth it. The police are on the way."

He immediately stopped and looked up at the house. His eyes moved from Secret to the upstairs window, as he locked eyes with Terrance and Tika.

"Victoria, I've reached my limit with you. Please do me a favor and go harass David for a change. I'm more than sure that he could be the father." Tarron turned away, after seeing Secret give him a signal to end the conversation. He began to walk toward the house. "Carry your ass home before you get hurt, tramp."

Secret resembled a deer in front of headlights. She asked herself several questions. *Did I just hear him say David is the father? Was that asshole fucking that slut too?*

When Tarron reached the front door, two police cars turned the corner with their sirens at the highest volume. He shook his head, as all the neighbors gathered in small groups to witness the action.

A male and female officer got out the first squad car. The second car was from the K-9 unit. "Damn, they even brought the dogs," Tarron mumbled.

"What seems to be the problem?" the overweight female officer asked.

"This woman is trespassing and disturbing the peace!" Secret shouted from the porch.

Victoria immediately worked on her Oscar performance. "I'm sorry officer."

"Sorry for what?" the male officer asked.

"I'm in love with that man standing over there," Victoria said, pointing to Tarron. "We're about to have a baby together, and I just found out he's a married man with children," she whimpered.

The female officer turned to her partner with a suspicious look, "You get her statement. I'm going up to the house to talk to the cheater and his wife." She slowly walked toward Secret and Tarron, to get their side of the story. After talking to them for a few minutes, she realized that her assumption was wrong. *Victoria was probably some fatal attraction type broad.*

Victoria was still pretending to cry when the female officer walked back. "I'm gonna need for you to leave the area," she said to Victoria, in a firm tone.

"Why, I need to talk with my baby's father!" Victoria yelled.

"The homeowner doesn't want to talk with you. So I'm going to ask you one more time to get in your car and leave, before I have to arrest you for trespassing," the officer replied.

Victoria's tears quickly turned to red horns as she stomped like a spoiled child to her car.

"Secret, you might've won this battle, but I'll win the war. When I have this baby, everything is going to change!" Victoria shouted. When she got into the car, her anger turned to the officer. I'm calling Captain Jackson to report your fat ass. You'll be on traffic duty by tomorrow, bitch."

Secret and Tarron just stood in amazement. Victoria had changed into a high school fatal attraction.

Tarron's cell phone vibrated. It was Mr. Shin's number on the caller ID screen.

"Hello, Mr. Shin," Tarron said, into the phone.
Secret watched Tarron with her arms folded across her chest. She became extremely irritated as Tarron whispered into the phone.

"He's so greedy. I knew if we added that huge bonus, he would jump for the deal. The only thing with big deals is that the fine print can kill you," Tarron said, with huge laugh.

"Daddy!" Tika shouted, from inside the house.

"Mr. Shin, I'll meet you in half an hour," Tarron said, and pressed the end button.

"I know we're going to talk about what just happened before you leave," Secret said.

"I'm going to speak to the kids, but I have to go after that," Tarron replied.

Tarron walked past Secret into the house. Tika jumped into his arms from the third step. Tarron began to twirl her around while making fart sounds in her neck. As he continued to play with Tika, Terrance made his way down the steps.

"How can you have that woman coming to our house like that?" Terrance asked.

Tarron looked up, "I know we've talked about you staying out of grown folks' business before, haven't we?"

Terrance folded his arms. "I'm going to need so much therapy, messing with you and Mom."

"Ha-Ha, you know I think you're missing your calling as a stand up comic," Tarron responded. "Now go upstairs before you get embarrassed."

Tarron's cell phone went off again. He looked at the number, and this time it was Shanice.

"What's up, Shanice?"

"We might have a problem. I think David found out that people are helping you. I think he overheard several of us going over the plan. You need to talk to Mr. Shin or Mr. Lee right away," Shanice replied.

"I'm on my way to meet with Mr. Shin now. Don't worry about anything. I'll talk to you later." Tarron hung up the phone. He kissed Tika on the forehead. He punched Terrance in the arm, then headed for the door.

"We need to talk, Tarron," Secret shouted as he opened the door.

"Give me three days, and I'll have all the time in the world," Tarron replied, as he gave her a kiss and closed the door.

Chapter 26

David continued to sit outside of Tarron's house over the next few days. He often tried calling Secret's cell phone, but she never answered, which really pissed him off. Leslie also held up her end of the deal, by calling Jay every time she saw David's limousine sitting at the end of the block. She watched the limo circle the block at least four or five times a day. Jay would ride through after Leslie's calls, but by the time he got there, David would be gone.

Both Jay and Tarron warned Secret to protect herself and the kids because of David's frantic behavior, and gave her a can of mace to keep in her purse.

"Make sure all your doors and windows are locked before you go to bed," Jay said.

"Do you really believe he'll try to hurt me?" Secret asked.

"Let me put it this way, David has really been saying some wild stuff lately," Jay replied.

"Like what?"

"All kinds of crazy talk, like why won't she answer my calls? If I can't have her, no one will. Tarron will be taken care of. Life is not worth living without Secret. You know, wild stuff," Jay said, making little circles next to his forehead.

One particular day, Secret looked out the window and saw David's limo sitting outside with her own eyes. She often wondered what he was up to, and why he watching her house. After that day she and the kids decided to stay with Tarron while Motherdear went back home. *No need to give that lunatic a free chance to do something stupid,* she thought.

✳   ✳   ✳

Tarron finally caught up with Shanice at the office after the firm had closed for the day. She gave him a folder with pictures used for evidence, and copied papers of billing forms. They talked for a few more minutes before Tarron left. As Tarron left the office, he looked at the pictures again and thought, *everything is coming together.*

What Tarron didn't know was that David had taken a client out to dinner when Shanice came to see if he'd left for the day. When David returned, he heard Tarron leaving, so he turned off the light in his office and hid in a corner. He peaked out the office window as Tarron walked past and noticed a folder in his hands. David waited for Shanice to go into Tarron's office before approaching her.

"What the fuck was in that folder you gave Mr. Jenkins?" David yelled.

"Oh shit, you scared me, Mr. Jordan. I thought you were gone for the day." She nervously put the used tape to the camcorder in her pocket. *I'm glad he didn't catch me changing the tape,* she thought. "Umm, the folder contained pictures of my wedding. Don't you remember, I got married two weeks ago," she lied.

"Do I look like a fool? I already know that you, Rodney, Tom and Shelly have been helping Tarron frame me." David began to point his finger in Shanice's face. "If you don't tell me what was in that folder, and all the stuff you've been helping him with, I'll …"

228

"I'm not helping anyone," Shanice said, pushing David's hand out her face.

David slammed the door. "You're going to tell me what was in that folder one way or another."

Shanice started to back up. David grabbed her arms and began to shake her forcefully.

"What was in that folder, bitch?" David repeatedly shouted.

"It was nothing. I swear Mr. Jordan!" Shanice shouted.

At that moment, Shanice tried to run for the door, but he snatched her back by her hair, throwing her into the desk. She swung her arms and kicked in defense, but it wasn't working. David fumbled around on Tarron's desk until his hand found a gold plated lamp. With all his might, he swung, and struck Shanice across the side of her face.

She fell to one knee, and was quickly pulled up by her hair like a rag doll.

"What was in that folder?" David asked again.

When Shanice didn't respond, David swung again, and her entire body fell to the floor. He hit her two more times, causing blood to splatter all over his face and clothes. David bent down and wrapped his hands around her throat and started to squeeze forcefully.

"You won't be the one to bring me down!" David yelled. He released her neck, and waited to see if she was going to move. "Go ahead and move, bitch. I've got more where that came from!" David yelled, to Shanice's unresponsive body. He checked the pulse in her neck, and the outcome was immediately confirmed. Shanice was dead.

David dragged her lifeless body into Tarron's closet and shut the door. He used a towel from Tarron's private bathroom to wipe up the trail of blood left behind. Somehow he hoped to blend the blood with the dark brown carpet. He continued to clean the blood off several more items before rushing out the office. He slowly opened the door, and looked from left to right, before walking out very calmly as if nothing had happened.

He went straight to his office to look for his car keys. He hadn't driven his personal car in months. David had to come up with a plan to get Shanice's body out of the office before anybody saw her. In the meantime, she would just have to be out sick.

He sped down 14th Street towards Secret's house, doing at least 100mph. He slammed on breaks, causing a loud screeching sound as his 745 pulled into the driveway. David jumped out of the car and knocked on the door repeatedly. He even rang the door bell a few times. He began to shout Secret's name at the top of his lungs, but there was no reply. David thought he saw the curtains in one of the windows move.

"I know you're in there!" he yelled, like a jealous lover.

When David's car made the unforgettable noise, Leslie and all the other neighbors looked out their windows. She knew something was about to go down, when she saw that David had parked crooked in the driveway. Leslie nervously called Jay. He didn't answer the first four times, so she continued to call until he picked up.

"Jay, you need to get here quick!" Leslie yelled into the phone, when he answered.

"What's going on?" Jay asked.

"That guy is back. He's yelling for Secret, and crawling through the bushes, trying to look through windows." Leslie said, breathing fast. "This doesn't look good, because normally he just parks up the street and sits outside, but tonight he's actually in the driveway. He's banging on the door and everything."

"I need you to keep watching, and if he breaks into the house, call the police until I get there," Jay replied.

"I should call the police now," Leslie said.

"No, I'm on the way. Call the police only if he gets into the house," he repeated.

Jay raced across town, running every red light and stop signs. He tried to reach Tarron several times, but was unsuccessful.

When he arrived, he saw David pouring gasoline around the house from a canister that Tarron always kept near the garage.

"What the fuck are you doing?" Jay shouted, jumping out of his car.

"I know she's in there. If she won't come out on her own, I'll burn her ass out!" David shouted back.

"Motherfucker, are you crazy? Put that damn gasoline down!" Jay said, running toward him.

When David saw Jay approaching him, he whipped out a nickel plated nine millimeter gun. "Stay right there," he said pointing the gunat him. "All of you think I'm fucking stupid. You, Tarron, and that bitch, Victoria. Don't think for a second that I don't know what games you're trying to play!"

Jay stopped in his tracks. He raised both hands, while giving David a confused look. "What are you talking about?"

"Don't try and play me, nigga! I know you and Tarron are up to something. I even saw your car parked over here the other day," David said, waving the gun.

"Man, I don't know what you're talking about. I was only here to check on my mom. I still don't have shit to say to my brother."

"Yeah right, motherfucker!" David shouted. "You think you're smart, huh? Well, I bet you didn't know that I was fucking your girl, Victoria?"

Jay gritted his teeth. *So this is the nigga she was meeting at the hotel,* he thought.

"That bitch gonna come and tell me I'm the father of her baby. Little does her dumb ass know that I can't even have kids," David said, interrupting Jay's thoughts. He reached into his pocket and pulled out a lighter, but it fell on the ground.

Jay immediately rushed David when he saw what was about to go down. Jay took the first hit, as they began to fight like two angry wrestlers in a ring. Jay managed to twist David's wrist, causing the gun to fall out his hand, but couldn't restrain him for good. They continued to exchange blows until they both fell on the ground. Jay saw the gun and tried to crawl toward it, as David held his legs tightly. He managed to dive over Jay's body and began crawling too. Unfortunately, they reached the gun at the same.

Boom! Boom!

Chapter 27

Leslie had been watching the entire fight, and ran into the house to call 911 when David pulled out the lighter. She was still on the phone when the shots rang out.

She screamed, "Oh, my God," and dropped the phone as she hurried back to the door. Her eyes bulged as tears welled up in her eyes. She ran back to the phone and cried until finally the operator answered. The sounds of tires peeling off could be heard, as she begged the dispatcher for help.

"Oh my God, I just heard gunshots!" Leslie yelled. "You have to help us, come quick," she said, dropping her cordless phone again. She looked out the window and let out a horrific scream.

"No, no, no!" Leslie said, jetting from the house, and running across the street like a track star. When she arrived, Jay was lying by the rose bushes, bleeding heavily. She silently cursed herself for not calling for help sooner.

Leslie used her hand to apply pressure to Jay's stomach as she screamed for help. One by one, each one of Tarron's neighbors came to help in any way they could. Suddenly the sirens from the police and ambulance echoed in the distance. When they arrived, it took two paramedics to pull Leslie away so they could work on Jay.

"Miss, he's losing a lot of blood, you have to move!" the heavy-set paramedic said.

"Well, work faster!" she screamed.

Several minutes later, they had hooked Jay up to several tubes, lifted him onto the stretcher, and rolled him in the back of the ambulance. Leslie jumped in, wearing a pair of jean shorts, white socks and a navy blue bra. A female paramedic handed her a paper gown as they sped off to the hospital.

✳   ✳   ✳

David called Mr. Shin on his cell phone as he raced down 16th Street. "Mr. Shin, I'm going to need a good faith payment of two hundred and fifty thousand dollars cash tomorrow morning at the merger."

"That's a large amount for a good faith payment," he replied.

"If you want to buy my shares of the company, I need that money in cash."

"I guess that won't be a problem, Mr. Jordan. I'll see you in the morning," Mr. Shin responded.

David hung up the phone as he pulled into the motel on New York Avenue. He walked to the office and paid for his room in cash, so his whereabouts couldn't be tracked. Once David was inside the dirty space, he closed the curtains and sat on the bed with his head buried in his hands.

"I can't believe I just did that," he said to himself. "If Secret's ass had opened the door, I wouldn't be in this shit!" He picked up his phone and dialed her number, but there was no answer. *If I leave a message, maybe she'll call back,* he thought.

"Baby, I need you in my life. I've done several things to make our future together a pleasant one. I have enough money for us to relocate anywhere your heart desires, but we need to leave tomorrow evening. We can start our lives fresh. Don't even

234

waste time packing. I'll buy you everything new when we arrive to our destination. I love you. Call me as soon as possible, David."

More Secrets More Lies

Chapter 28

The doctors immediately rushed Jay into surgery as soon as he arrived at the emergency room. Leslie continued to cry uncontrollably, when the police arrived at the hospital.

"Are you the woman who called 911?" an officer asked.

"Yes," Leslie answered, wiping her face.

"My name is Officer Stanton. I'm gonna need to ask you a few questions."

"Questions, what questions?" Leslie responded, defensively.

"Did you see what happened, or who shot the victim?"

"It was the man stalking my neighbor across the street," she whimpered.

"What's your neighbor's name?" Officer Stanton asked.

Leslie stuttered. "Secret Jenkins. She's Jay's sister-in-law."

"Who's Jay?" another officer said, writing in his notepad.

Leslie let out a loud scream. "He's the one that got shot, damn it!"

"Do you know how to get in contact with Ms. Jenkins?" Officer Stanton asked.

"What the hell! How should I know how to find her? Why don't you try knocking on her door? You know where Jay got shot at, so go! I don't want to answer anymore dumb ass questions. Just leave me the hell alone," Leslie said, standing up.

"We're sorry. We'll give you some space for you to check on your friend. I'll be back when you're feeling a little better," Officer Stanton replied.

✳   ✳   ✳

Jay stayed in surgery half the night. As Leslie paced back and forth in the waiting room, a doctor came over to talk about Jay's condition.

"He's lost a lot of blood," the young looking doctor said. "We removed two 9mm bullets from his stomach and side. The bullets bounced, causing damage to many of his internal organs. I removed the bullets without complications, but his bladder was another story. We did the best we could, so the next twenty-four hours may be critical. But don't worry, he should recover in time."

Leslie put her hands over her face and cried like a baby. "When will I be able to see him?"

"Mr. Jenkins is heavily sedated, and will be out for a few hours. Once we get him stabilized and into his room, I'll have the nurse come get you. Do you want a better gown to put on? Maybe a pair of scrubs?" the doctor asked.

"Yes, thank you."

The sun was beginning to rise when the nurse took Leslie to Jay's room. Leslie began to sob when she noticed the numerous tubes coming from several parts of his body.

"I'm sorry it took me so long to call for help," she said, rubbing Jay's hand." I'll never forgive myself if anything happens to you."

Leslie sat with Jay another hour, before looking for his personal belongings. She finally located a clear plastic bag that con-

238

tained his cell phone on a table. She looked through his contact list until she found the number for Motherdear.

After four rings, Motherdear answered. "Good morning, son."

"Is this Jay's mother?" Leslie asked nervously.

"Yes, who's this?"

"My name is Leslie Simmons. I live across the street from your daughter-in-law and son, Tarron."

"The little light skin girl Jay used to visit?" Motherdear replied.

"Yes, Mrs. Jenkins."

"What can I do for you, child?" Motherdear asked.

"I really don't know how to say this," Leslie said.

"Say what, child? Spit it out."

Leslie made a deep sigh before continuing. She wasn't sure how Motherdear would take the news. "Jay was shot last night, but please don't worry, the doctor said he'll be okay. We're at Suburban Hospital on Georgetown Road," she said.

"What! Jay was shot? When? Who? Why was my baby shot?" Motherdear asked, screaming into the phone.

"By some guy who's been hanging around Secret's house over the last few weeks. He tried to burn her house down last night and Jay confronted him. When they started fighting, the guy pulled out a gun, and Jay got shot," Leslie responded.

"Oh my goodness. Please stay with my son until I get there," Motherdear said, hanging up.

✳   ✳   ✳

Tarron was putting on his best suit and tie when the phone rang. He yelled for Secret to answer, but her hands was full of grease from Tika's hair.

Terrance decided to pick up the phone. "Hello."

"Tarron, your brother was shot."

"What happened to Uncle Jay, Grandma?" Terrance responded.

"Terrance is that you?" Motherdear shouted.

"Yes, Grandma."

"Give the damn phone to your father."

"Dad, its Grandma. She said get the phone because Uncle Jay got shot!" Terrance screamed out.

Tarron immediately grabbed the phone, and pressed speakerphone, so Secret could hear. "Jay got shot?" he asked, in shock.

"Yes, one of your neighbors just called me from Jay's cell phone telling me that the man who's been sneaking around the house shot my baby on your front lawn."

"Is he alright? What were David and Jay doing on my lawn?" Tarron asked.

Motherdear took a deep breath. "The girl said he'll be okay, but I need to see for myself. I don't know why they were on the lawn. Was this part of you guys' brilliant plan?"

"What plan?" Secret jumped in.

"Baby, they didn't tell you? My two sons have been sneaking around like thieves in the night, trying to get that man back."

"What have you two been up too?" Secret asked Tarron.

At first Tarron didn't speak. He took a few moments to clear his thoughts. Finally he responded to the situation, but ignored the question. "Mom, Secret and the kids will pick you up and take you to the hospital?"

"What? You're not going to check on your brother?" Motherdear asked, with an attitude.

"It's not that I don't want to, but I have a very important meeting that I can't miss. This meeting will change all our lives forever," Tarron replied.

"Boy, I don't care what kind of meeting it is. That's your brother in that hospital fighting for his life. You have to be there for him."

Tarron tried to calm his mother down. "Mom, please trust me on this one. David shot my brother, your son. I have to bury his ass in this meeting now more than ever."

"In that case, you rip his balls off!" Motherdear yelled.

"Motherdear, you're on speaker and the kids are in the room," Secret responded, covering Tika's ears.

"Girl, you should be in the car already. Hurry up and come get me so I can see my son," Motherdear responded, before hanging up the phone.

Secret hung up the other line, and rushed to get the kids ready. She gave Tarron a long stare. *Please Lord, don't let this be the last time I see him alive,* she thought.

"I love you, Tarron," Secret said, before leaving out the door.

"I love you too," he responded.

❋   ❋   ❋

Tarron entered the Viax-Shin Investment Firm building about an hour later. Several of his old co-workers stopped to talk with him in the lobby, as he made his way to the top floor. Even the gossiping security guard, Stanley, was glad to see him.

The big meeting had already started in the main conference room. Several members of the Marki Corporation and their lawyers were reviewing the terms of the deal with a fine tooth comb. They wanted to be certain David hadn't included any crazy terms or language.

Everyone in the conference room asked David if everything was alright as he paced back and forth. He looked as if he was

241

going on a long vacation from the bags under his eyes. The look on his face read frustration, fear and uncertainty. He was sweating profusely.

"Can we just sign the papers already?" David blurted out.

"It'll be another few minutes for my lawyer to go through everything. Don't worry, soon I'll be your business partner, instead of just another client," Mr. Shin replied.

Tarron walked towards Shanice's desk with a huge smile. It had been a while since he last saw her, and he wanted her to be there when the plan climaxed. When he arrived at her desk, she wasn't there. The pile of papers in her chair indicated that she'd been gone for a while. Tarron began to ask a few people if they had seen Shanice, and everybody responded with no.

Why wouldn't she come in today? Doesn't she remember what we planned? Maybe she's out sick, Tarron thought. He decided to peak in his old office and give her a call at home. When he opened the door to his old home, he immediately noticed everything out of place. *What's been going on in here?* Tarron sat at his desk and picked up the phone to call Shanice's house. No answer. He then decided to call her cell phone. A few seconds later he turned his head towards a ringing sound inside the closet.

"I must be tripping," Tarron said, as he dialed the number again. As the phone rang in his ear, he could also hear what appeared to be a phone ringing from inside the closet. This time he decided to investigate. *Shanice must've accidentally put her cell phone in her jacket. She was known to use my closet sometimes,* he thought, as he walked toward the closet. What he discovered was a pure nightmare. He opened the door to find Shanice's body bent like a pretzel, lying in a pool of blood. Tarron instantly fell to his knees and held her tightly.

"Oh, my God! Who did this to you?" Tarron yelled, stroking Shanice's blood soaked hair. He didn't even care about the stench from her body, he continued to caress her. Guilt rushed him like a ton of bricks. "I'm so sorry. I know this happened because you were trying to protect me," he cried out.

One of Tarron's co-workers heard Tarron yell, and walked into the office. "What happened to Shanice?" Eric asked, with his hands slightly covering his nose.

"Call the police Eric," Tarron responded.

"What about 911, doesn't she need an ambulance?"

Tarron looked back down at Shanice's face. "There's no need for an ambulance. She's gone. Now go!"

As Tarron heard Eric's heavy footsteps running back to his office, he thought about something. *The camera.* He gently placed Shanice's head back on the carpet, and followed the faint red light on his book shelf. He grabbed the small camcorder, and anxiously pressed stop and rewind. He couldn't believe it. Tears stared to fall as Tarron watched David beat his secretary to death with the gold plated lamp he'd gotten as a gift from her. *That motherfucker is going down,* Tarron thought. He grabbed the camcorder, ran down the hall at full speed to the conference room, and busted through the double doors wooden doors.

"You no good son of a bitch!" he yelled.

Everyone turned their heads toward Tarron. Tears continued to dash down his face. He was covered in blood.

"Why did you kill Shanice? What did she ever do to deserve such an ending?" Tarron said, moving toward David.

David moved to the other side of the conference table. "I don't know what you're talking about. Can someone please call security?"

"You know what I'm talking about, you punk motherfucker! You killed Shanice. I just found her body in my closet."

Everyone looked at David with their mouths open. "That's crazy, I haven't killed anyone. Are you on drugs, Mr. Jenkins," David asked.

"No, but I'll be on them soon enough, because I'm going to

destroy you. First you shoot my brother, now you've killed Shanice. The way I see it, you don't deserve to live either," Tarron said, running toward David.

Within seconds, security guards ran into the conference room and grabbed Tarron.

"Take him out of here. He doesn't even work here anymore. He has no right to be here!" David shouted.

"Oh, but he does," Mr. Shin said. "Tarron is now the CEO of our newest acquisition. I invited him to this meeting."

David looked back and forth from Tarron to Mr. Shin. "He's the what?"

"I'm the CEO of Viax-Shin Investment Corporation, and you're the one who no longer works here!" Tarron shouted, as he broke free from the guards.

David had so many thoughts running through his mind when the police walked into the conference room.

"I think this is all the evidence you'll need to convict this motherfucker of murder," Tarron said, handing one of the officers the camcorder.

The entire room stood still as sounds of David beating his former employer to death echoed through the room. "Cuff this asshole, and read him his rights," one officer said.

Tarron went back to his office and found the paramedics putting Shanice's body into a large black plastic bag. He held her hand as they pulled the zipper and closed the bag completely.

Chapter 29

Jay opened his eyes and found himself in a brightly lit room. He was still half-groggy from the medication. Jay looked around and found Leslie sleeping in a chair beside him. Still weak from the surgery, he tried to get Leslie's attention by talking, but only soft sounds emerged. Suddenly, Jay tapped on the side of the bed post, finally getting her attention.

"Jay, I can't believe you're awake so soon," Leslie said, jumping up. "I'm so happy that you're alive. I could've never forgiven myself if something happened to you."

"Where am I?" he whispered.

"You're in Suburban Hospital. You were shot two times by that lunatic, but you're going to be okay."

Leslie could see Jay's anger as he tried to sit up. "I'm going to kill that nigga when I see him," he said.

"Please don't get yourself all worked up. Nothing is going to come out of retaliation. He'll get what's coming to him," she said, rubbing his arm.

At that moment, Leslie had never looked so beautiful to him. Thoughts of them actually having more than a friendship entered his mind.

"My guess is that you've been here all night. You look like one of the doctors," Jay said, pulling on Leslie's scrubs.

"Yeah, I have."

"Well, go home and take yourself a hot bath, and change into some regular clothes. I'll be fine."

"Are you sure?" Leslie asked.

"Yes, please. You've done enough. Thank you for everything," Jay whispered.

Leslie decided to take his advice. She bent over his bed, and placed a soft kiss on his forehead. "I'll be back to check on you later on."

Jay didn't respond. All the talking had made him weak. He only gave her a thumbs up as she walked out the room. He laid there for several minutes, thinking about his life and how he ended up in this mess, but quickly realized it was for his family. *If getting shot to protect my family is what caused this to happen, then so be it,* he thought. *After all they've done for me, this is the least that I could do.*

Jay had dozed off for several minutes, when the door to his room opened. The person walked into the room, closed the door, and stood at the foot of his bed.

"Wake up sleepy head," Victoria said, with a huge smile.

Jay opened his eyes at the sound of her voice. As Victoria came closer, she had a look that meant trouble. He tried to sit up, but was unsuccessful.

"Look at my bad boy. The mean streets have finally caught up with you."

It hurt for Jay to respond. "The streets were nothing compared to a man loving a woman who doesn't love him."

"Who do you speak of? Hopefully not me. I did love you, I loved you with all my heart. You're the one who fucked that up. But it's okay we'll still be family because the baby I have grow-ing inside me belongs to your brother," Victoria said, rubbing her stomach.

I can't believe she's still telling herself that lie, he thought. "What about me or David? Are we not good enough to be the father?" Jay said, speaking softly.

"Well, I wanted David to be the father, but after he left me for that bitch, Secret, it's pay back time. Now as far as you're concerned, you were never, a candidate. I don't need a rapist to be the father of my child."

Jay turned his head away from Victoria. "At first I thought you deserved what I did to you. Now I know that no one deserves to go through that, so even though I know you'll never forgive me, I want to say I'm sorry."

"Boo hoo, motherfucker!" Victoria yelled. "You're right, I'll never forgive you for that shit!"

Jay tried to sit up again. "Then what are you here for? I didn't ask you to come and tell me all these lies. Get out!"

Victoria pulled the chair over next to the bed and sat down. "I won't leave. We have so much to discuss."

Jay rolled his head and looked into Victoria's eyes. "What do we need to discuss? You had me arrested. If I'm convicted, I'll go back to prison for the rest of my life. You say you loved me, but you were fucking David at the same time. Victoria, you don't love anybody but yourself. I've learned that you only use that word when it fits the situation. "You don't think I saw that note to the Judge, but I did. I knew what you wrote," Jay said softly.

"What are you talking about?" Victoria asked.

"The note to the Judge, when we had the first custody hearing for Terrance. You told the Judge that you remembered him from your club, and that he was the father of your unborn child."

Victoria lowered her head "Yeah, I fucked him at my club, but I only told him that so you could win the case," Victoria responded. "I only did what I thought I had to for you."

"Well, as you can see, it still didn't work, so you didn't do anything for me. Everybody is tired of your lies. Everything you do is for your own selfish desires. I don't think you even know who the father of your child is," Jay replied.

"You're the father," Victoria said, reaching for his hand.

"We're finally going to be a family."

Jay snatched his hand away and turned the opposite way. "You're sick. Didn't you just say I wasn't the father? Get out, before I call the nurse. I hate that we ever met, and I'm sure Tarron and David, hell even the Judge, feels the same way."

"Don't say that!" Victoria screamed.

"Get the fuck out my room." Jay reached for the button to page the nurse.

Victoria jumped up and pulled the cord out of the wall in a frenzy. Sweat poured from her forehead "You won't get rid of me that easily. If you think you can just fuck me, and throw me away like everybody else, you've got me mistaken." Victoria continued to mumble, as she fumbled through her purse

Jay knew the situation was growing uglier by the minute. He closed his eyes, hoping that when he re-opened them again, Victoria would be gone. She wasn't. Instead, Victoria stood trembling with a small .357 hand gun, pointed in Jay's face. Her expression showed her uncertainty about actually shooting Jay. Her neck rotated back and forth, as she closely watched both Jay and the door, again and again.

"Go on and do it!" Jay blurted out. "Maybe rotting in jail the rest of your life is what you need."

Instantly, Victoria thought about Jay's words. She never expected to resort to the gun anyway. On the way to the hospital, she'd told herself the gun would be used only if things got nasty.

"Do you hear me, crazy woman?" he asked, in the highest voice he could muster. "Pull the trigger!" he taunted. "Somebody will hear you! You're going to jail! Me, nor my brother, want anything to do with you,"he said, trying to raise his body up off the bed. "So shoot, damn it!"

Jay had a good bluff game going on, because he really wanted to scream for the nurse. Before he could decide what to do, Victoria threw the gun back into her purse, and covered his mouth with her right hand. Frantically, she started yanking out the needles from Jay's body.

"You're going to pay for what you did to me," Victoria whispered in his ear.

Jay tried to answer, but only managed to mumble something. Victoria's grip was too tight over his mouth. She quickly grabbed the pillow from underneath his head and smashed it over Jay's face. He was too weak to fight back.

Suddenly the door opened. As Secret and Motherdear walked into the room, they saw Victoria pressing the pillow on Jay's face. Instantly, Secret pulled Victoria back, causing her to stumble and trip over some of the cords hooked up to Jay's machines. Jay began to cough uncontrollably. Secret positioned her body to kick Victoria in the stomach, but Motherdear quickly grabbed her.

"Let me go! I told this bitch that I would kill her if she ever came around my family again!" Secret shouted, trying to pull away.

"Baby, she's not worth it. If you beat this pregnant girl, it would make you just like her. You're better than this poor child."

Secret turned her head to look Motherdear in the face. "I hate her. I just want to…"

Motherdear interrupted her. "I know you do, hell, I do too, but you have to find a way to control your rage. You have a family to take care of. Don't do anything to mess that up. Your children need you."

Motherdear let Secret go and rushed to check on Jay. Minutes later, two security guards walked into the room. They began asking all sorts of questions, but no one answered.

"Why are all of Mr. Jenkins' IV's disconnected?" a nurse asked, walking in behind the security guards.

"Ask her," Secret said, pointing to Victoria.

"Security, please escort all these women out of here immediately!" the nurse shouted.

The guards walked all three women to an empty room in the back of the security station. "If someone doesn't tell me what happened, we'll just wait until the police get here," a security guard said, closing the door. Motherdear, Secret and Victoria were left in the little room unsupervised.

"You're a stupid bitch," Secret said to Victoria.

Victoria raised her head. "I'm going to have both of you locked up. We'll see who the stupid bitch is when this is all over," she replied.

"If you file charges against us, and pursue the rape charges on my son, I'll file attempted murder on you for trying to kill him today," Motherdear said.

Victoria sat in silence. She thought long and hard about what Motherdear said, and about the gun concealed in her purse.

"Now we can tell the guards we were so happy to see each other, that when I came into the room, we ran to each other and hugged, then accidentally stepped on Jay's IV's, causing them to come out," Motherdear said, looking at Secret and Victoria. "Agreed?"

"That doesn't make any sense, Motherdear," Secret responded.

"Well, do you have any other bright ideas? We got to think of something before they call the cops."

After Secret and Motherdear tried to come up with the best possible lie, Victoria finally spoke up. "I'll take care of it. I've been seducing men all my life, so this should be easy to get out of."

When the security guard returned, Victoria asked to speak to him in private. Several minutes later, they both returned. He was smiling. She wasn't.

"You ladies are free to go," the guard stated. "Sorry for the inconvenience."

As they walked down the hall, Motherdear and Secret couldn't help but wonder what Victoria had said to the guard, but dared not ask. They watched her hold her head down all the way out the front door. Then they went back to check on Jay.

*   *   *

Tarron quickly walked to the entrance of the hospital. The closer he got, the more he recognized Victoria. Finally, they made eye contact.

"What are you doing here?" Tarron asked.

"I'm moving away, so I just wanted to tell your brother good-bye. We talked out our differences, so I'm going to drop the rapes charges," Victoria responded.

"Wow, I can't believe you're finally gonna do something good in your life for a change."

Victoria lowered her hand. When she finally looked back up, tears had flooded her eyes. "I'm really sorry for all the shit I put you through. The love I had for a stupid man caused me to do a lot of dumb things. It started off as just a business deal for David, but I started having feelings for you. I now understand the love you and Secret have for one another. I will never bother either of you again. Walk me to my car?"

Tarron was speechless. Maybe she'd changed, but he didn't know whether to believe Victoria or not. Besides, what harm could come from ending things peacefully. Before Tarron could respond, Victoria tugged on his shoulder, forcing him to walk along with her.

"It's our last goodbye," she said convincingly.

Victoria looked around several times as they walked toward her car. She walked quickly in silence, praying that Tarron would keep up the pace. The moment she laid eyes on her car, she looked once again, making sure no one was in sight. Her Benz was parked between a large black SUV and a dark green Volvo.

"Well, I guess it ends here," she said, shaking Tarron's hand.

Tarron extended him hand, and she yanked him close to the driver's side of her car. It was the perfect set-up. Nestled between the two other vehicles, Victoria opened her bag, and whipped out her gun. Closing her eyes, she gripped the trigger tightly.

"You owe me," she cried.

"For what?" Tarron responded, in shock. He held his hands in the air as if he were being robbed.

"For ruining my life," she responded.

"C'mon now, Victoria…" he begged. "You don't wanna do this."

"Aaaaaghhh…I do…I do…," she ended.

Her hands moved in a perfect motion, as she did what her heart instructed.

EPILOGUE

Seven Months Later

The long walk down the concrete cell block seemed endless. David walked slowly with his head down as the correctional officers escorted him to his cell. There was a loud banging sound when the iron door slammed behind him, as he was pushed into his new home for the next forty years. David looked around at the six by six foot cell, wondering where he'd gone wrong. He went from having a million dollar home, successful business, and chauffer driven limousine, to an iron bed, accompanied by a toilet and chair.

After all I've been through, she has to love me now, he thought. David pulled out the chair and began writing a letter to Secret. He wrote with so much emotion, that the pencil points kept breaking as he tried to write her name. His focus wasn't on how he was going to spend his last few breaths, but rather on how he could get Secret to understand his motive for committing suicide. David smiled as he reminisced about the romantic times he'd shared with her.

He hoped that his death would be considered heroic, and would finally make her love him. He finished his letter, and handed it to the officer he'd paid to help him carry out his plan. Although the officer stood with a solemn expression, as if he didn't want to go through with it, the thought of the thirty thousand dollars wired to his account was reason enough to go through with it. David held his head low and asked the correctional officer to mail it to Secret the next day. "Ask her does she love me now," David said, standing on the chair, as he prepared himself for the hanging.

The correctional officer turned and walked away, after supplying David with what he needed. Although sad about David's upcoming death, he ripped the letter into tiny pieces as he turned the corner.

＊   ＊   ＊

Tarron sped up the stairs to the portrait studio where Secret, Terrance and Tika had been waiting for over twenty minutes. He smiled as he rushed inside, to see his wife looking more beautiful than ever. Although upset, Secret understood that her husband was a busy man. After all, he was the CEO of the VIAX-Shin Investment Firm, and the general manager of the six new clubs opened by Ray, in several different cities.

Things were going well, and the money was rolling in. However, Secret and Tarron vowed to never let anything come between their marriage again; not work, money, and definitely not other men or women. They discussed the consequences of their dual infidelities. Tarron knew that Victoria allowing him to live was a gift from God, a second chance to treat his family right. He often remisced about how Victoria's gun remained pointed at his temple, and then suddenly lowered, as she told him convincingly he wasn't worth it.

Over the last seven months, Tarron and Secret started to behave like young lovers again. Every Friday, Motherdear would come over to keep the children, so that Secret and Tarron could date one another. From hotels, to dark parks, the fire has been resparked, and continues to burn strong.

Jay sat on his new front porch after he returned from cou₁
He was relieved that the rape charges were dismissed for lack
evidence, and that Victoria had also dropped all charges.
Strangely, she was a no-show. A part of him was glad that she
didn't show up, but another part of him wanted to confront her
about his child. Jay had a strong feeling that Victoria was carrying his baby, and had already decided he wanted to take part in
the child's life. Things surrounding his life were definitely starting to turn around for the better. The sky seemed to be shining
brighter, knowing that jail was no longer in his future. Besides,
Leslie made it clear that she wanted to be his present and future.
Jay felt in his heart that Leslie was the real deal. She didn't want
him for sex or money, she just wanted someone to be by her side.
Leslie knew all about Jay's fucked up past, but still loved him
unconditionally.

Moving forward, Jay had a lot to smile about; his woman, and
his new job as manager of the Lion's Den. Since Ray was moving
from place to place, setting up his new clubs in various cities, Jay
was the perfect man for the job.

❋   ❋   ❋

Victoria walked into a five star restaurant in downtown Los
Angeles, wearing a tight black mini skirt, five inch heels, and a
red lace shirt, that barely covered her protruding nine month
belly. She ignored the women who looked at her with disgust,
and blew kisses at the men who stared. *What? A pregnant woman
ain't supposed to strut her stuff,* she thought. Victoria lowered her

restaurant, until she noticed her client

rry. Do you have all the paperwork?"
.ng a seat.

ng is in order. All you have to do is sign on the
replied.

toria could sign, Jerry softly grabbed her hand.
e you want to go through with this? Because once
s, there's no turning back. I mean it. The moment you
.ie baby is no longer yours."

s, I'm sure," she replied. "Let's face it. You're a nobody in
own, if you don't have money, so selling this baby for two
.dred thousand dollars is a must. I never wanted children any-
ay."

Victoria shrugged her shoulders, reached into her purse, and
grabbed a pen from her upcoming job, Diamond Divas, the most
successful call-girl company in L.A. She quickly signed her
name on the paper and slid the contract back to her client.

"Now where's my damn money?" she asked.

He looked over the paper and smiled. "Here's fifty thousand
dollars now. You'll get the rest at the hospital once you deliver,"
Jerry said, sliding a briefcase under the table. "You are still being
induced on Friday, right?"

"I sure am," she said, preparing to leave. "It better be all
there, Jerry. Don't fuck with me."

As Victoria stood up, her client grabbed her hand again. "I
have to ask you this, so I hope you don't get offended."

"Well, what is it? Time is money," Victoria ordered.

"What about the father? Is he okay with this decision?"

"My child doesn't have a father. I was raped. Besides, that
motherfucker is broke anyway."